P9-BZI-104

WITHDRAWN

# PRAISE FOR *KILLER THRILLER*

"*Killer Thriller* grabs you from page one with brilliant wit, sharply honed suspense, and a huge helping of pure originality."
—Jeffery Deaver, *New York Times* bestselling author

"A delight from start to finish, a round-the-world, thrill-a-minute, laser-guided missile of a book."
—Joseph Finder, *New York Times* bestselling author of *Judgment*

"*Killer Thriller* is an action-packed treasure filled with intrigue, engaging characters, and exciting, well-rendered locales. With Goldberg's hyper-clever plotting, dialogue, and wit on every page, readers are in for a blast with this one!"
—Mark Greaney, *New York Times* bestselling author of The Gray Man series.

# PRAISE FOR *TRUE FICTION*

"Thriller fiction at its absolute finest—and it could happen for real. But not to me, I hope."
—Lee Child, #1 *New York Times* bestselling author of the Jack Reacher series

"This may be the most fun you'll ever have reading a thriller. It's a breathtaking rush of suspense, intrigue, and laughter that only Lee Goldberg could pull off. I loved it."
—Janet Evanovich, #1 *New York Times* bestselling author

"This is my life . . . in a thriller! *True Fiction* is great fun."
—Brad Meltzer, #1 *New York Times* bestselling author of *House of Secrets*

"Fans of parodic thrillers will enjoy the exhilarating ride . . . [in] this Elmore Leonard mashed with *Get Smart* romp."
—*Publishers Weekly*

"A conspiracy thriller of the first order, a magical blend of fact and it-could-happen scary fiction. Nail-biting, page-turning, and laced with Goldberg's wry humor, *True Fiction* is a true delight, reminiscent of *Three Days of the Condor* and the best of Hitchcock's innocent-man-in-peril films."
—Paul Levine, bestselling author of *Bum Rap*

"Great fun that moves as fast as a jet. Goldberg walks a tightrope between suspense and humor and never slips."
—Linwood Barclay, *New York Times* bestselling author of *The Twenty-Three*

"I haven't read anything this much fun since Donald E. Westlake's comic-caper novels. Immensely entertaining, clever, and timely."
—David Morrell, *New York Times* bestselling author of *Murder as a Fine Art* and *First Blood*

"The story of an innocent man caught in a deadly conspiracy has been told before, but Lee Goldberg takes it a step further in this rollicking, sometimes humorous, always deadly *True Fiction*.
Highly recommended."
—Brendan DuBois, author of *Storm Cell*

"Ian Ludlow is one of the coolest heroes to emerge in post-9/11 thrillers. A wonderful, classic yet modern, breakneck suspense novel. Lee Goldberg delivers a great story with a literary metafiction wink that makes its thrills resonate."
—James Grady, author of *Six Days of the Condor*

# KILLER
# THRILLER

# OTHER TITLES BY LEE GOLDBERG

*King City*
*The Walk*
*Watch Me Die*
*McGrave*
*Three Ways to Die*
*Fast Track*

## The Ian Ludlow Thrillers

*True Fiction*

## The Fox & O'Hare Series
## (coauthored with Janet Evanovich)

*Pros & Cons* (novella)
*The Shell Game* (novella)
*The Heist*
*The Chase*
*The Job*
*The Scam*
*The Pursuit*

## The Diagnosis Murder Series

*The Silent Partner*
*The Death Merchant*
*The Shooting Script*
*The Waking Nightmare*
*The Past Tense*
*The Dead Letter*

*The Double Life*
*The Last Word*

## The Monk Series

*Mr. Monk Goes to the Firehouse*
*Mr. Monk Goes to Hawaii*
*Mr. Monk and the Blue Flu*
*Mr. Monk and the Two Assistants*
*Mr. Monk in Outer Space*
*Mr. Monk Goes to Germany*
*Mr. Monk Is Miserable*
*Mr. Monk and the Dirty Cop*
*Mr. Monk in Trouble*
*Mr. Monk Is Cleaned Out*
*Mr. Monk on the Road*
*Mr. Monk on the Couch*
*Mr. Monk on Patrol*
*Mr. Monk Is a Mess*
*Mr. Monk Gets Even*

## The Charlie Willis Series

*My Gun Has Bullets*
*Dead Space*

## The Dead Man Series
## (coauthored with William Rabkin)

*Face of Evil*
*Ring of Knives* (with James Daniels)
*Hell in Heaven*

*The Dead Woman* (with David McAfee)
*The Blood Mesa* (with James Reasoner)
*Kill Them All* (with Harry Shannon)
*The Beast Within* (with James Daniels)
*Fire & Ice* (with Jude Hardin)
*Carnival of Death* (with Bill Crider)
*Freaks Must Die* (with Joel Goldman)
*Slaves to Evil* (with Lisa Klink)
*The Midnight Special* (with Phoef Sutton)
*The Death March* (with Christa Faust)
*The Black Death* (with Aric Davis)
*The Killing Floor* (with David Tully)
*Colder Than Hell* (with Anthony Neil Smith)
*Evil to Burn* (with Lisa Klink)
*Streets of Blood* (with Barry Napier)
*Crucible of Fire* (with Mel Odom)
*The Dark Need* (with Stant Litore)
*The Rising Dead* (with Stella Greene)
*Reborn* (with Kate Danley, Phoef Sutton, and Lisa Klink)

## The Jury Series

*Judgment*
*Adjourned*
*Payback*
*Guilty*

## Nonfiction

*The Best TV Shows You Never Saw*
*Unsold Television Pilots 1955–1989*
*Television Fast Forward*

*Science Fiction Filmmaking in the 1980s*
(cowritten with William Rabkin, Randy Lofficier,
and Jean-Marc Lofficier)
*The Dreamweavers: Interviews with
Fantasy Filmmakers of the 1980s*
(cowritten with William Rabkin, Randy Lofficier,
and Jean-Marc Lofficier)
*Successful Television Writing* (cowritten with William Rabkin)

# KILLER
# THRILLER

## LEE GOLDBERG

THOMAS & MERCER

This is a work of fiction. Names, characters, organizations, places, events, and incidents are either products of the author's imagination or are used fictitiously. Any resemblance to actual persons, living or dead, or actual events is purely coincidental.

Text copyright © 2019 by Adventures in Television, Inc.
All rights reserved.

No part of this book may be reproduced, or stored in a retrieval system, or transmitted in any form or by any means, electronic, mechanical, photocopying, recording, or otherwise, without express written permission of the publisher.

Published by Thomas & Mercer, Seattle

www.apub.com

Amazon, the Amazon logo, and Thomas & Mercer are trademarks of Amazon.com, Inc., or its affiliates.

ISBN-13: 9781503903562 (hardcover)
ISBN-10: 1503903567 (hardcover)
ISBN-13: 9781503904286 (paperback)
ISBN-10: 1503904288 (paperback)

Cover design by Mike Heath | Magnus Creative

Printed in the United States of America

First edition

*For Valerie and Maddie . . . and Oreo, too.*

# CHAPTER ONE

Ian Ludlow's UCLA creative writing professor insisted that the key to being a successful novelist was writing from personal experience. That's why the professor was the author of five unpublished novels about sexually frustrated novelists who toiled in obscurity while teaching talentless and ungrateful students how to write.

So Ian ignored his professor's edict and wrote escapist adventure stories that had nothing to do with his own mundane life. That's how he flunked the class but eventually became a writer for TV shows like *Hollywood & the Vine* (half-man, half-plant, all cop!) and the author of the internationally bestselling series of action thrillers about Clint Straker, freelance spy for hire.

"And that's how I ended up here," Ian said, standing in front of a hundred people at Seattle's Union Bay Books on a warm Saturday night. He was in his early thirties, dressed writer-casual in a loose-fitting polo shirt, jeans, and a pair of Nikes. Beside him was a table piled high with hardcover copies of his new novel, *Death in the Sky*. He gestured to the book cover, which featured a silhouette of Clint Straker (the publisher was too cheap to hire a male model) toting a rocket launcher against the backdrop of a 747 crashing into the Space Needle in a massive fireball.

"As you can see, I'm still writing outrageous stories about things that I know nothing about."

The irony was that this time he actually *did* write from personal experience. There were only two, possibly three, people still alive who knew that and he'd hoped that one of them, Margo French, would show up for his book signing. But she was a no-show. He couldn't really blame her for that. He'd pretty much ruined her life. She'd been his author escort, a fancy name for someone who drives out-of-town authors around to signings, in Seattle a year ago. That was when he discovered that a hypothetical terrorist plot he'd cooked up for the CIA, to prepare them for worst-case scenarios, had come true: Terrorists had hacked a plane and steered it by remote control into Waikiki, killing hundreds of people. But it wasn't terrorists. It was the CIA, or at least people who tricked him into believing they were with the Agency, who were responsible for the massacre. Those people came gunning for him to bury the truth. Margo got unwillingly swept up in his plight, a run for their lives that ended with the conspiracy being foiled, thanks to their unheralded efforts. He hadn't seen Margo since.

"Whatever happened to your creative writing professor?" asked a thin man with so much facial hair that it looked like an enormous vole was trying to swallow his head.

"I don't know, but he did come in and pitch me an episode of *Hollywood & the Vine* once," Ian said. "The story was about an incredibly talented but unappreciated creative writing professor stalked by a homicidal student. I gave him an assignment out of pity but he quit without finishing the script. He said he couldn't write a cop who was half-man, half-plant because he'd never been a shrub."

"So how did you write for the Vine?" a young woman asked. She was braless and spilling out of her tank top, so it took all of Ian's willpower to respond to her face and not to her boobs.

"By always keeping my mortgage and credit card bills next to my keyboard," he told her boobs. He'd never had much willpower.

"How do you write Clint Straker?" someone else called out.

"I imagine the man I wish I was, living the life of adventure I wish I had."

That answer was only half-true. He wanted to be as self-confident, resourceful, and attractive to women as Straker was but he didn't want to face the danger, violence, or the fate-of-the-world responsibility that his hero regularly took in stride. Once was enough for Ian. But at least he survived the experience and got a *New York Times* bestselling novel out of it.

He fielded a few more questions, signed a hundred new books along with fifty of his old titles, and an hour later he stepped outside, where Gwen, his new author escort, was sucking on an e-cigarette like it was a baby bottle. She was a graduate student in the University of Washington English Department who ferried novelists around town so she could pitch them her book, a civil war allegory set on a planet of unicorns, zebras, and horses.

She took the cigarette out of her mouth and exhaled some mist. "Shall I take you back to your hotel?"

"No, thank you. It's so nice out that I think I'll walk," Ian said. "See you tomorrow at the mystery bookstore."

"Would you like to meet early for coffee?" she asked. "I can show you my first chapter. Clint Straker shares more in common with unicorns than you might think."

"I'm sure you're right," he said. "Maybe another time."

Gwen forced a smile, got into her Prius, and drove off. He didn't really want to schlep a mile back to his hotel but it was better than being a captive audience for Gwen's story about unicorns at war with the horses that were enslaving zebras.

"Why are you so fucking polite?" a familiar female voice asked. "Tell her where to stick her unicorn. That's what Clint Straker would do."

Ian smiled as Margo stepped out of the shadows. She hadn't changed a bit. She was in her late twenties, thin and wiry, with short-cropped, crow-black hair that looked like she'd trimmed it herself with a box cutter. She wore a faded T-shirt, torn jeans, and Doc Martens.

"I'm not Clint Straker," he said.

"You could have fooled me," Margo said.

Ian gave her a hug and she squeezed him tight. "I'm glad you came."

"What else did I have to do? My dog-sitting business has dried up, all because of one negative Yelp review."

"You left the dogs alone with a pile of food, a bucket of water, and a corpse impaled with a fireplace poker." That was his fault, too.

"One time!" Margo said. "How often is that likely to happen?"

Ian laughed and gestured to the bookstore. "Why didn't you come for the reading and the Q and A?"

"Living it was enough. I'm still suffering from PTSD."

"Really?" Ian said.

"No, I'm fine. What we went through forced me to get my shit together. I'm focusing entirely on my music now," she said. "I'm writing songs. I play three nights a week at a steak house here in town and I do a lot of weddings, bar mitzvahs, that kind of thing."

"That's how Rihanna started," Ian said.

"I have a hard time picturing Rihanna singing 'Hava Nagila.'"

"I have a hard time picturing you singing 'Hava Nagila.'"

Two men in crisp business suits and wearing earpieces with wires that ran down under their starched collars approached them from either side. They had faces so rigid that they either were suffering from terminal constipation or were federal agents.

"Mr. Ludlow," the first man said. "Ms. French."

"Can you please come with us?" the second man said.

Ian and Margo shared a look. This couldn't be good. The two men herded them to a limousine parked on the corner. The first man opened the back door and motioned for them to go inside. Margo glanced at Ian for reassurance.

"He said 'please,'" Ian said. "That's a good sign."

"And it's a limo, not a hearse."

"So there's no reason to worry." Ian took a deep breath and got in. Margo followed.

One of the agents closed the door behind them. They found themselves sitting across from the lone occupant, who had Ian's new book on his lap. The man was in his early fifties, clean-cut and almost wholesome enough to be mistaken for a preacher or grade school teacher, if not for his military bearing and flinty eyes. He nodded at Ian, as if they'd met before, which they certainly hadn't, and then smiled at Margo.

"I'm sure Mr. Ludlow knows who I am, since he writes so much about espionage and government conspiracies," the man said to Margo. "But you may not. I'm Michael Healy, director of the Central Intelligence Agency."

He offered her his hand. She shook it. "Does this car have machine gun turrets and ejector seats?"

"No, I'm afraid not," he said.

"That's no fun," she said.

Healy turned his gaze on Ian. "I read your book. Scary stuff."

"Most of it's true," Ian said. "But you already know that."

"The president appreciates that you chose to tell your story as fiction. So do I. You did the right thing for your country."

"I wasn't being patriotic," Ian said. "I don't think the country would be too thrilled if they knew that what happened in Hawaii was my idea."

"That's why I'm here," Healy said. "Your fiction has an uncanny way of becoming fact. We could use people with imagination at the CIA."

Ian laughed. "Are you offering me a job?"

"How would you like to become Clint Straker?" Healy asked. "You'd still be a writer, traveling all over the world researching your international thrillers, but you'd also be working for us. It's the perfect cover."

"Author by day? Secret agent by night?"

"Something like that," Healy said.

"You can't be serious." Margo glared at Healy and then turned to Ian. "Have you forgotten that this is how you got into trouble before?"

"Relax," Ian said. "I didn't say I was going to do it."

"You didn't say no, either."

That was true. He didn't.

# CHAPTER TWO

Hong Kong. Fourteen months later, May 11. 9:15 p.m. Hong Kong Time.

"Hong Kong" means "fragrant harbor" in Chinese. The fragrance is the smell of money. First it was the boatloads of money earned by the British at the beginning of the nineteenth century from the sale of opium to millions of Chinese addicts. Now it was the money being earned by the Chinese from money itself—keeping it, investing it, laundering it, hiding it, and, of course, spending it. Hong Kong's crowded waterfront skyline of shoulder-to-shoulder skyscrapers was a monument to that sweet smell.

In a city where buildable land is scarce, the ever-increasing population density is among the highest on earth, and the only place to build is up, wealth and power are measured by how much of that airspace you possess. By that measure, or any measure really, Wang Kang was obscenely wealthy.

The billionaire lived atop a seventy-five-story harbor-front tower known locally as the Blade because the building was unusually thin, with only one large apartment per triangular floor, and had a long, razor-sharp edge that made it seem as if it had sliced itself into the skyline. In fact, it wasn't unusual to find the sidewalk littered with bisected birds that had flown into the leading edge of the Blade and were neatly cut in half.

It was a building that would have perfectly suited Warren Fung, if he could afford to live there, which he couldn't. Everything about him had a sharp edge. His eyes. His cheekbones. His fingernails. The cut of his business suit. The tips of his leather shoes. He walked across the black marble of the lobby to the guard who sat in the center of a circular desk embedded with security monitors.

"I'm Warren Fung with the *Wall Street Journal.*" He addressed the guard in flawless Cantonese. "Mr. Wang is expecting me."

The guard glanced at a monitor, which showed an X-ray of Fung, revealing his pen, a notepad, a cell phone, keys, a wallet, and no weapons. Fung leaned over and looked at the monitor.

"Cool," Fung said.

"Let's see some ID," the guard said.

Fung offered him his identity card. The guard scanned it, handed it back, and made a call. A moment later, one of the two elevators opened and a Caucasian woman came out, wearing black pants and a long-sleeved, white silk blouse with a squared Mandarin collar.

"I'm Emilia Farrow, head of Mr. Wang's security detail," she said in English and spoken with an Australian accent. "Please empty your pockets."

Fung emptied his pockets on the countertop. "You take security very seriously," he replied in English with the slight British accent befitting a man raised in Hong Kong under British colonial rule.

"Mr. Wang is one of the richest men in the world." Farrow examined the pen, scribbled on Fung's notepad with it, and then gave everything back to him. "Come with me."

She led him to the elevator and stepped inside. She positioned her eye in front of an iris scanner before hitting a button on the keypad. The elevator doors closed and the carriage shot up with astonishing speed and smoothness. The doors opened a moment later in Wang's marbled foyer. They were greeted by two muscular Caucasian men wearing the same outfit as Farrow, only their Mandarin-cut shirts were cotton instead of silk in deference to their strident masculinity.

Farrow led Fung past the two men into a vast office where Wang stood, his back to them, taking in the massive view to the north of Victoria Harbor, the densely populated Kowloon Peninsula, and the territories beyond, as if he owned it all. It was possible that he did. At least four of the massive skyscrapers growing like weeds across Kowloon carried his corporate logo in bright lights against the night sky.

His office was industrial, all concrete and steel. Even the desk was formed out of poured concrete. The couches were leather but looked like upholstered cinder blocks and were about as inviting.

"Mr. Wang," Farrow said. "This is Mr. Fung."

Fung stepped past her, held out his hand, and spoke in perfect Mandarin: "Thank you for seeing me."

Wang turned. The elegant sixty-year-old statesman wore a blue cotton Mandarin shirt under a classically square-collared black Tang jacket. He also replied in his native tongue. "It is my pleasure."

Wang shook Fung's hand and dismissed Farrow with a nod. She walked out, but Fung assumed there were cameras watching the room.

"We're profiling the ten most influential business leaders in Asia," Fung said. "You're at the top of the list."

Wang motioned him to sit on a couch. "It's an honor, one I'm sure I don't deserve."

"You're being too modest, Mr. Wang." Fung sat down on the hard couch, took out his pen and pad, and set them on the poured-concrete coffee table. "You own the majority stake in a dozen of China's top financial institutions. That makes you almost as powerful as President Xiao."

"That's hardly the case," Wang said in a tone that made it very clear that it was.

"If you make one misstep, the nation's entire economy could falter."

"There are many safeguards in place to prevent one man from having that kind of impact," he said, still standing so he could look down on Fung, who thought it was a petty power play. "Besides, I would never do anything to put those institutions at risk."

"Some would argue that you already have by making huge investments in money-losing US movie studios, electric car companies, and newspapers."

"I know what I am doing. I didn't get where I am by making bad decisions."

"We've heard rumors that there are members of the Politburo who want to crack down on you for flaunting your wealth and getting too cozy with the West," Fung said. "Many believe you moved to Hong Kong so the Chinese security services can't touch you without violating the 'one country, two systems' agreement."

"That's nonsense. I'm here overseeing the expansion of my movie studio complex in Kowloon." Wang gestured to the view across the harbor and something out there caught his eye. He stepped to the window to take a closer look. "My daughter Mei is costarring in an international thriller that starts production in July. Damon Matthews is the star. I want to be here for that, too."

"It doesn't worry you that over the last year a dozen business leaders have been kidnapped from Hong Kong and taken to Beijing?"

What Wang saw outside was a white helicopter streaking across the harbor from Kowloon toward the Hong Kong skyline. It was coming his way through the night sky like a guided missile.

"They weren't kidnapped," Wang said. "They went willingly to assist the government's anticorruption efforts."

"Aren't you concerned you might also be asked for assistance?"

"Not at all."

"So all your security precautions and your bodyguards, who just happen to be Australian and have no allegiance to China, are just for show?"

"I'm a billionaire, Mr. Fung. There are a lot of people who'd like to do me harm just for having money. I'm not going to make it easy for anyone to get to me."

"Yet here I am," Fung said.

Unnerved, Wang turned, and as he did, Fung pointed his pen at him and fired a dart into the billionaire's neck. Wang crumpled to the floor, where he lay twitching and half-conscious, his wide eyes bulging.

Fung pocketed his pen and notepad but made no move to rise from his seat. "You're so eager for publicity from the Western media that it's made you stupid and careless. You've seen Fung's byline but have you ever seen his face?"

Fung turned his head toward the door as Farrow and the other two bodyguards burst into the room holding guns. He leaned back casually, resting his arms expansively along the back of the couch.

"Here's what happened," Fung said in English to Farrow. "Mr. Wang fell ill. You called for medical assistance. Oh look, it's here." He tipped his head to the white helicopter that was close enough to the building now that they could clearly see it had the markings of a medevac unit.

"You aren't leaving this room and neither is Mr. Wang." Farrow aimed her gun at Fung's head for emphasis while her two men went to check on Wang, who was involuntarily wetting himself. They were lucky that he'd emptied his bowels earlier that evening.

"Wang is going to Beijing to deal with his medical issues and you're going carry him up to the helipad to meet the medevac chopper," Fung said.

"Why would we do that?" Farrow asked. At that same instant, the phone in her pants pocket began to vibrate.

"Because the Australian gaming company that is your security firm's biggest client doesn't want to lose their license to operate casinos in Macau and the billions of dollars in revenue they bring in." Fung pointed to her vibrating pocket. "That's your boss calling to tell you to stand down and do as I say."

Farrow reached into her pocket with one hand for her phone and held it to her ear while keeping her gun on Fung.

"Farrow . . ." Her face fell as she listened to the caller. "Yes, sir."

She lowered her gun and gestured to the guards to do the same. "Put away your weapons."

Fung rose from the couch and addressed the guards. "You two, pick up Wang and carry him to the helipad."

The guards looked to Farrow and she nodded, pocketing her phone.

The men holstered their guns, picked up Wang, and carried him out of the room as the helicopter came in for a landing.

Farrow watched them go and shifted her gaze to Fung. "You want us to be seen on the security camera footage taking Mr. Wang out of the building. That way Beijing can say that he left Hong Kong willingly."

"Just like you. You and your people have eight hours to leave the country and never come back. Or you can go home in caskets." Fung smiled, walked past her, and headed for the elevator. He paused in the doorway. "Oh, and one more thing. I was never here."

# CHAPTER THREE

The Cutting Board was a dimly lit wood-paneled steak house with booths upholstered in red leather. The air in the restaurant was stagnant and heavy with the smell of cigars, garlic, butter, and burning beef. The ambience was so masculine that infertile men could increase their sperm count just by walking in the door.

Senator Sam Tolan, wearing his trademark Stetson hat, sat in a corner booth cutting into a thick and very rare rib-eye steak. He'd killed his way into the US Senate by sending more men to death row in Texas than any prosecutor in the state's history. Texans liked that—unless they were black or Hispanic. He speared his fork deep into the morsel of meat, ran it through the blood on his plate, stabbed a french fry with the exposed tines, and shoved the combination into his mouth. He chewed it with relish, imagining the battle being waged in his bloodstream between the cholesterol in what he was eating and the horse-pill-size dosage of Lipitor that he took each morning.

Tolan looked across the table at Hamilton Nash, his dinner guest, who wore a Stetson in deference to the sixty-six-year-old senator and their home state, and who was cutting into his roasted half chicken.

"I don't see what you're so concerned about," Tolan said. "My bill doesn't end foreign investment in American companies—it simply requires our government to scrutinize those deals more closely for any potential national security risks. The president isn't even in my party and he supports the legislation. Do you know why?"

"Because he's a xenophobic protectionist," Nash said.

"Because he ran on saving American jobs and keeping our country safe," Tolan said. "Just like me."

"All I'm asking, Senator, is that you give the bill more thought before bringing it to the floor for a vote. What's the harm in that?"

"Because during every minute that we waste, another treasured American asset is taken by the Chinese." Tolan cut into his steak again, with some urgency this time, as if the Chinese might take his plate away, too.

"They aren't taking anything—they're saving companies and generating jobs that would be lost otherwise," Nash said. "Like my poultry company, our employees, and the thousands of chicken farmers we support in our state."

"You're talking about selling out to a foreign adversary."

"I'm talking about reaching 1.2 billion new consumers for American chicken."

"But they won't be American chickens anymore. They'll be Chinese and the profits will be going to Beijing, not Houston." Tolan ran his piece of meat through the blood again and stabbed another french fry. "Even worse, the Chinese are going to learn the trade secrets that made you a leader in the processed poultry business for a century."

"We'll be out of business if the Chinese deal falls apart and then what good will those trade secrets do us?" Nash pushed his plate away. He'd lost his appetite.

Tolan nodded and considered Nash's comment as he chewed. After a moment, he said, "Do you like this place?"

"Sure, it's nice."

Tolan picked up his napkin and dabbed at the steak juice that had escaped from the corners of his mouth.

"It's the best steak house outside of Houston. It's been around forever. They say this is where George Washington had his first meal with his wooden dentures. Every politician and lobbyist in town eats here. Even so, it fell on hard times. Two years ago, a Chinese company swooped in and saved it from closing."

Nash smiled and leaned back in his seat. "That's exactly my point, Senator. Thanks to the Chinese money, a Washington, DC, tradition will endure. Everybody wins."

"Especially Chinese intelligence, who've bugged the entire place, acquiring a gold mine of classified information that's sabotaged American foreign policy in Asia."

Nash leaned forward and lowered his voice. "Jesus. Is that true?"

"Damned if I know. But under my bill, the Chinese deal for this restaurant would have been rejected because of the potential for that frightening scenario to happen."

That statement didn't disturb Hamilton Nash nearly as much as it did the two dozen Chinese intelligence analysts in identical gray jumpsuits who were watching and listening to the conversation play out from their stations in a windowless situation room seven thousand miles away and twelve hours into the future.

✪

**Classified Location, Kangbashi District, Ordos, Inner Mongolia, China. May 26. 8:00 a.m. China Standard Time.**

Yat Fu stood in the back of the windowless situation room with his hands clasped behind his back, a thoughtful posture that thrust his potbelly out and ruined the utilitarian line of his dark-blue Mao tunic suit.

It was a pose he adopted whenever he was considering a move in the international game of espionage, a game in which he was acknowledged within China's Ministry of State Security as a grand master. Several rows of consoles, where his two dozen stiff-backed analysts worked diligently at their computers, separated him from the crescent-shaped wall lined with flat-screen monitors showing him multiple views of the Washington, DC, restaurant.

"Paranoia isn't healthy," Yat Fu said in Mandarin.

The analyst nearest to Yat Fu, a bald man with enormous ears named Pang Bao, understood the command and whispered an order of his own into his headset.

### The Cutting Board, Washington, DC. May 25. 8:02 p.m. Eastern Daylight Time.

Nash stared at Tolan and tried to contain his anger. "You'd destroy a century-old company and put thousands of your constituents out of work over a hypothetical scenario?"

"Don't worry, my legislation won't kill your deal," Tolan said. "But if it does, I'm sure you can find another investor in a friendly country. They eat chicken in Italy, don't they?"

Nash stood up, dropped his napkin on the table, and walked away without saying goodbye.

Tolan didn't care. The fact was, if the Chinese deal evaporated, the senator had another wealthy constituent ready to buy Nash's company at what would be a much lower price than it commanded now. Besides, Tolan didn't trust a man who ate chicken at a steak house, regardless of whether the individual was in the chicken business.

A waitress approached with a fresh martini on a silver tray. Tolan was so delighted to see the drink that he was willing to ignore that the waitress was Chinese. He didn't think of himself as a racist, but he felt strongly that the waitstaff should be white in a classic American steak house and Asian in a Chinese restaurant. But he'd overlook a lot given a martini at the right time. This was one of those times.

"You read my mind," Tolan said with a smile as the martini was set in front of him. She smiled, turned, and walked away. He guzzled down half his drink as he admired how her tight black slacks hugged her firm ass. His wife once had an ass like that. Now her ass looked like a couch cushion.

He put down his glass and was about to finish his steak when he felt a sudden tightness in his chest and then a stabbing pain like a spike being driven into his sternum with a mallet.

Tolan instinctively grabbed at his chest, as if he could yank out the invisible spike. His distress immediately drew the attention of the diners nearby. He opened his mouth to ask them for help, but something exploded in his chest and then he was aware of nothing. He pitched forward into his plate, his cheek against his steak, his eyes wide open and lifeless, his Stetson rakishly askew on the side of his head.

In all the commotion, nobody noticed the Chinese waitress walk slowly out of the restaurant and into the dark night.

# CHAPTER FOUR

An excerpt from the shooting script for *Straker*.

EXT. HONG KONG — KOWLOON — NIGHT

An exotic Chinese city balanced on the craggy precipice between past and future . . . its gleaming towers rising above Victoria Harbor, casting an otherworldly neon glow over a rats-warren of back alleys that haven't changed in centuries. We PAN DOWN to one of those alleys, through a tangle of neon signs in Chinese letters fighting for space above the streets, until we find a tiny restaurant no tourist has ever visited.

INT. RESTAURANT — NIGHT

It's smoky, dark, more like a bar than a restaurant. Straker is the only customer. The waitress is EVE CHAN. She is young, unbelievably beautiful, and moves with the grace of a ballet dancer. She brings him an array of exotic dishes—including Drunken Shrimp (a bowl of live shrimp swimming in alcohol) and Dead Alive Fish (a twitching fish that's deep fried except for the head, so it's essentially dying on the plate)—and three different red sauces. Straker speaks to her in flawless Cantonese ... but here's what we'll see in the subtitles:

> STRAKER
> I've been looking forward to this. It's been way too long since I've eaten anything that's still alive.

> EVE
> I don't know many white men with a taste for Zui Xia and Ying Yang Yu.

> STRAKER
> I also like Cap'n Crunch with Crunch Berries.

Straker uses a pair of CHOPSTICKS to catch a squirming shrimp, dip it in red sauce, and put it in his mouth. That's when THREE TRIAD KILLERS dressed IN BLACK come into the restaurant. They are each carrying nunchucks and exuding pure menace. KILLER #1 stays at the door while the other two approach Straker. Eve moves as far away as she can get. But Straker continues casually eating his plate of squirming shrimp, paying no attention to the killers. The one at the door speaks in English.

> KILLER #1
> You've disrespected the Wo Li Wo triad for the last time, Straker.

> STRAKER
> I'd like to eat my dinner before it dies. Wait for me outside and you can frighten me when I'm done.

> KILLER #1
> You will die before your meal does.

Lee Goldberg

> STRAKER

You're going to need more men.

> KILLER #1

There are three of us and one of you.

> STRAKER

You're still outnumbered.

Straker flings a dish of HOT SAUCE into the face of KILLER #2, who screams in pain and reaches for his eyes, dropping his nunchuck, which Straker catches. Straker whacks KILLER #2 across the knees with the nunchuck, knocking him to the ground, then sets the weapon on the table. KILLER #3 comes at him, nunchuck flying. Straker ducks and stabs KILLER #3 in the leg with a chopstick. KILLER #3 instinctively grabs for the chopstick, dropping the nunchuck, which Straker catches just as KILLER #2 comes at him again. He whips KILLER #2 in the face with the nunchuck, then whirls around and whips KILLER #3 in the face, too. Straker sets the weapon on the table as both men squirm on the floor. Our hero hasn't moved from his seat or disturbed his plate. He calmly reaches for a fresh set of chopsticks and looks at KILLER #1, who is stunned.

> STRAKER (CONT'D)

Can I finish my dinner now?

> KILLER #1

We'll be back.

> STRAKER

I'll be here, shaking in terror.

Killer #1 walks out. Straker returns to his meal as the two other killers struggle to their feet and stagger out of the place. Eve returns to his side with a fresh bowl of hot sauce. She is TREMBLING. He takes her hand. He speaks to her in Cantonese:

> STRAKER (CONT'D)
> You don't need to be afraid.

She answers in English.

> EVE
> It's not fear.

> STRAKER
> Then what is it?

> EVE
> Desire. I'm yours tonight . . . if you want me.

He smiles.

> STRAKER
> In that case, I won't be needing the dessert menu.

# CHAPTER FIVE

The Oakwood Apartments, Universal City, California. June 25. 11:00 a.m. Pacific Daylight Time.

*What a piece of shit.*

Ian Ludlow set the *Straker* script down on his lap, unable to endure another word, and looked around the pool. Nearly every chaise lounge at the Oakwood Apartments was occupied by someone reading a screenplay just like he'd been doing until only a moment ago.

The people with vaguely recognizable faces were actors, put up in a furnished apartment by one of the nearby movie studios while guest-starring on a TV show or playing a small part in a film. The rest of the good-looking people were aspiring actors, striking poses with their perfect bodies to attract any nearby directors or producers, who were the comparatively unattractive people, the ones with the pale, flabby bodies and roving eyes.

And then there was Ian.

"It can't be that bad," a woman said.

The remark came from a chaise lounge a few feet to Ian's left, where a twentysomething unnatural blonde in a string bikini was pretending to read a script. Her performance would have been more convincing if her script wasn't from a TV series that had been canceled two years ago.

"What can't be?" Ian asked.

"The script you're reading."

"Why do you assume it's bad?"

"The expression on your face," the blonde said. "You look like you just gave a hobbit a hand job. See, you're making that face again."

"You painted a vivid picture," Ian said.

"It's one of the visualization techniques I use to summon my emotions in a scene. Now you know my secrets and can be an actor, too."

"What makes you think that I'm not an actor?"

Ian knew it was the T-shirt and board shorts that he was wearing to hide his never-been-to-a-gym-since-high-school, it's-so-great-that-McDonald's-is-finally-serving-breakfast-all-day, damn-it-the-dry-cleaner-has-shrunk-another-one-of-my-polo-shirts body that gave him away. But he didn't know what else to say. If he were writing this scene instead of living it, he'd have no problem coming up with a witty one-liner.

She smiled. "You strike me as a behind-the-camera type."

"Guilty as charged."

"Are you a director?"

"Nope," he said.

"Producer?"

"Nope."

"Writer?" She said it warily and moved ever so slightly away from him, as if he might be contagious. That was because writers didn't have the power to hire anybody. In fact, writers were interchangeable and frequently discarded. The seven writing credits on the cover page of his *Straker* script were proof of that.

"Yes and no." He pointed to the line on the title page that read *Based on the novel by Ian Ludlow*. "I wrote the book that this script is based on, though they've made some big changes that I'm not wild about."

Now she looked like the one who'd given a hand job to a hobbit. "You're a *writer*?"

"A *New York Times* bestselling author."

"How nice for you," she said, deeply unimpressed. And with that she went back to pretending to read her script.

Ian wasn't surprised. He was used to the rejection. He'd heard that it was impossible for a healthy, single man not to get laid every night while living at the Oakwood. It was a big reason why he'd moved here nearly a year ago while waiting for his Malibu house, blown up in a gas explosion, to be rebuilt. But at least he could take some pride in achieving the impossible.

Ian got up, tucked the script under his arm, and headed back to his apartment to face the blank screen. He had a book to write. Reading the *Straker* script had been a pathetic attempt at procrastination.

He was nearly at his door when he was jolted to a stop by an unexpected sight. There was a homeless woman sitting on his doorstep and leaning against an enormous backpack, the kind that people carried to trek through Yosemite and not the concrete canyons of Los Angeles. It wasn't until the woman looked up at him that he realized it was Margo French.

"You didn't have a chance with that actress," she said.

"You saw that?" Ian asked as he approached her.

"I wish I could unsee it. It was cringe inducing. I'd have better luck with her than you."

"I don't think she's gay."

"You never know. From what I've heard, it's very trendy now for actresses to be 'sexually fluid.'"

Ian stood a few feet away from her so he wouldn't be looking down at her like a judgmental parent. "Did you hike all the way down here from Seattle to find out?"

"I took the bus and hiked from the Greyhound station in North Hollywood."

Ian was shocked by the news. Nobody walks in LA.

"That's ten miles away! You should have called me to pick you up or taken an Uber."

"I don't have your number and I can't afford an Uber," she said. "I spent my last dollar on the bus fare. Are you going to let me in?"

"Yes, of course, come in." Ian held his hand out to her, helped her to her feet, and then unlocked his door, opening it wide so she and her backpack could pass in front of him.

She stepped in and took stock of the place. The only furnishings that weren't bland rental pieces from what could have been called "the American Motel Collection" were two white dry-erase boards, propped up on chairs and covered with handwritten plot points for Ian's next Straker novel. The kitchen table was cluttered with cereal boxes and bags of potato chips.

"Geez, this is depressing," Margo said. "And I say that as someone who is homeless."

"You aren't really homeless."

"Yes, I am. I'm carrying my home on my back," she said, shrugging off her heavy backpack onto the floor.

He stared at the backpack, trying to make sense of what she was saying. "How can that be? The last time I saw you in Seattle, you told me you'd given up being a book escort and dog walker and that you were writing songs and performing."

"I lied. I can't write songs. I can't hold a job."

"Why not?"

She shifted her gaze, looking anywhere but at him. Her gaze fell on the cereal boxes on the table and she began browsing through them like books.

"Because I'm terrified all the time. The fear paralyzes me. Nobody understands what I'm going through and I can't explain it to them. I've used up my savings and lost my apartment." Margo stopped sorting through the boxes and looked at him. "I need a place to live."

"You want to live with me?" he asked, incredulous.

"I've got nowhere else to go."

"How about back to your parents in Walla Walla?"

"They haven't accepted that I'm gay. Do you really expect them to understand I have PTSD from being chased by the assassins who crashed a plane into Waikiki? They'd have me committed."

She had a point, but staying with him wouldn't solve her problems and would only create them for him.

"You need professional help," he said.

"Maybe I do. But who can I talk to who is going to believe my story? You're the only one who knows the truth." She looked right into his eyes this time and he saw her anger. "Because it's all your fault."

"That's not fair. I was a victim. I thought I was helping our country, not domestic terrorists. They tried to kill me, remember? They blew up my house with me in it. If anyone should be crippled with terror, it's me."

"Do you expect me to feel sorry for you? You got another book out of it and a million bucks. What did I get?"

He got a $250,000 advance but he wasn't foolish enough to correct her because she'd made her point. She got nothing. Was a check what she was really after? If so, he'd gladly write her one.

"Do you want money?"

"No, you idiot. I want a place to stay where I can feel safe," she said, and her anger seemed to lose its wind. "At least until I can get my shit together. You're lucky. You had Clint Straker to help you."

"He's a fictional character."

"He might as well have been your shrink. You were able to work out all your anxieties through your writing. You could make it seem like that woman we killed, like the people who tried to kill us, was all make-believe instead of something that happened to us, that scarred us."

"That's true," Ian said, and it wasn't the first time Straker had saved him from emotional pain or anxiety. But he didn't see how Straker could help her. Reading a book wouldn't be as therapeutic as writing one.

"I need to be with someone who understands what I'm feeling," she said. "Unfortunately for both of us, that's you, the least sensitive man on earth."

He'd have to be Straker for her. He knew he'd make a poor substitute.

"Well, when you put it that way, I'd be a schmuck to say no. Make yourself at home."

"Thank you," Margo said, opened a bag of Doritos, and took out a handful of chips. She offered the bag to Ian, and he declined with a wave of his hand. "I've got a question for you and I want an honest answer."

"Okay."

"The last time I saw you, the director of the CIA offered you a job. Did you take it?"

Ian laughed. "Do I look like a spy to you? I'd rather write about action heroes than try to be one. It's much less dangerous."

She gestured with a chip to the script under his arm. "Are you back in the screenwriting business?"

"I didn't write this. Pinnacle Pictures is making a movie out of *Death Benefits*. They're calling it *Straker*. Damon Matthews is the star."

Margo ate a few chips, then said, "He's five feet tall and fifty years old."

"He's five foot five and forty-nine years old."

"But Clint Straker is six feet tall and thirty. Matthews is totally wrong for the part."

"Damon is the number one box office action star on earth," Ian said. "That makes him totally right for it."

"*Damon?* You're on a first-name basis with him now?"

"We've never met. I'll be meeting him for the first time next week in Hong Kong, where they're shooting the movie."

"But the book is set in Texas," she said. "A drug cartel takes over a Texas border town and Straker goes in and saves them like a one-man *Magnificent Seven.*

He was flattered that she'd read it. "Most of the financing for the movie is coming from China so they've moved a third of the action there and cast a Chinese actress as the romantic lead. So now Straker is taking on a triad that's holding a Hong Kong neighborhood in a grip of terror."

Margo ate some more chips. "A movie crafted to fit a financial deal rather than tell a good story doesn't sound like a recipe for success to me."

"It's not," Ian said. "The script is horrible."

"Then why are you going there?"

"My publisher is sending me first-class to Hong Kong just to shoot some publicity shots of me with Matthews on the set. It will help sell books when the movie comes out and to capitalize on all that publicity, I'm setting my next Straker novel in Hong Kong. I'm going to use the trip, on their dime, to research my plot." He pointed to the dry-erase boards covered with his scrawl.

"Smart move," she said.

"Come to think of it, you picked the right time to show up."

"I did?"

"You can house-sit while I'm away," Ian said.

"Hell no," she said, wiping her hands on her jeans. "I'm going with you."

"Hell no, you're not. You said you needed a place to live. Now you have it."

"I can't stay here alone," she said.

"You'll be fine."

"You didn't listen to a word I said. I can't be alone." She took a deep breath and looked away from him for a moment. When she looked back, there were tears in her eyes. "I need you, someone I trust who knows what I went through, more than I need a roof over my head. You have no idea how hard it is for me to say that."

Actually, he did, and in that moment, he felt enormous affection for her. He had the sudden desire to hug her and tell her everything would be all right. But he fought the urge. He was afraid she might knee him in the groin if he attempted it.

She wiped her tears away, studied the dry-erase boards for a moment, then looked back at Ian. "I can help you. Talk me through your plot and I'll do the research. I'll find the locations and the experts you need to meet to make your story work. That way, when you aren't doing your PR shit, you won't waste any time figuring out where to go or what to do. I'll have done it for you."

He liked that idea a lot. The one thing he really missed from his TV days, besides the free lunches, was having an assistant to do his research and manage his schedule so he could be free to write. He'd thought about hiring one when he became a writer but he didn't want a stranger in his house and he didn't think he'd have enough work for an assistant to do. But in this situation, it made perfect sense. And maybe by the time they got back to LA, she'd be cured and would go straight back to Seattle.

"You have a deal," he said.

# CHAPTER SIX

**The White House, Washington, DC. June 26. 1:30 p.m.
Eastern Daylight Time.**

The president of the United States was enduring his weekly lunch in his private dining room with Vice President Willard Penny, who had just returned with food poisoning from a "friendship tour" of South America.

Penny nursed a 7-Up while the president dined on salmon that he'd caught himself fly-fishing in Missouri over the weekend. Seeing his vice president slurping his 7-Up reminded the president of their months together on the campaign trail and how Penny guzzled Diet Coke all day long. The carbonated soft drink made Penny so flatulent that they lived under the constant danger that he'd release a monster fart on stage, a nightmare that came true during the vice-presidential debates and nearly sank their campaign.

The president had sent Penny on the friendship tour of South America to meet with leaders from government and the business community "to reaffirm the president's commitment to deepening bilateral trade and investment ties with the region and continue the administration's support of security cooperation, business engagement, agriculture, and infrastructure development." The truth was the president wanted the pompous gasbag as far away from him as possible. But now the president needed the VP back in DC to cast a tie-breaking vote on an appropriations bill and, in two weeks, to be the warm body in succession while he went to Paris to attend the G8 summit.

"I'm sorry the food on your trip didn't agree with you," the president said.

"Neither did most of the leaders I met with after your incendiary tweets," the vice president said.

These private lunches were intended for candid conversation but the truth was the president didn't appreciate the candor. Penny made no secret of his disapproval of the president communicating to his base in blunt 280-character statements that often contradicted positions made by his vice president, his secretary of state, and other cabinet members.

"All I said was that too many South American countries are run by corrupt, power-hungry, cokehead politicians controlled by their drug cartel puppet masters, which is true. I didn't say they were all corrupt."

"You didn't say they weren't, either."

"They know who they are," the president said.

The president hated Penny's weakness and kowtowing to the political elite, here and abroad. He'd chosen Penny, the double-chinned former governor of Ohio who was ten years his senior, as his older and far less photogenic running mate to shore up party support and gain a wingman who could kiss Senate ass, something the president sure as hell wouldn't do.

The president had never held public office before winning the White House and both political parties viewed him as a threat to their way of life. He didn't get to the Oval Office, or create a financial services empire that made him the tenth richest person in the world at age fifty, by caring what anybody thought of him, least of all politicians.

"Speaking of geopolitical issues," Penny said, stifling a burp, "Senator Tolan's sudden death gives us an opportunity to reassess his foreign investment in the US legislation and its broader impact."

"Why would I want to do that?"

"Because with tensions ratcheting up in Asia, and with our own economy still on shaky feet, we need China as a political and economic partner for both our regional and domestic interests right now."

The only thing that Penny liked better than kissing Senate ass, the president thought, was kissing Chinese ass. Penny and Chinese president Xiao Guangchang were old buddies, going back twenty years when Xiao, then a lowly Chinese agricultural minister, came to Ohio to study farming and stayed with Penny, who was a state legislator at the time. Penny had visited Xiao in China often since then and never missed an opportunity to boast about his special relationship with Xiao, the third most powerful man on earth after Russia's leader.

"That was the attitude of the last four administrations and look what's happened," the president said. "The Chinese built military islands to take the South China Sea, they smuggled nuclear materials into North Korea, and now they're on a shopping spree buying up American companies. The next thing you know, they'll own McDonald's and turn it into Panda Express."

Penny flashed an unusually smug grin, downed his 7-Up, and set the empty glass on the table. "The fact is, with Tolan dead and without his influence in the Senate, there's nobody to champion his bill and the bipartisan votes aren't there for it, either. The ill-considered and dangerous protectionist movement he was trying to start in the Senate died with him."

"But there are empty seats on the Committee on Foreign Investment in the United States that I can fill with departmental appointees who will take a tougher line on China," the president said. "They'll find a reason to reject every Chinese acquisition, even if what they want to buy is a fortune cookie factory."

Penny gave him a cold stare. "That would be seen by the Chinese as a direct provocation."

"You mean a big fuck you," the president said, looking Penny in the eye. "And that's exactly what it is. Fuck them all."

"You're playing a dangerous game that you can't win. The Chinese own most of our multitrillion-dollar government debt. That's a marker you don't want them calling in."

"Your buddy Xiao does that and I'll slap a two-hundred percent tariff on every product coming into the US from China. But Xiao won't do that. You know why? Because he'd have to take on Europe, too."

"The EU isn't tightening rules on Chinese acquisitions or investment."

"They will be. The EU is going to back my play and prevent China from buying companies over there that do business in the US."

"Why would Europe do that?"

"So we'll keep defending them from the Russians."

"You'd pull out of NATO over this?" Penny asked, incredulous.

"No, but we might pack up most of our toys that we have over there and we might be slow to answer the phone, too, if they call for help," the president said. "That's what I'm going to tell the European heads of state at the G8 summit in Paris."

"You'll not only antagonize China but you'll enrage our European allies, too," Penny said. "I would strongly advise against that."

The president leaned across the table and pointed his fork at the vice president.

"I would strongly advise you to start thinking about your friendship tour to Africa."

The president was pretty sure Penny released a silent fart. He was tempted to order the Secret Service to arrest the vice president for trying to kill him with poison gas.

The vice president stood up. "Pretty soon, you're going to run out of continents to banish me to."

"Then we'll just have to start looking at islands, won't we?" The president grinned. "Seems to me that we've been neglecting Madagascar's strategic importance for way too long."

# CHAPTER SEVEN

The Oakwood Apartments, Universal City, California. June 26. 11:00 a.m. Pacific Daylight Time.

Ian stood in front of the dry-erase board, walking Margo through the plot of his new novel, what little there was of it. Margo sat on the couch, her bare feet resting on the *Straker* script on the coffee table.

"The basic premise of my novel is this," Ian said. "China is invading the United States with cash, not soldiers. They are buying key companies across our economy. Hotel chains, movie studios, drug companies, carmakers, agricultural seed companies, you name it."

"The economy is boring." Margo yawned to underscore her remark. "I thought you wrote thrillers. There's nothing thrilling about mergers and acquisitions."

"You have to look deeper." Ian pointed to a newspaper clipping, one of many taped to the dry-erase board. "For example, the Chinese own the second largest hotel chain on earth. They are bugging the rooms, acquiring every guest's credit card data, and infecting all their guests' computers with Trojan horses every time they connect to free internet. I bet you didn't know that."

"No, I didn't, because it's bullshit."

"There's more. Almost all of our electronics are being manufactured in China—iPhones, TVs, laptop computers—because the labor is so irresistibly cheap. But we're actually paying a very high price. All of those devices are being secretly hardwired to watch us and track our every move."

"Give me a break," she said. "You sound like Ronnie spouting his paranoid conspiracy theories."

She was referring to actor Ronnie Mancuso, the star of *Hollywood & the Vine*, who had fled Los Angeles to live as a survivalist in a remote corner of the Nevada desert, waiting for the end of the world, when Ian and Margo ran to him for help while they were being pursued by assassins. Ian had figured that Ronnie could teach them how to live off the grid and become invisible to their high-tech pursuers. Without Ronnie, Ian and Margo would never have survived their ordeal or beaten their adversary. Now, recently released from a mental institution, Ronnie was starring in a revival of *Hollywood & the Vine*.

"You're forgetting that Ronnie was right," Ian said.

"You're forgetting that he's certifiably nuts."

"The Chinese are trying to hack our minds, too."

"Of course they are." Margo sighed and massaged her brow. "Are you going to start wearing aluminum foil around your head like Ronnie to block their voices?"

"The Chinese are using a different approach to get into our heads. They're buying movie studios to spread their propaganda through films."

"Like your Straker movie?"

"Probably," Ian said.

Margo lifted her feet, picked up the script, and offered it to Ian. "Show me."

"It won't be on the page. It will be subliminal, embedded in every pixel."

Margo tossed the script back on the table. "I hope to God that you don't actually believe all this bullshit."

"I don't have to. I just have to make the reader believe that it's possible. It's what we call the willing suspension of disbelief."

"Okay, that's all dandy. What I'm not hearing is a story. What's Straker doing?"

"You've heard in the news about all those Hong Kong businessmen who have been kidnapped by Chinese authorities and taken back to Beijing?"

"Yeah. What's with that?"

"I don't know. But what if one of them is an old buddy of Straker's? So Straker goes to Hong Kong to investigate the disappearance and uncovers the invasion conspiracy. Now only one man—Clint Straker—stands between China and the hostile takeover of our nation. That's the story."

Margo leaned back on the couch and thought about it for a moment. "That's a nice logline for a book jacket, but what's the businessman's relationship to the conspiracy? More importantly, what's the ticking clock? Why is the takeover coming to a head now? And how does Straker stop it?"

"Those are very good questions and I don't have answers for any of them," Ian said. "I hope to come up with them in Hong Kong."

"In other words, you have nothing."

"I always start with nothing," Ian said, taking a seat next to her on the couch. "That's what makes my job so terrifying."

"No, that's what makes your job *hard*," she said. "What makes it *terrifying* is when someone takes your story, turns it into reality, and tries to kill you to cover it up."

"True," Ian said. "But how often can that happen?"

# CHAPTER EIGHT

Iskenderun, Turkey. June 27. 10:45 p.m. Turkey Time.

The Chinese man who'd called himself Fung in Hong Kong was now Simon Chen. He sat alone in a tiny bar at the corner of Yavuz Sultan Selim and Kanatli Caddesi in central Iskenderun, an industrial eastern Mediterranean port city in the Hatay Province of southern Turkey. The bar had the ambiance of a Chevron station mini-mart and the odor of someone deep-frying fish in a men's locker room.

Iskenderun had been around since 330 BCE. It was established by Alexander the Great, after his victory over the Persians on the Plain of Issus, as a place to work on his tan and eat oranges. Perhaps Iskenderun was nice then, but now it was street after street of square, featureless concrete storage units for human beings. The buildings resembled prison blocks with neon-lit, street-level storefronts. What the city had then and still had now was strategic significance. It was thirty-two miles from the Syrian border and was the nearest port to Aleppo, a mere sixty-one miles away.

As a result of the city's proximity to a country ravaged by a devastating war, the bar was teeming with smugglers, terrorists, refugees, and mercenaries all nursing what looked like glasses of milk—actually raki, licorice-flavored alcohol that turned milky white when mixed with cold water—and eating meze, sarma (rice-stuffed vegetables), and sliced melon with their dirty, calloused fingers while doing business with either the Syrians or the rebels or the refugees. There was blood-soaked money to be made here.

Chen was dressed in a loose-fitting white shirt, tan linen jacket and slacks, and leather penny loafers, the outfit of a cocky but stupid businessman who'd wandered into the wrong bar. He sat at a table with an untouched glass of raki, bought to rent his seat while he waited for his contact to arrive. There was a briefcase on the floor beside his feet. Many men cast glances at the briefcase and thought about taking it from him. He could see their intentions in their shifty eyes, the twitch of their cheeks, and the nervous tapping of their feet. But these were violent men, and despite his clothes, they knew a killer when they saw one. He had the gaze of a man who saw death everywhere he looked. No one bothered him.

A small, dented panel van pulled up outside and Batu, his Turkish contact with the Syrian rebels, was at the wheel. It had taken months of working with the bony, skull-faced little man to get to this moment. Batu had no allegiance to anything but money and was getting a fee from both parties for arranging the deal. But Chen expected the Turk would try to rip him off at some point in the transaction.

Chen picked up his briefcase, walked outside, and got into the passenger seat of the van. He could feel every spring in the seat cushion. Batu smiled, showing off a mouth of missing teeth, his gums so rotted that it was nearly impossible for a tooth to stay rooted in place. His breath smelled like a corpse left too long in water.

"This is the big night," Batu said in English.

"Tomorrow you can buy yourself a mouthful of gold teeth," Chen said.

Batu laughed, nearly spitting one of his remaining teeth at Chen, put the van into gear, and pulled away from the curb. They headed north, then took the palm-lined Cengiz Topel Caddesi southwest along the waterfront until they left the city behind and reached a dead end. But they kept going, through a rotting cyclone fence and into a weedy lot dominated by an abandoned, half-completed five-story building, the cinder block and rebar ruins of a condo development project that ran out of money years ago.

Batu steered the van into the center of the ruins, where four Syrians, each wearing sweat-stained khakis and armed with automatic weapons, stood in front of four wooden crates that resembled coffins and a large van that was used to deliver the cargo. The space was lit by the head-lamps of their two vans and a bright moon.

Chen got out and approached the leader, Tarek, a rebel who was lucky to be alive since his strong body odor surely made his presence on the battlefield known to the enemy from a hundred yards away, two hundred yards if they were downwind. Batu remained inside the van so he could make a quick getaway if things went bad.

"Do you have the money?" Tarek asked in English.

"Show me what I'm buying," Chen replied.

Tarek nodded to his men, who used a crowbar to open the crates, while he kept his weapon loosely aimed at Chen. The men brushed aside a layer of straw and removed several rows of raki bottles to reveal the component parts of a portable antitank missile system.

"A Russian-made 9K135 Kornet-EM antitank guided missile launcher, compact and easy to assemble," Tarek said like *The Price Is Right* announcer describing the final showcase. "Used by Syrian rebels against the corrupt Assad regime and smuggled out of Aleppo before the city fell. Note the original Russian markings."

It worried Chen that Tarek thought the markings added value for him. Chen crouched down and examined the missile system, which was comprised of three basic parts: the missiles, the tripod launcher, and the sighting system. He checked the launch tube, about the length of a bag of golf clubs, to make sure it wasn't bent and that the wires weren't corroded. It was good. He wasn't worried about the sighting system. He intended to upgrade and retrofit it anyway.

"It's easy to carry, fast to assemble, and can be freestanding or mounted on any vehicle or boat. Two people can carry the whole thing." Tarek continued his sales pitch while Chen examined the goods. "It fires a thermal-sighted, laser-guided missile tipped with a high-explosive warhead and has a range of five miles."

Chen moved to the next crate and examined the two missiles—each about four feet long, a half foot in diameter, and weighing seventy pounds—for bulging and sweating, both big problems with aging ordnance left in the desert heat. A bulge meant the explosives inside the missiles had expanded and moisture was a sign that they were breaking down into a liquid as unstable as nitroglycerin. These missiles were sweating more than Tarek and his men.

"It's an excellent weapon," Tarek said. "Bargain priced at thirty thousand American dollars."

Chen stood up. "No deal."

"We were told you were a serious buyer," Tarek said, his voice edged with anger. "We brought this to you at great personal risk."

"You certainly did." Chen got into Tarek's face, nearly nose to nose. Tarek's men tensed up but the Syrian held them back with a raised hand. "One bump in the road with this shit and you could have blown yourself up. You would have deserved it, too, for trying to rip me off. What kind of asshole do you think I am?"

Tarek smiled and shrugged. "Obviously a more discerning and knowledgeable one than I am used to dealing with."

Chen smiled, too, dissipating the tension. "You must not get many repeat customers."

Tarek laughed and waved at two of his men. "Bring my new friend the other crates."

The two men set down their rifles, went to the back of the van, and pulled out two more crates. They set them down in front of Chen and

Tarek, opened them with crowbars, and revealed four more missiles. Chen examined them. No bulges, no sweat.

"That's more like it," Chen said, rising to his feet.

"Do we have a deal now?" Tarek said.

"We do." Chen went to Tarek's van, placed the briefcase on the hood, and opened it up.

Tarek picked up a random stack, flipped through the bills, and then placed it back in the briefcase, closed the lid, and snapped it shut.

"Seal the crates and load them into this gentleman's van," Tarek ordered his men, who did as they were told. "See, I do like some repeat customers."

"You didn't like me so much a few minutes ago."

"I've never had a Chinese customer before. I didn't know what to make of you," Tarek said. "Now I do. I will remember you."

Chen didn't like being memorable. He gestured to the briefcase. "Don't blow that all at once."

# CHAPTER NINE

Batu drove quickly away from the half-completed building, glancing repeatedly into the rearview mirror as if he expected Tarek to come after them.

"I told you I'd come through for you," Batu said.

"You did."

"You didn't trust me."

"I don't trust anyone," Chen said.

"When do I get my cut?"

"Soon."

The word was barely out of Chen's mouth when the building behind them exploded, rocking the roadway and startling Batu, who swerved wildly in surprise. He would have steered them right into the sea if Chen hadn't grabbed the wheel.

Batu came to a hard stop and looked over his shoulder just as a massive fireball rose up into the night sky and the building collapsed.

"What happened?" Batu asked.

It was a much bigger explosion than it should have been. That's because when Chen rigged the briefcase with a modest explosive, he hadn't anticipated that there would be two crates of rotting missiles in Tarek's van. If he'd known, Chen could have used a firecracker instead and achieved pretty much the same result.

"Tarek must have opened the briefcase for one more look at the cash before he drove off," Chen said. "I told him not to blow it all at once."

"You put a bomb in the briefcase?" Batu turned and stared at Chen in disbelief. "Why would you burn thirty thousand dollars?"

"It was toilet paper, counterfeit cash from North Korea," Chen said. "It's their most popular global export."

Batu narrowed his eyes at Chen. "My cut had better be real."

"It is." Chen stabbed him in the liver, severing his hepatic artery, and twisted the blade, holding it in place. "Feel it?"

Batu was in too much pain to speak. Chen reached across Batu with his free hand, opened the door, and pushed him out onto the roadway, removing the knife from his body as he fell and leaving him on the crumbling asphalt to bleed out.

Chen tossed the knife on the street, slid into the driver's seat, and closed the door. He put the van into gear and leisurely drove up the coast, passing several speeding fire trucks and police cars going in the opposite direction. He passed the waterfront plaza where a statue of Mustafa Kemal Atatürk, Turkey's first president, stood pointing his finger up at the sky, presumably at a future of freedom and liberty, but Chen thought it was more likely at the seagulls who'd been crapping on him for years. A short distance past the plaza, Chen made a left turn toward the man-made harbor, where dozens of fishing boats, a few small sailboats, and a handful of yachts were tied up along the breakwater that served as the dock.

The breakwater also doubled as a road and parking lot where the boats could load or off-load their cargo. Chen parked his van in front of a sleek eighty-foot designer yacht with a cantilevered flybridge over the aft deck and wraparound windows along the pointed, forward-leaning bow that made it look more like a starship than a boat. He got out and was greeted by a sea-tanned middle-aged Italian couple who sat at a teak table on the rear deck, enjoying cocktails, a white-uniformed crew member standing nearby, ready to attend to their needs. The couple appeared to be wealthy, retired tourists but they were actually Corsican smugglers that Chen had met through his triad contacts.

"Did you see the fireworks?" Lucio asked, nodding toward the south. He was dressed in a white shirt, a blue blazer with an elaborate nautical insignia of some sort on the breast pocket, and a captain's hat with an embroidered golden anchor on the front. It was a yachting outfit that bordered on cartoonish.

"No," Chen said. "Is tonight a special occasion?"

"Only if funerals count," Fina said, tapping one of her glossy-red talonlike nails on the rim of her Stefano Ricci stone bur–engraved crystal champagne flute. Her body was also engraved, her breasts and physique surgically sculpted to resemble someone twenty-five years younger. She was also dressed in a nautical theme in a white turtleneck, navy-blue peacoat, and white capri pants. "It was an explosion. Someone almost always dies when there's one."

"At least in our experience," Lucio said.

Chen knew Lucio and Fina had plenty of experience with violence. They'd planted their share of car bombs and had been known to dismember rivals with an antique two-handed blubber-mincing knife used in whaling.

"I have your crates of raki," Chen said.

"We'll bring them on board." Lucio snapped his fingers at the nearby crew member, who disappeared into the cabin.

"And we'll try not to drink it all before we get to Marseille." Fina winked so hard she nearly broke an eyelid.

"I'll see you there in five days," Chen said.

Six crew members got off the yacht, went to the back of Chen's van, unloaded the crates, and carried them on board. He watched them while they worked.

"Are you sure you don't want to come with us?" Lucio asked. "It's a wonderful trip."

"I wish I could, but I have more business to do." Chen reached into his coat, pulled out an envelope stuffed with euros, and tossed it to Lucio, who caught it and slipped it into his jacket. This time the cash was real. Lucio was a professional who wouldn't be fooled by North Korean counterfeits, certainly not with five days to examine the bills. "You'll get the second half on delivery."

"Of course," Lucio said. "I hope the rest of your business goes well."

Fina pointed one of her talons to Chen's right. "Coca-Cola is great for getting blood out of linen."

He'd used his right hand to stab Batu. Chen glanced down and saw a tiny fleck of blood on his right sleeve. Fina had owl eyes to go with her talons.

"I'll keep that in mind," Chen said. "Have a safe trip."

Chen got into his van and drove off, heading north to a secluded, dark stretch of waterfront roadway. There were no other cars around and no homes or buildings nearby. He lowered his window, floored the gas pedal going into a curve, and headed for the railing. The van burst through the barrier, went airborne, then landed in the ocean. He'd achieved exactly the loft and distance he'd hoped for.

He calmly unbuckled his seat belt, removed his coat and shirt, and kicked off his shoes, while freezing water poured into the van. The cold, rising water didn't bother him—he found it invigorating after all the boring business of the evening—but the total darkness unnerved him. The blackness was all-consuming, an icy, physical force. It was as close to death as he could get without actually being dead. He took a deep breath from the tiny air pocket that remained and, once the van was completely submerged, he opened the driver's side door, then swam up to the surface and onward to the shore.

Chen emerged from the water in a tiny inlet and strode to a gravel lot, where he'd parked an old car earlier that day. He found the key he'd hidden under a rock and unlocked the car's trunk, where he'd stowed a carry-on suitcase that contained a towel, clean clothes, a passport, a wallet, and a burner phone. He stripped and dried off, got dressed, and drove to the Hatay Airport to catch his flight to Paris.

# CHAPTER TEN

Boeing 777-300, somewhere over the Pacific. July 1.

Ian reclined in his first-class seat, crossed his outstretched legs on the leather ottoman, ate another artisan cracker slathered with Venetian caviar, and washed it down with a sip of Krug Grande Cuvée. This little cubicle, with its teakwood accents, fresh orchids, fifteen-inch TV, and wardrobe closet instead of an overhead bin, was far more elegant than his Oakwood apartment, which he'd been sharing for the last week with Margo French.

He'd been worried about having her as a houseguest and getting pulled into her troubled life. But that didn't really happen. Instead, she'd thrown herself into putting together his Hong Kong research itinerary. And, to his surprise, he liked having her around. He didn't realize how lonely he was until she showed up on his doorstep.

So now, comfy in his airline-provided cotton pajamas and slippers, he felt a little guilty about being in first class for the sixteen-hour flight while she was stuck in premium economy. It wasn't by choice. The movie studio had paid for his ticket long before she showed up on his doorstep. He'd bought Margo's ticket out of his own pocket and he certainly wasn't going to spend $10,000 on a first-class seat or half that for business class. The prices were insane. He got her the seat he would have bought for himself if he'd been paying for his flight.

But he still felt like he owed her something to make up for the glaring difference in their travel experience. So when the ravishingly beautiful Chinese flight attendant came by to transform his seat and ottoman into a seven-foot-long bed, Ian took the remaining caviar, his bread basket, and a glass of champagne back to Margo in the premium economy section.

He found Margo in the second seat of a four-seat row, a woman breastfeeding a baby to her right and on her left a snoring, overweight man spilled over the confines of his armrests into her space. The seat in front of Margo was reclined so far back that the passenger's head was practically in her lap. But Margo was oblivious to it all. Her eyes were covered with a sleeping mask, her ears were stuffed with neon-yellow earplugs, and he was pleased to see that she was asleep.

Ian remembered her first night at his apartment, when she woke up screaming with night terrors. He ran out of his bedroom and held her on the couch until she stopped shaking, her face nuzzled against his neck.

"If I was writing this," he said, stroking her hair, "this is where we'd make love to soothe your fears."

Margo sniffled. "I'm a lesbian with a nose full of snot."

"If I was writing this, that wouldn't make a difference."

"Are you so horny that you'd make a move on a lesbian suffering a severe emotional and psychological meltdown?"

"Well, when you put it like that, it sounds sleazy," he said. "If I was writing this, I'd say our incendiary passion burned away the barriers between us until all that was left was a shared need that was primal and true."

"Yuck," she said.

He'd kept holding her until she fell asleep and then he slipped back to his bedroom. Now it occurred to him that maybe all she'd needed to sleep was a lot of noise and discomfort to distract her from her inner turmoil.

Ian reached across the overweight man and opened the table on the seatback in front of her. He set the caviar, bread basket, and glass of champagne on the table and then he went back to his first-class cabin. He hoped that the stewardess would be waiting naked in his bed for something primal and true.

If he were writing this, she would be.

The Chinese liked to expand their islands, or create entirely new ones, by shearing off the tops of mountains and dumping the soil into the sea. That's how they joined Chek Lap Kok and Lam Chau, two small islands twenty miles outside of Hong Kong, into one and then built a vast international airport on the new, flat land in between them.

The Boeing 777-300 banked over the sheared hilltops of the two islands and landed at the airport in the early evening. Ian watched the landing from his window and also on his TV screen, which showed him the views from the forward-facing cameras mounted on the nose and high tail of the aircraft.

Since Ian was in first class, he was also first off the plane when it landed. He could have sailed through the VIP lane at Chinese customs and been halfway to Hong Kong while Margo was still waiting in line to get her passport stamped.

Instead, he graciously waited for her in the terminal right outside of the jet bridge. She shuffled out with dark circles under her eyes, messy hair, wrinkled clothes, and sticky skin. Unlike Ian, she hadn't been given pajamas.

"You look rested," Ian said.

"You mean dead," she said. "Thank you for bringing me the champagne, caviar, and bread. It was a nice surprise to wake up to."

"You're welcome," he said and led her down the long hallway to customs. It was always a long hallway, he thought, no matter where in the world he went.

"Did giving me your table scraps relieve any of the crushing guilt you felt for sticking me in the cattle car with a canvas blanket," she said, "while you relaxed in a bed with fifteen-hundred-thread-count embroidered Egyptian sheets?"

"They were only five hundred threads and I told you before, I had no choice. The studio was required to buy me a first-class ticket. It's Writers Guild of America rules. It was a nonrefundable ticket or I would have cashed it in for two business-class seats. My hands were tied."

"With velvet handcuffs," she said. "You could have bought me a first-class ticket."

"You're lucky I bought you a ticket at all. You're getting a free trip to Hong Kong," Ian said. "Besides, what are you complaining about? You slept well for the first time in months."

"I have one word for you," Margo said. "Ambien."

"Why didn't you take that before to stop your night terrors?" Ian said. "You could have slept through them and stopped your life in Seattle from imploding."

"Because I didn't think that becoming addicted to sleeping pills was a practical solution to my problem."

"How do you know until you try?"

"Asshole," she said.

Ian smiled to himself. Giving her a hard time was fun. He brought her with him through the VIP line at Chinese customs without a problem and his suitcases, and her backpack, were waiting for them on the luggage carousel when they got past the checkpoint.

They put their things on a luggage cart and wheeled it out into the terminal, where they were greeted at the door by a young Chinese woman holding up an iPad with Ian's name on the screen.

The woman wore a black pantsuit with a white blouse, her incredibly red, glossy lips standing out like candy apples. She was nearly bursting with pent-up enthusiasm as they approached. If she'd been a puppy, her tail would have been wagging furiously and she'd have jumped all over them, covering them with licks. Ian was afraid she still might do it.

"Welcome to Hong Kong, Mr. Ludlow. I'm Susie Yip," she said excitedly, holding out her hand and bouncing on her feet. "It is such a pleasure to meet you."

Susie spoke with a perfect, proper British accent and Ian was instantly infatuated with her.

He shook her hand. "Call me Ian and the pleasure is all mine."

Margo groaned with annoyance and offered Susie her hand, too. "I'm Margo French, Ian's researcher and conscience. He apologizes for leering."

The remark seemed to fly over Susie's head or she didn't hear it as she took their cart and led them to the terminal exit. "I'm a publicist with your UK and Australian publisher. We also publish your book in Hong Kong. I'll be coordinating your photo shoot and seeing to all of your needs."

"I'm very needy," Ian said.

Margo swatted Ian's arm. "Stop it."

They stepped outside. It was like walking into a heavy towel soaked in boiling water. Ian broke out in an instant sweat but was distracted from his discomfort when he saw the green Rolls-Royce limousine parked at the curb in front of them and the uniformed, white-gloved driver who stood beside it. He wouldn't be sweating for long.

"Impressive," Ian said, admiring the car as he approached it.

"The Peninsula Hotel has a fleet of fourteen Rolls-Royce Phantoms," Susie said. "All of them in their trademark Brewster Green."

"They know how to treat their guests." Ian decided he could get used to being on a studio expense account. He'd never been in a Rolls-Royce before and, after this ride, it would probably make his C-Class

Mercedes feel like a Ford Fiesta every time he got inside. But it was a risk he was willing to take. He stepped up to the back door of the Rolls and glanced at the chauffeur to open it for him.

That's when Ian saw Susie holding open the back door of a red-and-white Toyota taxi that was idling at the curb in front of the Rolls. *That* was their ride.

Ian flushed with embarrassment, but he was confident it would be mistaken for a reaction to the oppressively humid heat. He peeked in the window of the Rolls and smiled at the chauffeur.

"A fine automobile," Ian said. "I always like to take a moment to admire exceptional craftsmanship when I see it."

He nodded approvingly once more at the Rolls, then walked over to Margo, who said, "Someone got spoiled on the flight."

"I was examining the car for research purposes. I knew we weren't staying at the Peninsula."

"Of course you did," Margo said.

They got into the taxi with Susie, who sat up front for the forty-five-minute ride on the freeway and over several bridges into Kowloon, where the movie studio and their hotel were located.

"Damon Matthews and the director, P. J. Tyler, got here a couple of days ago," Susie said. "But the second-unit crew has actually been in Kowloon for the last two weeks shooting portions of the big chase sequence with stunt drivers."

"So now that the actors are here," Ian said, "the director will shoot pieces of the chase with the stars to cut into the second-unit footage."

"That's scheduled for later this week," she said. "Hair and makeup tests, costume fittings, and the table read of the script with the cast are tomorrow. Principal photography begins the following day at the Big Wheel."

"The Big Wheel?" Ian asked.

Margo spoke up. "That's the Ferris wheel on the Hong Kong waterfront overlooking Victoria Harbor and Kowloon. It's on my list of sites to see for your research."

"It's a great location for the movie," Susie said. "That's also where we'll be doing your photo shoot with Damon."

"Will they give Damon a box to stand on," Margo asked, "or will Ian have to crouch?"

Susie looked over her shoulder and smiled at Margo. "You're a troublemaker. I'm going to have to keep an eye on you."

# CHAPTER ELEVEN

The red-and-white Toyota taxi that brought Ian and Margo into Kowloon was one of thousands just like it that clogged the narrow, congested streets. It seemed to Ian that everything in Kowloon was crowded together and fighting for room—the buildings, the cars, the people. Even the airspace above the streets was a battleground, crammed with neon signs that reached out over the roadway from the stores and restaurants on either side. The blazing signs overhead, with their red, orange, and yellow Chinese symbols, lit up the night with a sordid glow that was as bright as day.

Ian rolled down his window to see what the atmosphere was like outside. The hot, humid air poured in, thick and heavy, reeking of exhaust fumes, fried food, raw fish, and flowery perfume, blaring with the cacophony of car horns, music, and Chinese chatter, and crackling with the friction of all the activity on the teeming streets. It was too much for him. He began rolling up the window but it was a grind, the old gears struggling to push the pane of filthy glass through the sticky air.

"I like it here already." Margo stared out her window in wide-eyed wonderment. "It makes Manhattan seem dull and quiet by comparison."

She liked it, Ian thought, for the same reason she was able to sleep on the plane and not at home. It was hard to hear your demons when all of your senses were being bombarded. He thought that he might like Hong Kong's energy, too, once he'd conquered his jet lag. When his internal clock was out of whack, everything felt surreal even when he wasn't in a strange new place.

The taxi pulled up outside of the Nine Dragons hotel, a blue-tinted glass tower on the Victoria Harbor waterfront. Susie took Ian and Margo into the lobby, which had a high, vaulted ceiling with a waterfall that spilled smooth and clear down a four-story wall like an undulating sheet of glass.

"I already have your keys," Susie said. "I'll show you to your rooms."

She led them to a bank of elevators that whisked them up to the thirtieth floor in seconds and then they followed her to Ian's suite. The instant his door opened the lights came on, the stereo system played something bold and orchestral, and the window curtains parted automatically like the opening of a show. And that's exactly what it was. The windows presented a spectacular view across Victoria Harbor to Hong Kong's dense forest of skyscrapers, each one displaying its own elaborate, animated light show.

Ian was so distracted by the dramatic view that he didn't notice anything else about the room until Susie spoke up.

"I've left a shooting schedule and the new draft of the script on the bar," she said. "That way you'll be completely up to speed when you get to the studio tomorrow."

Ian turned and saw his room had a fully stocked wet bar with four stools, a living room with a leather couch, a matching easy chair, a writing desk, and a flat-screen TV. Sliding doors separated the living room from the bedroom, where he could see a king-size bed. He was tempted to finagle a way to stay here for the entire shoot rather than go back to his bleak Oakwood apartment.

His gaze drifted back to the script with dread. Every time a change was made in a final shooting script, the new pages were printed on colored paper, each color representing a new draft, starting with blue and then on through pink, yellow, green, goldenrod, buff, salmon, and cherry, with the release date noted on the title page and the header of every page. If there were more revisions after that, the cycle of colors started over with second white, second blue, and so on. This draft was entirely yellow. The script he'd brought with him in his bag was the second cherry draft. That made this one the third yellow and the twenty-third complete rewrite.

"This is an amazing view," Margo said, standing in front of the window. "I'm not sure I'd ever leave my room if I had this to look at."

"You do," Susie said. "Your room is right next door."

"Really?" Margo smiled at Ian. "I thought for sure I'd be on the second floor with an unobstructed view of the trash dumpsters."

"You can thank the studio," Ian said. "They have a block of rooms set aside just for the *Straker* cast and crew."

"I want to see it," Margo said, turning to Susie. "Can you show me?"

"I'd be glad to." Susie glanced at Ian. "I'll pick you up in the lobby at nine a.m. and take you to the studio."

"I'm looking forward to it," Ian said.

The two women left. Ian ordered a selection of dim sum from room service, moved the easy chair in front of the window, and sat down to enjoy the show.

# CHAPTER TWELVE

An excerpt from the third yellow draft of *Straker*.

EXT. KOWLOON — NIGHT

One of those ubiquitous RED & WHITE HONG KONG TAXIS moves north on Lai Chi Kok Road, a major thoroughfare divided by a low K-RAIL that is only interrupted at intersections. [Production note: Vehicles are left-side drive in Hong Kong, so you might be a bit disoriented, no pun intended, following the driving action that's coming . . .]

INT. TAXI — NIGHT

Eve is in the back seat . . . lost in thought . . . oblivious to:

EXT. LAI CHI KOK ROAD — NIGHT

The four MOTORCYCLE-RIDING ASSASSINS clad in ALL BLACK, from helmet to toe, who are charging up behind her car. ASSASSIN #1 roars up alongside her taxi.

INT. TAXI — NIGHT

Eve turns to look and ASSASSIN #1 pulls out a GUN and aims it at her. At the same instant he's about to shoot, A CAR cuts off the taxi. The TAXI DRIVER slams on the brakes and THE ASSASSIN roars past the stopped TAXI, his BULLETS HITTING THE DRIVER instead of Eve.

THE TAXI DRIVER

Slumps over, pulling the wheel to the left, his HEAVY FOOT now FLOORING THE GAS PEDAL.

THE TAXI

Shoots into the left lane, sideswiping the K-RAIL and SHOOTING UP SPARKS as it charges down the road, veering to the right and sideswiping A BUS. The TAXI is now speeding along pinned between the K-RAIL and the bus.

EVE

Leans over the front seat and grabs the steering wheel, just as the car shoots past the bus and into traffic. She tries to steer the RUNAWAY TAXI . . . weaving around the cars ahead of her. Behind her, ASSASSIN #1 SURGES FORWARD, firing his GUN at her.

EVE

Ducks for cover . . . and LETS GO OF THE WHEEL . . . as bullets RIDDLE THE TAXI and the REAR WINDOW shatters.

THE TAXI

Clips the LEFT REAR BUMPER of the CAR ahead of her like a POLICE PIT MANEUVER, sending it spinning sideways, right in front of

ASSASSIN #1

Who T-BONES into the car . . . sending him cartwheeling over the vehicle and smack into traffic, where he's IMMEDIATELY RUN OVER. Crunch!

EVE

Sits up, grabs the wheel again, and fights to regain steering control of her SPEEDING TAXI, sideswiping vehicles. But she has other problems. She glances in the REARVIEW MIRROR and sees the OTHER THREE MOTORCYCLE ASSASSINS closing in . . .

ASSASSIN #2

Charges forward, gun out, and starts firing at her.

EVE

Wrenches the wheel hard, squeaks past a car, and careens straight into the cross traffic of

A BUSY INTERSECTION

The TAXI barely avoids getting hit on the passenger side by A TRUCK, which comes between her and the motorcycles behind her.

ASSASSIN #2

Slides sideways UNDER THE TRUCK and comes back up on the other side to continue the chase.

ASSASSINS #3 & #4

Swerve around the truck . . . and follow ASSASSIN #2.

EVE

Looks back. The ASSASSINS are closing in . . . but then she sees an incredible sight:

SOMEONE ON A WHITE MOTORCYCLE

Is riding ON THE K-RAIL behind her. It's—

CLINT STRAKER

He rides to the end of the K-RAIL, FLIES OVER THE TRAFFIC, rolls across the top of a bus . . . and lands in the street, right behind

ASSASSIN #4

Who turns to look at what's behind him just as

STRAKER

Grabs him and YANKS HIM OFF HIS MOTORCYCLE, flinging him into

THE BUS

Which smacks into him and then smashes into his motorcycle, sending it spinning RIGHT OVER STRAKER'S HEAD.

ASSASSIN #2

Is closing in on the taxi.

EVE

Swerves, trying to evade collisions with the cars in front of her and the bullets being fired by the assassin who's chasing her.

ASSASSIN #2

Is taking aim at her head when

A CAR

Smashes into her, sending her car spinning out of control, bouncing like a pinball off the K-RAIL before she regains control.

ASSASSIN #2

Barely avoids being caught in the melee and speeds PAST the TAXI. Meanwhile:

ASSASSIN #3

Turns and starts shooting at

STRAKER

Who rears his motorcycle up on one wheel and charges past ASSASSIN #3 to a TRUCK filled with BARRELS ahead of them. He lands his cycle and pulls the latch on the rear of the truck. DOZENS OF BARRELS tumble out into the path of

ASSASSIN #3

Who smashes into them and goes flying, his motorcycle smacking into the K-RAIL and EXPLODING.

STRAKER

Jumps his cycle back atop the K-RAIL and speeds after the TAXI.

EVE

Regains steering control of her smashed-up TAXI. She sees Straker charging up the K-RAIL alongside her car and, ahead of her, she sees ASSASSIN #2 turning and charging back toward her, against traffic, his gun out.

STRAKER

Is atop the K-RAIL and alongside the taxi . . . and heading for an INTERSECTION, where the K-RAIL comes to an end. At the last possible instant, he leaps off the motorcycle and onto the TAXI, grabbing hold of the center pillar between the front seat and the back seat . . . while his

MOTORCYCLE

Goes aloft like a missile and straight into

ASSASSIN #2

Taking him out in a FIREBALL.

STRAKER

Opens the front passenger side door, reaches in, and yanks out the cab driver, throwing his body into traffic . . . and releasing the pressure on the gas pedal.

INT. TAXI — NIGHT

Straker slips into the front seat and behind the wheel, just as the taxi, all smashed up with bullet holes and shattered windows, glides to a stop at

EXT. HOTEL — TAXI STAND — NIGHT

In front of an ELDERLY AMERICAN COUPLE with suitcases. They look at the taxi in total shock. Straker smiles at them through the broken window.

> STRAKER
> Where to?

> ELDERLY MAN
> We'll take the next one.

# CHAPTER THIRTEEN

Ian tried to sleep but, as tired as he was, he couldn't manage it. So he got out of bed, opened his laptop, logged in to the hotel's Wi-Fi, and caught up on his email. That killed an hour. Then he turned on the TV and channel surfed between CNN and BBC, both channels full of pundits debating what the president of the United States meant by his latest tweet (he praised the first lady's boobs as being "natural and all-American") and trying to predict what outrageous thing he would say or do to embarrass his country at the G8 summit. That killed another hour. Finally, with nothing else left to do, Ian read the new draft of the *Straker* script. Yellow was the perfect color for this draft because the writers had pissed all over his book. The only thing they kept was Straker's name. But Ian didn't care. The studio's check had cleared and that's all that mattered.

He showered, got dressed, and watched the sunrise over Hong Kong, checking the clock every few minutes to see whether it was too early to disturb Margo. He was antsy and eager to get out of his room. At 6:00 a.m., he convinced himself that she must be awake and as antsy as he was. He went into the hallway and knocked on Margo's door.

She opened the door a crack. She was wearing a Nine Dragons terry cloth bathrobe that was too big for her.

"What's the matter with you?" she whispered but still managed to put a harsh edge on her voice. "It's six a.m."

"I know that," Ian said.

"Then why are you knocking on my door so early?"

"I couldn't sleep. I've got jet lag. I figured you had it, too."

"I don't," she said.

"What about your night terrors?" he asked.

"I took an Ambien."

"You seem awfully alert for someone who took a sleeping pill."

"You're a pharmacist now? Go away."

Margo closed the door as hard as she could without actually slamming it. But she made her point. Ian turned to walk away and accidentally kicked a room service tray of dishes beside her door that he hadn't noticed before. He looked down and saw two glasses and two plates.

*Two?*

He crouched down and saw bright red lipstick on the rim of a glass.

*Susie's lipstick.*

No, that couldn't be possible, he thought. Could it?

Ian went down to the lobby, got a cup of coffee and copies of the *South China Morning Post*, *USA Today*, and the *Wall Street Journal*, and found a seat that allowed him to stake out the elevators while he read.

At about seven thirty, Susie emerged from the elevator with matted hair, wearing no lipstick and the same clothes she'd had on the previous night. He held up his newspaper to obscure his face and peeked at her from the edge of the page like a detective in a bad movie. He'd always thought it was a stupid thing for a detective to do but it worked. She didn't see him.

The instant that Susie left the hotel, he dropped his newspaper and took the elevator to the thirtieth floor, marched to Margo's room, and knocked insistently on the door. Margo practically yanked the door off its hinges when she opened it. She was still in her bathrobe.

"What is wrong with you? You're going to wake up everyone on the floor."

"I can't believe you," Ian said.

"I'm not the one banging on doors all morning."

"You're the one banging my publicist all night."

"Were we that loud?" Margo asked. "Is that what kept you up?"

Ian couldn't believe how casual she was about what she'd done, like it was no big deal when it was a *very* big deal.

"No," Ian said.

"Then what's your problem?"

How could she not understand? "We weren't even in Hong Kong for an hour and you got my publicist into bed."

Margo smiled. "Are you jealous?"

"Yes." Ian startled himself with his honesty. It had to be the jet lag.

"Good. Now go away. I have to take a shower before breakfast." She started to close the door.

"Wait," Ian said. "I've got to know."

"Know what?"

"How did you do it?"

She leaned against the door. "You mean how did I, smelling like a wet dog after sixteen hours on an airplane in cattle class, manage to seduce a gorgeous woman I'd just met into her first experience with the joy of sapphic sex?"

"It was her *first* time?"

"Of course not," Margo said. "I just wanted to see you start panting. She's definitely been with other women before I flew into town."

"Even so . . ."

"Yeah, it's still pretty amazing, isn't it? I can't believe it myself. The truth is, she seduced me. I wasn't hard to get, either, not after a year of unwanted celibacy." Margo sniffed her underarms and frowned. "It must have been my horny pheromones that made me irresistible. God, I need a shower. I reek."

"Maybe you shouldn't shower," Ian said. "You could seduce every lesbian in Hong Kong."

"You have a point," she said. "I'll meet you downstairs."

And with that she closed the door.

Ian was in the hotel restaurant, finishing his self-styled Asian-American-fusion breakfast of dim sum, fried eggs, white rice, bacon, and an assortment of fresh melon when Margo, her hair still wet from the shower, took a seat across from him at his table.

"I decided to have mercy on the lesbians of Hong Kong," Margo said as she waved at the waiter to get his attention and held up her coffee cup. "You don't have to look so glum."

"I'm not," Ian said as the waiter approached with the coffeepot. He waited for the waiter to fill Margo's cup and go away before he continued speaking. "It's just that Susie is my publicist. If one of us is going to sleep with her, it should be me."

She sipped her coffee. "You are aware of how childish, stupid, and pathetic that sounds."

"Yes."

"Then there's still hope for you as a human being." Margo looked past him and smiled at someone approaching. "Susie is here. Please don't embarrass her."

Susie joined them a moment later and stood beside their table. She'd changed into a different pantsuit, fixed her hair, and reapplied her glossy candy-red lipstick. "Good morning. How was your night? All rested?"

"I didn't sleep a wink," Ian said.

"Neither did I," Margo said.

"That's a shame," Susie said with a sly smile.

It was more than Ian could take. He abruptly stood up.

"Let's go," he said. "We have a long day ahead of us."

# CHAPTER FOURTEEN

Kangbashi District, Ordos, Inner Mongolia, China. July 2.
9:15 a.m. China Standard Time.

The Western media called Ordos a ghost city, one of several largely uninhabited urban centers that the Chinese government hurriedly built over the last decade, supposedly in anticipation of a population boom that hadn't boomed. Instead, the city's skyscrapers, vast apartment blocks, wide boulevards, shopping malls, theaters, schools, and hospitals remained empty. Outsiders believed the construction of the ghost cities was a desperate ploy by a corrupt government to artificially fuel China's economic growth. That was partly true, but spymaster Yat Fu knew there were other reasons.

At least this unwanted city in the middle of a desert wasn't a cheesy replica of Manhattan (like Yujiapu with its miniature Rockefeller Center) or an embarrassing faux Paris (like Tianducheng with its rotting Eiffel Tower). Those places looked like abandoned amusement parks. Yat Fu believed that Ordos had true character that was reflected in the daring abstract architecture of the vacant performing arts center, its two derelict stadiums, the bare cultural museum, the unused mosque, the forsaken horse-racing track, and the hollow national library. What it didn't have was people, businesses, an industry, or any apparent reason to exist.

Yat Fu liked walking the empty streets of Ordos, as he did on this gray, hazy morning, past the unoccupied skyscrapers and apartment buildings, to Genghis Khan Square to gaze upon the giant statues of two horses rising to face one another on their hind legs, their bodies creating a dramatic arch that framed the skyline.

At times like this he felt like the last man on earth, the only survivor of a great apocalypse. He found the idea oddly peaceful and relaxing. People only caused him misery. That was why he didn't feel, like many of his underlings here did, that he'd been exiled to this place. To him Ordos was paradise. No crowds. No fighting for space. No smells of sweat, cooking grease, or piss. No dogs or cats. There was barely any life at all. Not even insects.

The best thing of all was the silence. It was nearly absolute, giving him the quiet he needed to think, to envision grand schemes like the one unfolding now that would change the world. That silence was broken by the footsteps of Pang Bao coming behind him. The irritation must have shown on Yat's face because Pang bowed ever so slightly for his superior's mercy.

"I'm very sorry to bother you, sir," Pang said. He had an iPad tucked under his arm. "But it is urgent."

"What is it?"

"Our automated bots continually scan our acquired data for key words and phrases so we can zero in on any communication or information of interest to us."

The term "acquired data" referred to the information that they gleaned by hacking into emails, phone calls, databases, and personal devices on a global scale. Those millions of devices and countless streams of communication were constantly being monitored by entire buildings full of servers—the seemingly empty skyscrapers that surrounded him now. Ordos wasn't really a ghost city. It was a city of servers, the largest "server farm" ever built, constantly crunching a planet's worth of raw data.

"I'm aware of what our automatic surveillance does and how it does it," Yat said. "Are you here to tell me what I already know?"

The underlings always assumed that their superiors were bureaucrats, interested only in results and completely ignorant of how they were obtained. What none of Yat's underlings knew, because it was top secret, was that he designed the global hacking technology hidden within this city.

"My apologies, sir," Pang said. "A guest at the Nine Dragons hotel in Hong Kong logged in to the Wi-Fi with his laptop last night. Our bot invaded his device and exposed his data to us. We found a very disturbing file on his hard drive. It might be nothing, but . . ."

Pang handed the iPad to his boss so he could see the file for himself. Yat took the iPad and walked a few steps away so he could read without his underling looking over his shoulder.

The document, written in English, was a detailed report of China's efforts to control the United States, its industries, and its people through strategic purchases of key companies and by ensuring, through low labor costs, that devices that connected to the internet were manufactured in China. Those electronic products, including children's toys, were hardwired with a "back door" that allowed the Ministry of State Security to gather personal data on millions of Americans and keep them under constant surveillance. All that was left to uncover, according to the report, was the nature and timing of "the inciting event" that would allow China to take total control of the United States economy and its people.

Yat Fu couldn't believe what he was reading. It was frighteningly accurate. Whoever wrote this report was one discovery away from sabotaging their plan and destroying decades of meticulous and expensive work.

"Who is the hotel guest who had this file?" Yat asked his underling.

"An American novelist named Ian Ludlow," Pang said. "He arrived in Hong Kong last night for the start of principal photography on *Straker*, a movie based on one of his books."

"Isn't that the movie being financed by Wang Kang for his daughter?"

"Yes, it is," Pang said.

Yat turned his back on Pang and took a moment to consider the details of the report, the timing of Ludlow's arrival, the links to billionaire Wang Kang, and what it all meant.

Clearly, Ian Ludlow was an American spy and the Ministry of State Security was absolutely right to be concerned that Wang's relationship with the West was far too close. Perhaps Wang was a CIA mole. That was a frightening thought given Wang's knowledge, the secrets he knew, and his hold on the Chinese financial industry. It was a good thing they already had Wang in custody and cut off from the outside world.

What Yat found intriguing, and a reason for hope, was how they'd obtained the dangerous report and what those circumstances revealed.

If Ludlow truly believed everything in the report, the spy wouldn't have logged in to the hotel Wi-Fi and opened his computer up to his adversaries. That mistake told Yat two important things:

1. Ian Ludlow's mission in Hong Kong was to verify the intelligence in the report; and
2. the spy didn't believe that the report was credible . . . at least not yet.

The second point was particularly interesting to Yat. Perhaps the Americans had purposely selected an agent skeptical of the report to ensure he wouldn't be swayed by weak evidence. Either way, the discovery of the report and the spy's arrival in Hong Kong actually offered Yat a great opportunity.

He would follow Ludlow's investigation, and plug every leak the spy unknowingly revealed to him along the way, thereby assuring that Yat Fu's ongoing operation, and its imminent conclusion, wouldn't be endangered.

And then he would capture, torture, and kill Ian Ludlow.

"It might just be a coincidence," Pang said, "a story the author is researching for one of his thrillers. But given the timing, and Wang's involvement, I thought you should see it."

"You did the right thing." Yat turned to face Pang again. "I appreciate it. Who else knows about this file?"

"Right now, only you and me."

"Keep it that way." Yat didn't want this intelligence failure to get back to Beijing before he could demonstrate that he'd solved it. Otherwise, Yat was afraid that President Xiao might abort the final stage of their operation, after decades of work and billions of dollars in expense, even though they were so close to success.

"But I want Ludlow under constant and total visual, audio, digital, and personal surveillance," Yat added. If anybody in Beijing asked about it, he'd explain that it was part of his ongoing investigation into Wang Kang's activities, which wasn't far from the truth. Those were always the most effective lies. "Mobilize every resource that we have."

"Including the assassins?"

"Especially the assassins," Yat said.

# CHAPTER FIFTEEN

Wang Studios, Hong Kong. July 2. 9:45 a.m. Hong Kong Time.

The Wang Studios lot in Kowloon was just as drab and industrial as any movie studio complex in the United States, at least the ones that didn't double as amusement parks. The studio was made up of a dozen sound-stages, several office buildings, and a "backlot" of fake Hong Kong streets and building facades, all safely tucked away behind the high wall that surrounded the property.

Susie handed Ian and Margo each a lanyard with an ID badge as they walked from their car in the parking lot to the soundstages.

"Wear these lanyards around your neck while you're here," she said. "They will give you access to the entire lot and get you through security when we are shooting on location in the city."

"Cool," Margo said.

Susie stopped in the road that ran between one of the soundstages and a four-story office building.

"This soundstage is where they keep the stunt cars and motorcycles. P. J. is in there now, meeting with the second-unit director. P. J. is expecting you. My office is over there." She gestured to the office building.

"Third floor, room 303, if you need anything or simply a couch to crash on."

"I could crash right now," Margo said.

"We have work to do." Ian tugged Margo by the strap of her big shoulder bag and headed for the soundstage door.

Margo went along with him but watched Susie go into the office building.

"What work do I have to do?"

"You're supposed to be researching my next novel," he said, "not a lesbian sex manual."

"I've got your research itinerary all planned out but there's nothing for me to do until you're done here."

"That's not true." Ian opened the soundstage door. "Seeing what they're doing on the Straker movie might give you some ideas for my novel."

He walked inside and she followed him. The soundstage was essentially a large warehouse that was ordinarily used for filming scenes on sets. But now it was being used to hold the various stunt and camera vehicles. At the far end of the soundstage, a group of men were huddled around a bank of monitors, watching footage.

Ian walked past several motorcycles and four red-and-white Toyota taxis, one of which had a roll cage on top of the passenger cabin. The roll cage had a driver's seat, a steering wheel, and gas and brake pedals. He hadn't seen a rig like this before.

"You're just cock blocking me," Margo said.

"You don't have a cock."

The taxi was also fitted with a camera mount and a seat for the cameraman on the outside of the driver's side door. There was another stationary camera mount on the hood.

"I have a rubber one," she said.

"You brought a dildo to China?" Ian asked.

"I never leave home without it." Margo gave her shoulder bag a shake and flashed a mischievous smile.

That's when the director, P. J. Tyler, spotted Ian and called out to him.

"Ian, you made it! Welcome to the eye of the storm."

P. J. came over and pulled Ian into a hug, nearly breaking Ian's sternum with the camera viewfinder that the director constantly wore around his neck, even when he wasn't shooting a movie. The director claimed it was because he never knew when inspiration would strike for a shot, but he wasn't fooling anyone. It was so everybody, especially women, would know that P. J. was a director. P. J. looked over Ian's shoulder at Margo, let go of him, and offered her his hand.

"I'm P. J. Tyler," he said.

She shook his hand. "I'm Margo French, Ian's muse."

"Mine is right here." P. J. clapped Ian on the back. "It all starts with the words. Did you read the new draft of the script?"

"I haven't had a chance," Ian said. He didn't want to get pulled into a discussion about the script at that moment, or ever, though he had his copy in the messenger bag that was over his shoulder in case there was no way to avoid it.

"You're in for a thrill ride. It's much more visceral than the last one. This new team of writers really gets it. They worked with me on *T.J. Hooker: The Movie* so they understand how I think. I want all of my movies to be an extremely visceral experience."

"I watched *T.J. Hooker* on the plane," Margo said. "I definitely had a visceral reaction. I was glad that every seat came with a—"

Ian gave her a warning look from behind P. J.'s back and she said: "—seat belt."

Ian signed with relief. He was certain she was going to say *barf bag*.

"Chris Pine should have gotten an Oscar as Hooker," P. J. said, "but the Academy is biased against action movies."

P. J. turned, put his arm around Ian's shoulders, and led him over to the bank of monitors, where three burly-looking American stuntmen were intently watching bits and pieces of the taxi chase through Kowloon.

"Most directors would settle for what these guys have already shot, film the actors in a parked car in front of a green screen, and use CGI to cut them into the action. Not me. I'm going for a more visceral experience." P. J. gestured to the taxi with the roll cage on top. "I'll be filming Wang Mei at the wheel during her wild, explosive ride. I like the actors to physically experience every smash and every crash. The secret is that they aren't actually in control of the cars. Our stuntmen are driving the vehicles from the cages on top."

"Even so," Ian said, "the actors could get killed."

"That's the key. If it's visceral for the actors, it will be visceral for the audience. That's how I make movies." P. J. clapped Ian on the back again like they were old pals, which they weren't. Ian had met him briefly only once before. They had lunch at a taco wagon in Santa Monica and P. J. spent half the time looking at women with his viewfinder. "I've got to let you go. I've got to prepare for some camera tests with Wang Mei. We're filming her shots in the chase later this week. Have you met her?"

"Not yet," Ian said.

"She's the Asian Jennifer Lawrence." P. J. leaned close to Ian's ear. "Though I would have preferred Jennifer Lawrence. But it's the Chinese financing from her father's studio that got this movie made, so we compromised."

"Is she good?" Margo asked.

"Yeah, but let's just say that nobody is ever going to call Jennifer Lawrence the American Wang Mei." P. J. shifted his attention back to Ian. "Will you be around later for the table read?"

"I wouldn't miss it," Ian said, though he really wanted to.

"Of course not. They're your words."

"Actually, they're not," Ian said.

"They are in the sense that they are different words that say the same thing as your words, only with extra intensity, so the effect is much more—"

"Visceral," Ian said.

"Exactly. You ought to go say hi to Damon. He's in his trailer, right outside the soundstage, doing a wardrobe fitting." P. J. pointed to another door, on the far side of the soundstage.

"I won't be intruding?" Ian asked.

"He can't wait to meet you. He carries your book with him every-where he goes."

# CHAPTER SIXTEEN

Ian and Margo exited the soundstage into a roadway lined with trailers—small motor homes for the actors and much larger, specialized wagons where their hair and makeup were done. They were barely out the door when they nearly collided with Wang Mei and her two Chinese bodyguards as they were coming in.

Wang Mei was in her early twenties and had a fragile beauty, as if she might shatter into a thousand radiant pieces if she fell. The two stocky, thick-necked men in business suits who flanked her made no effort to hide their profession. They wore stony expressions and they each had an earpiece that kept them in contact with other operatives elsewhere.

"Excuse me, Wang Mei?" Ian asked.

The two men immediately blocked her, becoming a great wall of Chinese muscle.

"Step back," one of the bodyguards said, but Ian didn't actually see his lips move.

"I'm Ian Ludlow, the author of the Straker books."

Wang Mei smiled and reached her arm between her two bodyguards to offer Ian her hand. "Oh yes, I heard you were coming. I'm delighted to meet you."

"Likewise." Ian took her hand, practically pulling her forward, forcing the two men to part and let her through.

She glared at the bodyguards. "I apologize for my bodyguards. They can be overprotective."

"It's understandable," Ian said, releasing her hand. "They must be edgy ever since your father was kidnapped."

"My father wasn't kidnapped. That's Western media propaganda," Mei said. "He's in Beijing being treated for a very serious medical condition."

It was almost word-for-word what the Chinese government said in its press release. And Yat Fu, watching from 1,500 miles away in Ordos, was pleased that she quoted it so accurately.

## Classified Location, Kangbashi District, Ordos, Inner Mongolia, China. July 2. 10:30 a.m. China Standard Time.

"Wise answer," Yat Fu said, standing in his control center, looking at the image on the big screen being transmitted from the button cameras on the two Ministry of State Security agents who were acting as her bodyguards. He was getting a chest-eye view of Ian Ludlow, Margo French, and Wang Mei's back.

"Do you think she knows that we're listening?" Pang Bao asked from his seat at his console. The other operatives in the room worked silently at their keyboards, panning through the mud of hacked data from around the world for flecks of intelligence gold.

"No, but she knows that her bodyguards are," Yat said.

Actually, the two bodyguards weren't paying any attention to the conversation. Their mission was to keep Wang Mei in custody without actually locking her up. She was a dog on a very short leash.

## Wang Studios, Hong Kong. July 2. 10:31 a.m. Hong Kong Time.

"But you're right about one thing, Ian—they are here to protect me," Wang Mei said, then got a mischievous glint in her eye. "Otherwise, I could be abducted and sold to some deranged Arab sheik for his harem of Asian sex slaves."

"That sounds like it could be the plot of one of Ian's novels," Margo said.

"I know," Mei said. "I've read them all."

Ian doubted that, but it was nice of her to say.

Margo offered Mei her hand. "I'm Margo French, Ian's personal trainer."

Mei shook it. "I've heard that all Americans have one."

"We all have personal chefs, too," Margo said.

"You can't believe anything Margo tells you," Ian said. "The only chef I have is Chef Boyardee."

Mei smiled politely. Ian realized that she had no idea what he was talking about. "I hope you are not too disappointed with me."

"No, no, of course not." Ian immediately regretted his remark. "It was an obscure reference to a brand of canned spaghetti. It was a stupid thing for me to say. I'm disappointed in myself for saying it."

"I wasn't talking about that," Mei said. "I know Chef Boyardee. It's one of the brands owned by Conagra Brands in Chicago, which outbid my father to acquire TaiMei Potato Industries in Shangdu, becoming the biggest potato processor in the region. I remember because my father doesn't often lose."

"Then I don't understand. Why would I be disappointed in you?"

"Because I'm not a twenty-two-year-old, sixth-generation Texan with a truck driver's vocabulary, a poet's eyes, and a pole dancer's body."

She really had read his books, at least the one that *Straker* was based upon. Hearing his own prose recited to him made Ian self-conscious. He knew that nobody would ever mistake his writing for Hemingway's.

"Don't worry about how I described Eve in my book. James Bond wasn't Scottish in Ian Fleming's books. But actor Sean Connery was, and will always be, the best 007. The same goes for you," Ian said. "You're far better than the character that I imagined."

"That's nice," Mei said. "But I think that's what you were planning to say to Damon if he asks you if he's too old and too short to be Clint Straker."

Margo laughed. "I think you're right."

They both were, but Ian didn't think it was wise to admit that. Instead, he said, "He'll never ask me that."

"And if he does?" Mei asked.

"I'll tell him that Marlon Brando wasn't Italian and was only fifteen years older than Al Pacino in *The Godfather*. But Brando was still believable as Pacino's father and was the perfect Don Vito Corleone, just like you will go down in movie history as the definitive Clint Straker."

Mei nodded with approval. "He'll like being compared to Brando."

"But I won't get the chance to answer the question," Ian said. "He doesn't have your humility."

"Or my insecurity," she said.

Margo spoke up. "I wouldn't be so sure about that. You're not the one who is going to be standing on a stepladder in your scenes together."

# CHAPTER SEVENTEEN

Yat Fu watched as Wang Mei and the bodyguards entered the sound-stage, leaving the American spy and his assistant behind.

"Curious that Ludlow would mention a spy novel to Wang Mei," Yat said. "There's more to this conversation than it seems. Get a tape of it to cryptology for analysis."

"Yes, sir," Pang said.

The screen now showed the bodyguards' point of view as Mei walked up to the director.

"I don't want to see this," Yat said. "I want to see Ludlow and his assistant. Do we have any cameras on the studio lot?"

"Only the ones on Mei's bodyguards and the devices they planted in her trailer."

"Can we access the studio's security cameras?"

"We can, but they are only pointed outside the property and sound-stages, not inside or on the backlot. Studios don't want footage leaking out of their actors or their films."

"Very well," Yat said. "Show me our satellite view."

Pang hit a few keys and the images on the screen were replaced by a surprisingly clear, tight shot from earth's orbit of Ian and Margo walking among the trailers.

⊕

Ian and Margo approached a trailer that had "Damon Matthews" handwritten on a strip of blue masking tape affixed to the front. As they neared the open door, they could see Damon inside, standing on a wooden box, being fitted for a tuxedo by a young and harried Chinese seamstress.

Damon was 50, though his age was stated as 49 in his press materials and was likely to be for years to come, but he still had a boyish quality that would probably keep him looking youthful well into his eighties. He was in the midst of a heated argument with a balding American man with a four-hair comb-over and a sagging face that made it appear as if he were melting.

"Why does she get bodyguards, Larry, while I'm left totally unprotected?" Damon said. "I'm a global superstar. I'm more valuable to this production than she is."

Ian assumed the other man was Larry Steinberg, the line producer, the man responsible for the actual nuts-and-bolts production and keeping the film on time and on budget.

"I don't know who's paying for those guys, but it's not us," Larry said. "They've been glued to her since her father was taken to Beijing. I'm told that the only time they aren't going to be with her is when she's shooting."

"I still want protection," Damon said. "If she has two guys, I probably need four."

"It's not in the budget," Larry said.

Now Ian was certain Larry was the producer and saw a way to score some points with the guy who was paying for his trip. Ian spoke up, directing his remarks to Damon.

"Not only that, but it wouldn't look good for the movie, or your action star image, to be seen with bodyguards," Ian said, both Damon and Larry noticing his presence for the first time and probably wondering who the hell he was. "People want to believe that you can take on a dozen ninja assassins single-handedly."

"I can," Damon said, defensive. "I just don't want to take paychecks from the stuntmen."

"And that's why you're the guy I saw in my mind when I created Clint Straker," Ian said by way of introduction.

"Ian Ludlow!" Damon stepped off the box to greet Ian and Margo at the door, which was two steps above Ian, and leaned down to fist-bump him. "I've been looking forward to meeting you. I'd invite you in but this Chinese trailer is too Goddamned small." He turned to Larry. "Where is my motor home?"

"We shipped it from Los Angeles by boat, but it's been delayed at sea by a storm," Larry said. "It should be here in a day or two."

Damon looked at Ian. "My personalized motor home is so big we could have the Last Supper in it. It's got push-outs on push-outs." Then Damon turned back to Larry. "There must be bigger trailers than this in China. You're the producer. Find one for me until mine gets here."

"I'll see what I can do." Larry walked out of the trailer and, his back to Damon, rolled his eyes in frustration for Ian to see.

"Damn producers, all they care about is money," Damon said. "They forget this is an art." He spotted Margo. "I'm sorry, we haven't met. I'm Damon Matthews."

"I thought you looked familiar," she said. "I'm Margo French, Ian's sober companion."

Damon fist-bumped her, too. "Word."

"I don't know what that means," Margo said.

"It's going to be a struggle keeping Ian clean. I'm sure he has to face his demons every time he writes. That's how he finds the hard truths. I know. I'm an artist, too." Damon went to the kitchen counter behind him and came back to the doorway with a well-worn paperback copy of *Death Benefits* and held the book up like a preacher waving his Bible. "I take your book with me everywhere I go. I'm constantly going back to it for inspiration. It's the sacred text."

"The screenwriters don't seem to think so," Ian said. "The script doesn't resemble it much."

"That's why I keep the book with me," Damon said, "to make sure we stay true to the integrity of what you wrote. It's the soul of the movie."

"Thank you," Ian said and he meant it. "It's great that you have so much respect for the writing."

"Hell yes, man. Without the words, I wouldn't have the foundation I need to become the character and create the dialogue."

Ian took a second to parse what Damon meant by that last comment, which didn't quite jibe with all the respect the actor claimed to have for his book. When he figured it out, it made him a little queasy. "You're improvising your lines?"

"It's so much more than that."

"Of course it is," Ian said, trying hard to hide his contempt.

"I channel the character, body and soul, so every word I speak in performance is truer than anything the writer can achieve as an observer. You're gonna be blown away."

"I'm sure I will be," Ian said.

Damon fist-bumped him again. "Catch you later."

Ian walked away with Margo, who waited to speak until they were out of Damon's earshot. "I don't know how you can stand this business."

"I can't. That's why I quit screenwriting and became an author," Ian said. "Let's get out of here before I really do need a sober companion."

# CHAPTER EIGHTEEN.

Port Ouest, Marseille, France. July 2. 6:00 a.m. Central European Summer Time.

On a mountainous, sparsely developed stretch of coastline called Les Riaux, northwest of the Marseille city center, was a small port that mostly served fishing boats and pleasure craft. The port was backed against a narrow, winding road and steep chalky-white cliffs that were topped by a vast abandoned quarry.

The docks were busy at this early hour as fishermen prepared to head out to sea. Chen's panel van was just one of many and his arrival in front of Lucio and Fina's yacht went unnoticed by the locals.

He got out of the van and found the Italian couple having breakfast on their port deck. They were in matching silk pajamas and bathrobes and were enjoying their eggs, ham, berries, and yogurt with a bottle of champagne. Chen thought that they probably screwed with champagne glasses in their hands, too.

"Right on time," Lucio said. "To the second."

"It was surprisingly easy." Chen stood on the dock and tipped his head toward the tiny guard shack at the roadside entrance to the port. "The guards at the gate never even looked at me. Just waved me through."

"They are only there for show," Lucio said.

"Like flowerpots," Fina added.

"Our Corsican friends here, La Brise de Mer, have run the ports in Marseille for a century." Lucio snapped his fingers at the servant who stood at his side and pointed at Chen's van. "Bring Mr. Chen his crates."

"Marseille is the most corrupt city in France," Fina said. "If not all of Europe."

Two of the yacht's crew members emerged from the boat carrying Chen's crates, brought them onto the dock, and walked past him to his van, which he'd left unlocked for them.

Lucio popped a berry in his mouth. "This is the gateway for all the South American cocaine and Moroccan hashish into Europe. But you can run anything through here."

"And we do," Fina said. "Drugs, cars, jewels, weapons, sex slaves, chemicals, even an occasional Bengal tiger."

She shared a smile with Lucio at the fond memory and took a sip of her champagne.

"The French government hasn't cracked down on what comes in and out of Marseille after the terrorist attacks in Paris and Nice?" Chen asked, watching as the two deckhands closed his van and returned to the yacht.

"On the contrary," Lucio said. "As other trade routes by land and air have been choked off due to tighter security, Marseille has become the focal point for European smuggling, which is a key pillar of the entire European criminal economy."

"Surely the French government knows that," Chen said.

"They do," Fina said. "That's why they will always lack the manpower, the resources, and the balls to lock down the port. It's too big a part of the economy to jeopardize."

"La Brise de Mer controls the docks by recruiting the same poor, disenfranchised immigrants that ISIS radicalizes everywhere else in

Europe," Lucio said. "But we have something to offer that's stronger than ideals or religion."

"Money, honey." Fina raised her glass in a toast and took another sip.

"Speaking of money . . ." Lucio said, letting his voice trail off.

Chen reached into his coat pocket and tossed Lucio a thick envelope full of euros. Lucio caught the envelope, glanced inside, then slipped it into the pocket of his bathrobe. "We can do more than transport sensitive cargo for you. We can handle all of your needs, from acquisition to delivery."

"You won't have to get any more blood on your sleeves," Fina added with a mischievous twinkle in her eye. Or perhaps she was just loaded.

"You don't know what my needs are," Chen said.

"We took a peek at your cargo." Lucio gave him an apologetic shrug. "We like to know what we are carrying. We can get you everything from Kalashnikovs to nuclear materials."

"Or a Tasmanian devil," Chen said.

"If that's what you'd like," Fina said. "They are adorable creatures and marvelous at disposing of corpses."

"Every home should have one," Chen said. He liked her, which was a shame. "When do you go back out to sea?"

"This afternoon, after we stock up on French wine and cheese," Lucio said, then added with a smile: "Our pockets are burning with cash."

### Mong Kok, Hong Kong. July 2. 1:15 p.m. Hong Kong Time.

The Mong Kok neighborhood was on the western edge of the Kowloon Peninsula and was a place where anybody could buy almost anything, legal or illegal, moral or immoral, real or fake. Ian had passed through here on his taxi ride into the city from the airport and it was no less dense and frenetic in the daylight than it was at night.

He'd just emerged with Margo from the Mong Kok subway station and she was taking him on a walking tour, explaining as they went what she'd gleaned from her research.

Mong Kok was known for having entire blocks that were dedicated to a single product or service. There was the photocopying street, the ladies market, the goldfish street, the shoe market, the tile street, and the flower market, to name a few.

Some of the streets, like the one dedicated to bootleg clothes and accessories, were closed off to traffic during certain hours and filled with market stalls, a mix of pop-up tents and portable sheds with corrugated metal roofs, where long folding tables were piled high with fake Polo shirts, Vuitton bags, and Hermès scarves.

But gentrification was creeping into Mong Kok from all sides in the form of gleaming skyscrapers with massive malls full of international brand-name stores selling real Polo shirts, Vuitton bags, and Hermès scarves. Those places, Ian thought, weren't nearly as much fun or full of character as the street markets.

"Mong Kok is where old, traditional Hong Kong and the contemporary, future-leaning city collide like a speeding Lamborghini into a bus full of retirees on their way to a bingo parlor," Margo said as they moved through the crush of people in the bootleg market.

"You should leave the metaphors to the professionals," Ian said. "But I get your point. It's a stunning contrast."

"It's also one of the most densely populated neighborhoods on earth."

"I can feel the energy," Ian said.

"That's probably just a pickpocket's hands in your pants," she said.

Ian looked up at the canopy of neon signs that arched over the roadway. He could already imagine using the signs in an action sequence. Perhaps Straker could be in a fight with a killer on top of a moving bus while trying to avoid being hit by one of the signs. Or, better yet, maybe Straker could be swinging from sign to sign, like Tarzan using vines, to avoid pursuers. There was no shortage of action possibilities to be found here. But it was one thing to see it and another to describe it.

"This is what a lot of people imagine when they think of Hong Kong," Ian said. "For a film, it's great. But it's hard to capture the big picture in a book without pages of description. So I'll need to find the colorful flourishes, the individual brush strokes that will allow the reader to create the painting himself."

Margo gave him a critical sideways glance. "Is that an example of a professional metaphor?"

"It's not as belabored as yours."

"Yeah, but it's not very visceral. Maybe P. J. is onto something," Margo said. "I've found a place that's uniquely Hong Kong that I think you'll like. Follow me."

Ian did, and so did a dozen security cameras on the street and a satellite in earth's orbit.

# CHAPTER NINETEEN

Yat Fu entered the Ordos command center, stood beside Pang Bao, and took a moment to survey the multiple live video feeds of Ian and Margo in Mong Kok while he thought about the call he'd just received from his man in Marseille. The weapons had arrived safely from Turkey and the operation was right on schedule. Yat did not tell him about the CIA intelligence report that exposed almost everything or the American spy they were tracking in Hong Kong. He didn't want anything to distract the operative from his mission.

Yat spoke to Pang but kept his eye on the screens. "Status report."

"Ian Ludlow and the woman took the subway to Mong Kok. They are now walking along Flower Market Road."

"Just two tourists taking in the sights."

"We have three teams tracking them, one behind, one ahead of them, and another in the bird market. More teams are standing by on Duke Street, Boundary Street, and Sai Yee Street."

"Don't get too close and keep the teams in heavy rotation. Ludlow is a highly trained professional. He'll spot a tail. Let's rely on electronic surveillance whenever possible."

"We've tapped every camera in the area, government and private," Pang said. "We're also tracking them by satellite."

"Good. Do we have audio?"

Pang shook his head. "Not since Ludlow's conversation with Wang Mei outside the soundstage."

"I think those references to James Bond and *The Godfather* mean something. What do our cryptographers say?"

"If it was some kind of code, it's eluding them."

"That's the point of a coded conversation." Yat's face tightened with anger. He hated incompetence more than anything. "Tell them to stay on it until they can explain to me what it really means."

Sometimes he wished there was a button he could push that would instantly vaporize people who were too stupid to live. He'd use it to vaporize the idiot cryptographers right now. Perhaps a kill-the-morons button would be his next project. Sure, it seemed impossible to achieve, but at one time, so did the idea of China taking over the United States without a war. And he was about to pull that off.

The Yuen Po Bird Garden in Mong Kok was both a tiny park and a market for songbirds, their cages, and other bird-keeping accessories. Old men took their caged birds for walks along the tree-lined garden paths, passing other old men huddled with their friends, smoking cigarettes and playing cards, while their birds sang from cages that hung from low-lying branches in the trees. Free birds flocked here, too, filling the branches around the cages, taunting their more colorful, pampered, and imprisoned brethren with incessant chirping.

In the center of the park was an open-air pavilion crammed with market stalls selling hundreds of live birds, elaborate bamboo cages, hand-painted porcelain feeding cups, live crickets and grasshoppers, bins of birdseed, imitation birds, and anything else a bird owner might need.

Margo led Ian into the pavilion. "All of this was originally on Hong Lok Street, known for decades as the Bird Street, until it was all mowed down in the 1990s to build Langham Place, a sixty-story office building and a separate fifteen-story shopping mall. All of the merchants were moved here and their aging customers came with them. Collecting and caring for songbirds is a dying art, not many young people are getting into it, so this market will probably be demolished soon, too, for an office building or an apartment tower. In the meantime, I thought this would be a cool place for Straker to make a drop or pick up a package from a secret contact who doesn't want to be exposed."

"It's narrow, cluttered, noisy, and exotic," Ian said. "You're right, it's a perfect spot for a clandestine exchange."

"I'm full of good ideas."

Ian began taking pictures with his iPhone, drifting away from Margo and passing a couple of young Chinese tourists who were using their phones to take a video, which was being live-streamed to the command center in Ordos. The man and woman also had flesh-colored transmitters in their ears that allowed Yat Fu to tell them:

*"Stay with him. This could be a meet or an exchange."*

Ian stopped at one of the stalls, where a ten-thousand-year-old Chinese man sat on a wobbly wooden stool surrounded by hundreds of birdcages and bamboo baskets filled with bird supplies and trinkets.

Ian browsed through a basket of tiny, stunningly lifelike imitation birds made of Styrofoam and feathers and an array of white-and-blue-painted feeding cups. He chose a fake thrush and a water cup and paid the ancient seller, who put the items into a paper bag that was as wrinkled as his face and had the same texture.

Margo joined Ian and gestured to his paper bag. "What are you going to do with those? You don't have a birdcage."

"They're souvenirs to have on my desk when I sit down to write the book." Ian stuck his purchases into his messenger bag. "Sometimes having a visual cue that brings back memories helps me get into a scene."

"And if that doesn't work?"

"I sacrifice a goat."

Yat Fu pointed to the screen. "I want that bag and whatever message was just passed to Ludlow by that old man. I also want the old man apprehended and brought in for interrogation."

"Do we take Ludlow, too?" Pang asked.

"No, not yet," Yat said. "Make the grab for his bag look like a mugging. It's okay if Ludlow gets roughed up, but not too much. He's no good to us if he's in a hospital. He needs to be able to walk."

"He's not going to believe it was a mugging."

"He will if our agents pay no attention to him and only to his bag," Yat said. "As a spy, his fear is that he'll be abducted or killed. If our men run off with his bag and leave him on the street, he'll believe that his cover is still safe."

"Understood," Pang said. "The team will take the bag at their first opportunity."

# CHAPTER TWENTY

Ian and Margo left the bird garden and headed down Tung Choi Street, known locally as Goldfish Street. Both sides of the street were lined with storefronts that overflowed onto the sidewalks. Hundreds of baggies filled with water and live goldfish hung from corkboards at the doorway of each store. There were also buckets of colored gravel, buckets of coral, and shelves spilling over with plastic galleons, treasure chests, anchors, and other knickknacks for decorating aquariums.

"I've never seen an entire street devoted to goldfish before," Ian said.

"The Chinese believe that having an aquarium is good *feng shui*. It brings wealth and luck."

"This would be the perfect place for a Straker fight scene."

"Maybe if this was Chainsaw Street or the knife market," Margo said. "But there's nothing dangerous about a baggie full of goldfish."

"That's why it works. Readers love it when Straker turns a harmless object into a deadly weapon. That said, is there a Chainsaw Street or a knife market?"

"Not that I know of, but you could create them."

"I prefer my fiction to be based in reality."

She rolled her eyes. "Is that so? In one of your books, you had Straker give a woman an orgasm so intense that she went into a coma for three days."

Ian and Margo were so busy talking that neither one of them noticed the two men walking toward them, not that there was anything suspicious about them besides their laser focus on Ian. One man had a pockmarked face from a youth spent picking at his acne. The other man had a once-broken nose that looked like it was trying to climb over his left cheek.

"You love using that scene as an example whenever you talk about a Straker book," Ian said. "You must have really liked it."

"It was memorably awful."

"That's not it," Ian said, a chiding tone in his voice. "The truth is, it turned you on. That's why you remember it."

"Don't flatter yourself."

"I'm not the one who keeps bringing up the scene," Ian said. "By the way, the ancient erotic art of *Seiteki chōetsu* that Straker used to give her that orgasm is real."

"No, it's not."

"How do you know?"

"Because I looked it up," she said. "I couldn't find it anywhere."

"Aha!"

"Aha what?"

"You were so aroused by what I wrote, and so eager to learn how to experience *Seiteki chōetsu* for yourself, that you rushed out to find everything you could about it. But you won't find anything on Google or in any library. It's a technique that's taught only through experience. You have to find a *Seiteki chōetsu sensei* to teach you."

"And I suppose that's you."

That's when the pock-faced man charged forward, grabbing Ian's messenger bag from his shoulder and knocking him off his feet.

In that same instant, Margo whipped out her rubber dildo, whacked the thief across the face, then spun and hit the second man in the groin. She spun again, clubbed the thief across the back of the head, then hit the second man once more across the face, breaking his nose. Both men dropped to the ground. She ended her spin in a defensive karate stance, brandishing her dildo like a short *bō* staff.

Ian was still on his back, shocked by the mugging and even more so by Margo's physical prowess, when a third man charged out of nowhere, wielding a knife.

The third man stabbed at Margo, who swung her dildo to protect herself. The blade sliced the dildo in half, leaving her exposed. Margo quickly grabbed two bags of goldfish, tossed them in the man's face, and then kicked him in the gut, sending him backward into the store.

Just as the guy with the knife was about to charge Margo again, Ian grabbed a bucket of aquarium pebbles and spilled them out on the sidewalk in front of the man's feet. The pebbles were like marbles. The attacker slipped and fell backward, his head smacking against the sidewalk, knocking him out.

Ian stood up, grabbed Margo by the arm, and pulled her into the street. "Run!"

They rushed down the street, leaving the three men and Ian's messenger bag behind. They dashed into an alley and onto another street market teeming with people browsing through piles of new athletic shoes. Ian didn't stop running until he was sure that nobody was chasing them.

He stopped to catch his breath at a stall selling bootleg Air Jordans and looked at Margo. "What the hell was that?"

"Muggers," she said, breathing hard.

"I'm not talking about them. I'm talking about you and what you did back there. When did you become Wonder Woman?"

"Don't exaggerate. What you saw was pure desperation."

"It was more than that," Ian said.

"I took a few self-defense classes after everything that happened to us. I thought it would make my fear go away," Margo said. "It didn't."

"I never knew a dildo could be used as a weapon."

"It was all I had."

"I'm glad you had it," Ian said.

"It was my favorite one, too. I'm going to miss it." That's when Margo realized that she was still clutching the half dildo that remained. She gave it a wistful look, then tossed it in the street. "Sorry they got your bag. Was there anything valuable in it?"

"No, just the *Straker* script and the bird souvenirs. Certainly nothing worth dying for. I'll buy another bag here," Ian said. "But I was right."

"About what?"

"Goldfish Street is a great place for a fight scene."

# CHAPTER TWENTY-ONE

There was silence in the command center. All of the operatives were staring at the screen in shock except for Yat Fu and Pang Bao.

Yat was red-faced with rage. He'd never seen anything more pathetic than the conduct of his agents, beaten into submission by a civilian waving a dildo. It would have been comical if it wasn't so utterly disgraceful.

But Pang seemed more contemplative than shocked as he studied the various angles of Ian and Margo on multiple screens.

"They are on Fa Yuen Street," Pang said. "They appear to be calmly browsing for shoes."

"Maintain surveillance but keep our people back," Yat said, his voice tight and even as he tried to keep his anger in check. It wasn't just the way the embarrassingly inept bag snatch unfolded that pissed him off—he was also troubled by Pang's analytical expression. What was his underling thinking?

He hadn't picked Pang as his right hand. The operative was assigned to him by others within the small number of people at the Ministry of State Security who knew the details of Yat Fu's operation beyond merely the global data mining and intelligence gathering. It was done to ensure that Pang's ultimate loyalty would be to the state, not to him.

"If Ludlow is a professional spy," Pang said, "why didn't he defend himself and why did he run?"

Yat's first reflex was rage. How dare his underling question his assessment of the situation, especially now, in front of everyone, after such a humiliating display of incompetence by his men. On the other hand, the question also revealed the limitations of Pang's intellect. His underling could only see what was in front of him and lacked the ability to extrapolate the consequences or, in this case, greater meaning. It was that intellectual deficit that would keep Pang from ascending to Yat's status as a spymaster who reported directly to the president.

"It would have blown his cover in front of his assistant if he displayed his skills," Yat said in his most patronizing voice. "She doesn't know he's a spy."

"But he let our people get away with his bag."

"Think it through," Yat said, still patronizing him. "It means that Ludlow already reviewed the message and either he thinks it will be meaningless to anyone who finds it or it is no longer in the bag."

An image came up on-screen of the broken-nosed agent in a car using his cell phone camera to speak to them. He held a napkin to his bloody nose as he spoke. "We have the bag."

Yat glowered at the screen, though the agent couldn't see him. "You were nearly defeated by a frightened civilian wielding a sex toy."

"She took us by surprise."

"You sicken me," Yat said, then turned to Pang. "I don't want to see his face or hear his voice."

Pang hit a button and the image disappeared. Yat leaned close to Pang and spoke sharply into his ear. "I want the bag and its contents analyzed immediately and those three incompetent agents reassigned to janitorial services for the rest of their worthless lives."

"Understood," Pang said.

"Destroy all the records, audio and visual, of today's operation. It's humiliating. If anybody in Beijing ever sees it we'll *all* be cleaning toilets or summarily executed."

Pang swallowed hard. It pleased and reassured Yat to see that Pang appreciated the danger of the situation for both of them. They were in this together now.

"Consider it done," Pang said. "Those three men will certainly never speak of it, either."

Yat knew that was true. He straightened up and tugged on his Mao coat. "If they had any dignity, they'd kill themselves."

And if Pang was smart and ambitious, as Yat had been at his age, he'd take the initiative and have them killed so there would be no dirt on him that anybody could use against him in his rise to power.

But Yat doubted that Pang would take the hint. Such a shame.

## Les Riaux, Marseille, France. July 2. 4:00 p.m. Central European Summer Time.

Chen crouched at the edge of the abandoned limestone quarry atop the chalky, windswept cliffs of Les Riaux that overlooked the town of L'Estaque and the Bay of Marseille. He trained his binoculars on Lucio's yacht, which was headed out of port and into the Mediterranean.

"It looks about two miles out to me," he said in Mandarin.

"Closer to three," Tan Yow responded in the same language. She'd flown to Paris after poisoning Senator Tolan in Washington, DC, and had been waiting for Chen in the van at the Marseille airport when he'd arrived from Turkey.

"That's even better." Chen turned to Tan, who'd assembled the missile launcher on its tripod and was aiming the targeting laser. Although she was adept at covert ops and assassination, her primary skill set was in electronics. "Are we ready?"

Tan slid out from under the firing tube, which extended out at both ends over the tripod. The shooter was safe underneath the weapon, but anyone standing behind it when the missile was launched would be blown apart by the back-blast. She'd seen it happen more than once on the battlefield.

Chen rose to his feet and took a moment to openly admire her. She was in a tank top and tight jeans that accentuated her lean, perfectly muscled body. He knew from experience how strong and flexible she was. Last night she'd used his erection like a gymnast on a set of parallel bars. His groin still ached.

"We're good to go," she said, being just as open about appraising his body. He knew she found it to her liking. "It's pretty much point and shoot. The rocket will go wherever you point the targeting beam, even after launch."

"So I can track a moving target." He handed her his binoculars and she handed him a pair of headset earmuffs that matched the pair around her slender neck.

"Or change your mind about what you want to destroy."

"I won't," he said, putting the earmuffs around his neck and sliding underneath the tripod.

Tan crouched beside him and he felt a new ache in his groin as he began to harden, aroused just by the nearness of her body. He could almost feel the heat radiating from her smooth skin and taste her on his tongue.

"In the unlikely event that we are caught or killed before we can act, Yat Fu has ordered me to retrofit this with a timing device that will automatically fire the missile in our absence." She pointed to where she'd installed the new device on the weapon's central housing, below the firing tube and above the viewfinder.

"We'll be there to fire it." Chen peered in the viewfinder and saw the laser beam reaching out to the yacht. He slipped on his earmuffs, indicating that he was ready.

Tan put on her earmuffs, laid down on the ground beside him, and looked out to sea with her binoculars.

Chen fired. There was a loud crack and a whoosh. The missile's front and rear fins unfolded as it blasted out from the firing tube and rode the laser beam to its target at 250 meters per second.

The yacht exploded in a fireball that utterly obliterated the craft. Chen knew it was overkill, like using a stick of dynamite to blow up a Styrofoam cup, but he needed to be sure that the weapon system worked. He was sorry to see Lucio and Fina go, though. They were a fun couple. But he couldn't let anyone live who could lead investigators back to him and, by extension, China after the mission was completed.

Chen removed his earmuffs and glanced at Tan. "It will do."

Tan smiled and it was like she'd flicked his glans with the tip of her tongue. She knew it, too. He could see it in her mischievous eyes.

It took them five minutes to dismantle the weapon, put its two remaining component pieces into the van, and then drive off, Tan at the wheel for their eight-hour journey to Paris.

He had no problem being a passenger. She was more familiar with the roads in France than he was. And it was painful driving for hours with an erection.

# CHAPTER TWENTY-TWO

An excerpt from the third yellow draft of *Straker*.

EXT. BIG WHEEL — CABIN — NIGHT

Straker and Eve are standing alone in a glass cabin on the Big Wheel . . . an enormous Ferris wheel by the Hong Kong ferry terminals. The view of the Hong Kong skyline on one side, and Victoria Harbor on the other, is spectacular . . . and romantic.

> EVE
>
> I don't understand you.

> STRAKER
>
> Nobody has ever accused me of being a complicated person.

> EVE
>
> You came here to avenge your friend's death. You did that. Why are you still here?

STRAKER

Because I need to set things right.


EVE

No, you don't. The triads have been here for over a century and they will be here long after you're gone.


STRAKER

Not in your neighborhood. Not anymore. Not ever.


EVE

You live half a world away. What do you care what happens here?


STRAKER

Because my friend did. And because you do.


He moves in and kisses her, her back against the glass that faces the
bay. But as their passion increases, Straker looks over her shoulder and
sees a HELICOPTER closing in. She leans back from him, sensing his
distraction.


EVE

What is it?


The TRIAD KILLER is in the chopper, holding an AK-47 . . . and opens fire.
Straker forces Eve to the floor as the cabin is riddled with bullets.


STRAKER

Stay down.

He takes out his gun, rises to his feet, an open target, and fires three times at the chopper . . . hitting the pilot.

The CHOPPER weaves out of control, its tail swooping PRECARIOUSLY CLOSE to their CABIN, before it drops into the harbor and EXPLODES. Straker lowers his gun, lifts up Eve, pulls her close, and says—

STRAKER (CONT'D)

Where were we?

And they kiss.

## Wang Studios, Hong Kong. July 3. 3:27 p.m. Hong Kong Time.

P. J. Tyler, Damon Matthews, Wang Mei, Larry Steinberg, all the department heads, the primary cast members, and Ian and Margo sat around a long table in a conference room for a reading of the script. It was essentially a sitting rehearsal, giving everyone a chance to see how the script played out and to make note of any production or creative issues. P. J. read the scene directions and the actors performed the parts, sometimes engaging in pantomime to convey action absent props. The two stars had just finished reading the scene at the Big Wheel. Damon had Mei pinned against the wall and he was kissing her with such gusto that it bordered on molestation.

"That was great," P. J. said.

Damon let go of a red-faced Mei and waved the script at the director. "I have a problem."

Mei gasped for air and glowered at Damon's back.

"What's that?" P. J. asked.

"Why does it take three shots for me to bring down the helicopter? All I need is one."

"It humanizes him if he misses first."

"It makes me a pussy." Damon shifted his gaze to Ian. "What do you think?"

Everybody was looking at Ian now. If Ian contradicted Damon, it would be the same as calling the global superstar a pussy. If he sided with Damon, then he would alienate a superstar director and probably get thrown off the set. It was a no-win situation. But Ian wasn't worried. If anything, he saw the predicament as a challenge.

"I think it would take six shots," he said.

Damon's eyes widened in surprise and his face flushed with anger. Nobody ever contradicted him. But before the actor could explode, Ian spoke up again, confident and relaxed.

"Straker fires the first five shots while bullets from the chopper are riddling the cabin around him. Maybe he even gets hit in the shoulder. Now he's wounded, blood streaming down his arm, his hand shaking, and the chopper is coming around for another pass. He's down to one bullet and one chance in hell of surviving. Straker takes aim and hits the shooter, who falls back into the chopper, firing wildly in his death throes, killing the pilot, shooting up the cockpit. The chopper blows up in an enormous fireball. One of the dismembered chopper blades spins wildly toward Straker. He casually ducks as the blade sheers off the top half of the cabin . . . and then, the wind whipping him, blood seeping from his wound, he rises up with the Hong Kong skyline as his backdrop, pulls Eve to him, and says: 'Where were we?' They kiss, a kiss for the ages, and as the Straker theme builds to a crescendo, we fade to black, the end."

The room was silent for a long moment, everyone as still as marble statues, until finally Damon blinked hard and spoke.

"Holy shit," Damon said. "It's iconic. I love it."

Now that Damon had told everyone what their opinion would be, the director chimed in.

"So do I. To make it even more visceral, we could mount a camera on the broken chopper blade as it spins toward Straker's head."

"A flaming chopper blade," Damon said.

"Yeah." P. J. looked at Ian. "That was a great note."

Everyone applauded, except for Larry Steinberg. He gritted his teeth and a huge vein throbbed under the skin of his forehead like a parasitic worm squirming over his skull. Ian assumed it wasn't a sign of profound happiness but he chose to ignore it.

"Thanks, I'm glad I could help." Ian closed his script, stuffed it into his new messenger bag, and stood up. "I hope the rest of your table read goes well. I want to get in some research for my next book before the photo shoot tonight."

Margo stood up, too. Damon came over, gave Ian a big hug, and clapped him on the back even though it meant everybody in the room would see how much shorter the actor was than the author.

"We're making movie history, bro." Damon broke off the hug and approached Mei as Ian and Margo headed for the door. "We need to rethink the staging of that kiss. It's lacking eroticism."

Mei crossed her arms under her chest. "What do you think it needs?"

"Boobs."

That was the last word Ian heard as he walked out the door. He was glad he wouldn't be there for whatever came next.

As they stepped outside the building, they were nearly run over by the red-and-white taxi, the one outfitted for filming the chase sequence, as it sped by. There was a helmeted stunt driver in the roll cage on top and a helmeted cameraman sitting on the platform mounted on the passenger side of the car. A woman was in the driver's seat as a stand-in for Mei.

"What are they doing?" Margo asked.

"A camera test for tomorrow's chase scene."

"I wouldn't want to be Wang Mei," she said. "That's a lot of trust to put in a guy driving on the roof, especially with cars and motorcycles flying at you."

"That's why I'm glad I only have to write this shit and not live it."

Larry burst out of the building and gave Ian a shove, startling him. "Do you realize what you just did?"

Ian feigned ignorance. He knew exactly what crime he'd committed from Larry's point of view and he didn't care. "I came up with a little change that makes it a better action sequence than what you had before."

And he'd won over both the actor and the director, which was an amazing feat given the position he'd been put in.

"This is why I never invite writers to the set," Larry said, the vein in his forehead pulsing. "Your 'little change' is going to put us a million dollars over budget and add days of green screen work on the soundstage."

Margo raised a finger to make a point. "But it will be so much more visceral, Larry."

If looks could kill, then Larry would have just dismembered Margo, doused her with gasoline, and set her ablaze. He shifted his death gaze onto Ian.

"Your photo shoot is tonight at the Big Wheel. That's the only reason we brought you to Hong Kong, not to offer script notes. So after tonight, you're done," Larry said. "You can stay one more day and then you're on the first plane back to LA."

Larry marched off. Ian watched him go and then saw Margo studying him. "What?"

"You were just messing with them, weren't you? You came up with the most expensive, stupid scene you could think of just to see if you'd get away with it."

"Yes," Ian said. "And I did."

Margo nodded, impressed. "You really might make movie history."

"Worst scene ever shot?"

"It's a strong contender," she said.

# CHAPTER TWENTY-THREE

Classified Location, Kangbashi District, Ordos, Inner Mongolia, China. July 3. 4:15 p.m. China Standard Time.

Yat Fu sat in his office looking out at the dozens of identical, hollow, twenty-story apartment towers, some still topped with rusting construction cranes, in the desolate residential neighborhood below. Wind-blown sand spread over the unused streets and parks and piled up high against the bases of the buildings. He wondered how long it would take before the buildings were buried.

"What did the lab get from Ludlow's bag?" Yat turned away from the beautifully postapocalyptic view to look across his desk at Pang Bao, who sat in the chair facing him.

"Nothing. The bird and the feeder have been examined under a microscope and x-rayed as well and they have found no objects or messages. They've even tried to find unconventional methods for conveying information. For example, they examined the feathers to see if the pattern might resemble a bar code. They've come up with nothing."

"Then the message is gone," Yat said. "What have we learned from Ludlow's contact at the bird market?"

"The interrogator is waiting on secure channel five to give you his report."

Yat picked up a remote control on his desk and aimed it at a flatscreen monitor on his wall. The monitor flicked on to reveal the elderly merchant tied to a chair, naked and bloody, his head slumped on his bony chest. It was a startling image, not because of the blood or the broken fingers and toes, but because of the old man's skin, so weathered and thin and stretched that it was almost translucent. If there were more light in the dank torture chamber, a basement in Hong Kong, Yat was certain they'd be able to see the man's withered and bruised internal organs.

The interrogator stood off camera, wary of being captured on video with a victim of his vicious ministrations. Yat couldn't blame him for his camera shyness. One never knew who was watching or when or where an incriminating video might show up.

"What information have you extracted?" Yat asked.

"The man insists that he knows nothing about any message," the interrogator said. "The American was just another tourist."

Yat wasn't satisfied. "You need to use more extreme methods."

"He's very old and feeble," the interrogator said. "Anything more might kill him."

Was that compassion that Yat heard in the interrogator's voice? Unlikely. That was an emotion so forbidden in the interrogator's profession that it was considered profane. Perhaps the interrogator was simply being practical. Very well—Yat could work with that. He'd done his share of interrogations in his youth.

"There's a simple work-around. Torture someone he loves who is young, strong, and has more stamina. In my experience, women are best. They aren't shy about expressing their agony," Yat said. "That should loosen his lips."

Yat disconnected the call and glanced at Pang, who shifted uncomfortably in his seat. The color had drained from his face and he appeared ill at ease.

"What is your problem?" Yat asked. "You don't have the stomach for enhanced interrogation techniques?"

"It only bothers me if it's unnecessary," Pang said. "Perhaps the old man is telling the truth."

Yat's first thought was that Pang was a coward, but then he realized it took courage to offer an opinion that contradicted his superior's orders. No, Pang's problem wasn't cowardice. It was spinelessness. They were both variations on a theme, but Yat believed that there was a subtle difference. Cowardice was the fear of doing something because of the risk to one's personal safety—be it physical, emotional, or professional. Spinelessness was the lack of the inner strength to endure the anguish or pain required to overcome a major obstacle or a difficult challenge.

"What are you saying?" Yat demanded. "That Ludlow isn't a spy?"

Pang shifted in his seat again, as if he had a burr in his ass. Perhaps it was hemorrhoids, the bane of supervisors who spent most of their time in a seat watching instead of doing. Yat's own butt itched just thinking about it. "We may have misinterpreted the intelligence."

Yat revised his assessment of Pang. It took backbone to question your superior's judgment. So he wasn't spineless after all. He decided that Pang's affliction, in addition to hemorrhoids, was arrogance. But Yat had to admire Pang's use of "we" instead of "you" to take the edge off his disrespectful suggestion. It showed a hint of political prowess.

"You started this," Yat said. "You read what was on Ludlow's computer and were concerned enough to bring it to me."

"Maybe the report was actually conjecture," Pang said. "The elements of a story for another one of his books rather than an intelligence document."

Yat tried to make sense of Pang's contradictory behavior. The underling had been bright enough to see the danger in the information they'd found in Ludlow's computer. But now that agents were making blunders in the field, and blood was being spilled in a torture chamber, Pang was second-guessing his initial instinct that the report was dangerous.

Yat decided the problem was that Pang was an analyst, not a field operative. He was fine with data on a page but was incapable of handling the dirty business of spy craft. It was the action that was distracting him from the facts. All Pang needed was a reality check to focus him again on the data and put him in his comfort zone.

"You found a report that accurately states the objectives of our top-secret operation on the computer of an American. This man came to Hong Kong to work on a movie that's financed by Wang Kang, a Chinese billionaire we've imprisoned to mitigate the danger he poses to our country," Yat said. "Do you honestly think those connections are just a coincidence? And that it's a coincidence these events are happening right before the most critical point in our operation?"

"It's unlikely," Pang conceded. "But what if we're seeing things that aren't there, or are misinterpreting the facts, precisely because we are at such a critical point in our operation and are being overly vigilant?"

"Don't be a fool. Ignoring what we're seeing wouldn't just be an act of sheer stupidity, it would be dereliction of duty worthy of execution by a firing squad. It's like seeing an army marching toward your border, telling yourself they are just out for a stroll, and then watching in shock as your country is invaded," Yat said. "There's no such thing as a coincidence in our business. Your initial instincts about this were correct. I urge you to wise up fast and focus on the potential threat. The future of China and the new world order is at stake."

The intercom buzzed on Yat's desk. He hit the speaker button. "Yes?"

One of the command center operatives spoke. "Ludlow is on the move."

# CHAPTER TWENTY-FOUR

Victoria Peak, Hong Kong. July 3. 4:37 p.m. Hong Kong Time.

Before the age of skyscrapers, the obscenely rich British colonials escaped the heat, squalor, and rampant malaria in Hong Kong by building their mansions in the cooler, fog-shrouded mountains overlooking the harbor, the Kowloon Peninsula, and the South China Sea. It was so nice that the British declared Victoria Peak off-limits to the Chinese—except, of course, for their servants and the coolies who carried them up the steep trails to their homes in sedan chairs, a fancy name for a wicker seat tied between two bamboo poles.

A funicular tramway, completed in 1888 and still running today, made it much easier to get to the Peak, so more wealthy British moved up there. By the late 1940s, the restriction against Chinese homeowners was lifted and anybody who could afford it could live in the clouds and pretend to throw lightning bolts down on the sweating populace below.

Today the Peak was one of the priciest, and most exclusive, places to live on earth. The handful of remaining mansions, many of them overlooking even Hong Kong's tallest skyscrapers, were selling for $100,000 a square foot. And yet anybody with five dollars for a Peak

Tram ticket could join the seven million tourists a year who flocked to the wok-shaped Sky Terrace observation deck and shopping mall to see the spectacular view and enjoy such quintessentially Chinese experiences as the Madame Tussauds wax museum, Kentucky Fried Chicken, and Sunglass Hut.

Ian and Margo were among the mob of tourists that day standing atop the Sky Terrace, marveling at the 360-degree view and trying not to get hit in the face with a selfie stick. Most of the tourists spent their time with their backs to the view, trying to capture it and themselves with their stick-mounted cameras rather than seeing it with their own eyes. But who needs memories, Ian thought, when you can have Instagram likes?

"This may be the best view I've ever seen," Ian said to Margo, who stood at the railing beside him and had just given him the snide history lesson on the Peak. "Even better than the Grand Canyon."

"I've never been there," Margo said.

"I drove out there one day a few years ago. It was an eight-hour drive from LA. But once I got there, I spent ten minutes looking at it before I got bored and drove back. But I could stand here looking at this all day. What does that say about me?" Ian didn't have the answer, but he'd explore that question when he put Clint Straker here in the book and use it to flesh out the character a bit.

"I have no idea," Margo said. "I brought you up here to get you oriented to Hong Kong. No pun intended."

"Of course it was," he said. "You've been waiting all day to say it."

She didn't argue because he was right. Instead, she continued to play tour guide as they walked beside the railing and the row of coin-operated telescopes.

"The apartment towers below us, on the rise to the Peak, are in an area known as the Mid-Levels. It's a very expensive place to live. The competition is particularly fierce for the apartments that are above the pollution layer."

"You're making that up."

"I wish I was," Margo said. "The area in the flats below Mid-Level is Central, the main business and financial district of Hong Kong, much of it built on landfill that used to be the waterfront. That's where most of the skyscrapers are. To make the commute to work and play easy for the Mid-Level residents, there's a half-mile-long outdoor escalator system that's raised above the streets and goes nearly all the way down to the center of Central, not far from the waterfront and ferry terminals."

"That must have killed the sedan chair business."

"It had already been dead for thirty years when the escalators were built in the 1990s. The Mid-Level escalators are the boundary between Central and the Western District, where all the best clubs and restaurants are." Margo put a coin into a telescope, peered through it for a moment, searched around for something, then offered it to Ian. "A lot of the apartment towers have pools and tennis courts on top. Take a look."

Ian leaned forward and peered into the telescope, which Margo had pointed at an apartment tower with an infinity pool on the roof. The pool had a transparent bottom that was cantilevered over the edge of the building so anybody in the water would have the sensation of swimming in midair.

He panned the telescope to other buildings and then out to the harbor, which was a freeway of ferries, ocean liners, fishing boats, barges, Chinese junks, cargo freighters, and yachts going in all directions. It amazed him that there weren't multiple collisions and sinkings each day. It was an exhilarating and inspiring view.

Ian leaned back from the telescope, took in the sight for a few moments with his naked eye, and began visualizing a scene, seeing it play out in front of him.

"You know what would be exciting? A paraglider chase and gunfight between Straker and triad assassins that starts right here and then goes on amid those towers. Straker narrowly avoids smacking into the buildings but a few of his pursuers aren't so lucky. It could end with him over the harbor, landing on one of those floating restaurants, sauntering casually up to the bar, and ordering a martini."

"That's ridiculous," Margo said. "Why would they be up here on paragliders?"

"I don't know but I guarantee you that I'll think of something."

"Why can't you just enjoy the view without cheapening it with an idiotic action scene?"

"Because I'm writing books, not movies. You can't see a view in a book."

"You could describe it. Isn't that what writers are supposed to do?"

"Writers tell stories. To translate this to the page," Ian swept his arm out at the vista in front of them, "I need to get my characters and the reader *into* the view so they experience it rather than see it. Action is how I do that."

"In other words, you want to make it visceral," she said. "You're just like P. J."

Holy shit, he thought, she's right.

Margo saw the realization on his face, smiled to herself, and gave him a reassuring rub on the back. "It's not so bad. Look at the bright side. At least now you know he's the perfect director for *Straker*. I'm also learning something from this."

"That I'm blind to my own staggering hypocrisy?"

"Everybody knows that. I'm beginning to think that maybe there's more to what you do than sitting in your underwear, eating Doritos, and fantasizing."

"I'm going to take that as a compliment," Ian said.

As Margo and Ian walked away, they ducked under another selfie stick, but the camera on the end wasn't focused on the young couple striking a pose against the backdrop of Hong Kong. It was focused on Ian.

# CHAPTER TWENTY-FIVE

Classified Location, Kangbashi District, Ordos, Inner Mongolia, China. July 3. 4:50 p.m. China Standard Time.

Yat stood in the control center and watched Ian and Margo leaving the Sky Terrace observation deck from the point of view of the fake tourist couple's phone and the numerous security cameras mounted throughout the facility. It was an event covered from more angles than the Super Bowl and yet there was nothing to see.

"Why did they come here?" Yat asked.

It was a rhetorical question, but Pang offered an answer anyway. "Maybe it was for the view."

"They aren't here on holiday," Yat said, each word dripping with disdain at Pang's stupid comment. "They came here to make contact with someone, or to retrieve a message, or to leave a message behind. Everything Ludlow is doing is for a covert purpose."

"We haven't seen any interactions with individuals or any opportunities for an exchange," Pang said, undeterred by the disdain. "The only thing they touched was the telescope and there's no place on the device to leave a message."

Yat was about to chastise Pang but stopped himself. Something clicked in his mind and he chastised himself instead.

It had become a reflex to dismiss Pang's comments, but now Yat realized, in a moment of stunning clarity, that it was wrong to do so. There was wisdom in some of Pang's observations, even if the underling didn't realize it himself.

"You're right," Yat said. "Ludlow went there for the view."

Pang turned in his seat to study his superior. When he decided that Yat wasn't being sarcastic, he said, "What did he go there to see?"

"Now you're using your head."

"Was he checking the location of his next meet to see if it was secure?"

"I don't think so. I believe there was a message posted out there in the city somewhere, perhaps in a window or on the rooftop of one of those apartment buildings, and he needed the telescope to see it. The message told him where to go to meet someone or to make an exchange."

"How do you know?"

"I don't know for sure. But we will soon find out," Yat said. "Don't lose Ludlow. I want eyes and crosshairs on him at all times."

✥

**Hong Kong. July 3. 6:07 p.m. Hong Kong Time.**

Ian and Margo took the Peak Tram down to Central, then walked to Lan Kwai Fong, where the narrow streets and alleys were packed with bars and restaurants that catered to the young, rich, and bored. Most of the places opened wide to the sidewalk, and people spilled out into the streets every night, creating the carnival atmosphere that was the neighborhood's main attraction.

But now, in the hour or so before dark, the customers were mostly tired office workers, freed from their cubicles in the nearby towers and unwinding (or perhaps fortifying themselves) with a beer before making the trek up the streets, staircases, or Mid-Level escalators back home.

Margo took him up a narrow staircase in an alley between two tall buildings to Wyndham Street. It was a busy street lined mostly with new skyscrapers or gentrified older buildings. If you took the Chinese signs away, Ian thought, central Hong Kong wasn't really any different than any big, modern city. He could be standing in Seattle, London, Frankfurt, or Sydney.

But he only held that opinion for half a block. That's when he came to a skyscraper that was under construction and surrounded by bamboo scaffolding that was tied together without nails or screws. It was such an antiquated way to build scaffolding that it seemed utterly out of place in the construction of new, cutting-edge architecture.

Margo read his baffled expression and explained: "Bamboo is faster to put up than steel and withstands typhoons better. It's also a cultural thing."

Ian was sure he'd use the bamboo scaffolding in a book. It was too weird not to. He took a few pictures and they continued along the street to the Mid-Level escalators, a covered, pedestrian overpass that was inclined uphill, or downhill depending on your perspective.

They took a staircase up to the pedestrian bridge. Inside, there was a moving walkway going uphill that was beside a walkway that was graduated every few feet with four-step stairs.

"The escalators go downhill in the morning and uphill the rest of the time," Margo said as she led him down the graduated walkway. "There are three moving walkway stretches like this and the rest is made up of twenty escalators."

Ian looked over the bridge railing at the traffic below and across the rooftops of some small buildings. He could envision Straker in a foot chase that took him across the rooftops, onto the Mid-Level escalators, and into the traffic below.

They only walked a block or so on the Mid-Level escalators, just enough for Ian to get a feel for it, before Margo led him down a staircase to Gage Street, which was packed with flower and fruit vendors, their produce displayed on tables and open crates on the sidewalks. The vendors were wedged between fast-food stands, spice markets, and other stores, their street signs arching over the roadway. Aging, dirt-caked, water-stained buildings with rusted air conditioners in every window were shoulder to shoulder with sleek, gleaming skyscrapers.

"I like this neighborhood," Ian said. "It's a clash between old and new, but the new seems to be winning."

"I thought you'd like it, but that's not why I brought you here," Margo said and then did a strange thing. She took a *Wall Street Journal* out of her shoulder bag and stuck it under her arm as they walked. "There's someone I want you to meet. He's a reporter who's been covering politics and business here for the last five years."

That explained the newspaper under her arm. It was so he'd recognize them. "You've lined up an expert to give me background and some local color."

"It wasn't easy for me to get him to talk to you."

"So I shouldn't ask him what would be the best guns to use in a paraglider gunfight."

"Don't be an ass," she said, scanning the crowd.

"If that's how you talk to your employers," Ian said, "it's no wonder you can't hold a job."

She spotted someone. Ian followed her gaze and saw a Chinese man with a *Wall Street Journal* tucked under his arm standing at the corner of Gage by an outdoor market that ran down Graham Street, a glorified alley that was closed to traffic.

The man was in his thirties, dressed in a jacket, tie, and slacks, like one of the office workers they'd just seen nursing beers in Lan Kwai Fong. He acknowledged them with a slight nod and crossed the street to meet them.

Margo offered him her hand. "Mr. Fung, thank you for meeting us."

# CHAPTER TWENTY-SIX

Classified Location, Kangbashi District, Ordos, Inner Mongolia, China. July 3. 6:16 p.m. China Standard Time.

Yat shifted his gaze from the big screen and multiple angles of Warren Fung to Pang Bao, sitting at a console beside him. "I suppose it's coincidental that Ludlow is talking to the reporter that our operative impersonated to abduct Wang Kang."

"I agree that it's a troubling development," Pang said.

It sure the hell is, Yat thought, then addressed everybody in the room: "Everyone stop what you are doing and listen to me."

The two dozen data-mining experts in the room swiveled in their seats to face him and sat as rigid and expressionless as mannequins.

"Your priority now is Warren Fung. Hack his computer, his email, his bank accounts, everything. Do a global data search using all of our bots," Yat said. "I want to know what he knows and who he has been talking to since he emerged from his mother's womb."

They nodded, almost in unison, swiveled back to their terminals, and began typing furiously at their keyboards.

Yat looked at Pang. "Where are our operatives?"

"We have two on foot and two in cars on Wellington. Two more are on the Mid-Level escalators at Wyndham. Two more are in cars on Gage and on Peel," Pang said. "We have two snipers, one on Gage, another on Wellington, waiting to see where Ludlow goes."

"Ludlow won't go far now," Yat said. "Tell the snipers to find good firing positions and be prepared to execute my kill order."

⊕

"Thank you for meeting us, Mr. Fung," Margo said. "I'm Margo and this is Ian Ludlow."

Ian shook the reporter's hand. "I appreciate it."

"Call me Warren." The reporter looked around anxiously. "Officially, I'm interviewing you for the *Journal* about your new movie and what it means for the globalization of the Hong Kong film industry."

"Sounds like a good story to me," Ian said. "I'm glad to answer your questions if you'll answer a few of mine."

"Let's walk and talk." Warren tipped his head to Graham Street, which was a packed outdoor market filled with butchers, fishmongers, spice sellers, and scores of fruit and vegetable stands. Shoppers and tourists clogged the center of the narrow roadway, which was closed off to vehicular traffic. The entire street was covered with a ragged patchwork of awnings, tarps, and umbrellas that sheltered the vendors and their customers from the elements.

Warren walked into the market and Ian and Margo joined him. The air was redolent with the clashing aromas of dead fish, blooming flowers, fresh vegetables, spices, and incense, all infused with the strong scents of cleanser and rot from the constant stream of foul water that ran down the street from the market's melting ice, leaking buckets, and washed-out stalls.

"Why are we meeting in a busy outdoor market and not your office"—Ian raised his voice to be heard over a butcher they passed who was hacking away at a slab of meat with a cleaver—"or someplace more private and quiet?"

Warren walked slowly. He was in no hurry to leave the tight, noisy, smelly, sheltered confines of the market for this conversation. He also spoke softly, just loud enough for him to be heard by Ian and Margo.

"My office is bugged and meeting somewhere private would only make it easier for something bad to happen to us. It's safer for us to be in a crowded, public place."

That didn't make any sense to Ian. "I didn't know it was dangerous for a *Wall Street Journal* reporter to talk with a novelist about his book."

"It is when the subject is China's abductions of billionaire businessmen like Wang Kang."

"That's only one small aspect of my research. I might not even use that in the book."

"You don't know the whole story."

Yat couldn't see Ludlow, Fung, or the woman anymore. There were only a few surveillance cameras on Graham Street and they were positioned above the awnings and umbrellas that covered the vendors. But even when the cameras could get a clear view of the street, Ludlow and Fung were frequently obscured by signage and the crush of people.

"We're losing them," Yat said, frustrated. "Get our people on foot into the market. I want eyes on Ludlow and Fung."

"Understood." It was one of the many control room operatives who'd spoken, but all Yat could see from his vantage point were the backs of everybody's heads, so it was a disembodied voice.

Yat looked at Pang. "Where are we with the hack?"

"Fung's email accounts, his files at the *Wall Street Journal*, and the files on his home computer are encrypted. They can be breached but not quickly. So I'm trying an alternative strategy that will yield immediate benefits," Pang said. "His iPhone was manufactured in Zhengzhou. I'm accessing our back door to get control of his microphone and camera."

Pang was showing some initiative under pressure. Yat liked that. But decisive old-school methods might be necessary here.

"Where are our snipers?" Yat demanded of the room.

"On either side of Graham Street, sir," another disembodied voice said. "I'm putting their sniper scope views on screen. You will see what they see and you are now in direct audio communication."

A video screen on the big wall now showed a rooftop sniper-scope feed that was labeled SNIPER #1. His crosshairs and laser-targeting beam moved over the sea of tarps and awnings to the occasional openings over the center of Graham Street, where a river of people moved. It was difficult for Yat to make out any distinct individuals. For an instant, Ludlow briefly appeared, then he disappeared again. Sniper #1's voice came over the control room speakers.

Sniper #1: *"I can't get a clear shot on any of them."*

The video feed from Sniper #2's scope appeared on another monitor. He was positioned in the window of an office that also overlooked Graham. His view wasn't any better than Sniper #1's.

Sniper #2: *"I can't get a clear shot, either."*

"Don't try to target all of them," Yat Fu said. "Concentrate on the reporter."

On the screen, Sniper #2's crosshairs found the top of Warren Fung's head.

Sniper #2: *"Wait. I got him."*

But the words were barely out of his mouth when Fung stepped under another awning and was safe again.

The threesome stopped briefly in front of a vendor selling salted duck eggs, quail eggs, chestnuts, and blocks of tofu that looked like gelatinous concrete. Warren pretended to browse the selection and spoke softly to Ian and Margo.

"The Communist Party congress is being held this fall and that's when key members of the ruling Politburo are selected. President Xiao Guangchang wants to consolidate his power before that happens," Warren said, then continued his stroll. "Xiao can't risk any political or economic instability, so he's abducted business executives suspected of corruption or of supporting the Hong Kong democracy movement."

"But Wang Kang doesn't fit that profile," Ian said. "He's not corrupt and he's been loyal to the government."

"He's done something worse," Warren said. "He went on a spending spree in the West, taking on enormous debt that has leveraged against his majority stakes in Chinese banks and financial institutions. He's just one bad decision away from crashing the Chinese stock market and crippling the economy. But even that shouldn't have led to his abduction."

"That's not enough?" Margo said, stopping briefly in front of a vendor selling all kinds of egg and rice noodles.

"Wang owns banks, so he knows how much money the Politburo and Central Committee members have, where it came from, and where it's hidden. That sensitive knowledge should have made him untouchable," Warren said. "But it didn't. That means something else is going on besides Xiao consolidating his power, something with enormous stakes for China."

Which was why the three of them were in the crosshairs of two snipers, both armed with lightweight Nemesis Vanquish rifles loaded with .308 Winchester cartridges and fitted with sound suppressors . . . and why four Ministry of State Security agents, two on either end of Graham Street, all of them armed with silenced Glock 17s and Ka-Bar tactical knives, were closing in on them, too.

# CHAPTER TWENTY-SEVEN

Classified Location, Kangbashi District, Ordos, Inner
Mongolia, China. July 3. 6:42 p.m. China Standard Time.

"Does anybody have eyes on them?" Yat demanded. The replies from
the ground team and snipers came over the speakers.

Ground Team 1: *"Not yet."*

Ground Team 2: *"I think I can see their backs."*

Sniper #1: *"I have Fung's head. No. Wait. I lost him. Reacquiring."*

Technically, the sniper's report was redundant. Yat could see the
sniper scope views if he wanted. But Yat couldn't pay attention to every
camera at once. Things were moving too fast.

"Sir," Pang Bao said energetically. "I've activated the microphone
on Fung's phone."

"Let's hear it," Yat said.

The live conversation played on the speakers.

Ian Ludlow: *"Maybe President Xiao wants to use the dirt Wang has on
the Politburo members to shore up his power."*

Warren Fung: *"That's certainly possible. But there's more at work. My
sources tell me that Wang recently discovered that his studio has wired large
sums of money to nonexistent vendors in Turkey and Italy and opened a*

*production office in Paris for a fake movie. Why? One day after Wang started asking questions about that, a reporter showed up at his penthouse for an interview. That was the same night Wang fell ill and was taken to Beijing."*

Ian Ludlow: *"Money being embezzled from a movie studio isn't as compelling to me as political intrigue."*

Warren Fung: *"The reporter was posing as me."*

Ian Ludlow: *"That's creepy, but it's still not grabbing me."*

Margo French: *"How do you know all of this?"*

Warren Fung: *"Some of it came from one of Wang's Australian body-guards, a woman who was expelled from Hong Kong hours after the abduction. She got a photo of the guy impersonating me from the security camera footage, which was subsequently erased. She sent that photo to my phone . . . right before she was killed in a car accident in Sydney."*

Yat didn't know what else Fung had to say but he knew he didn't want Ludlow to hear it. "Ground teams, I want that phone. Does anybody have Fung in their crosshairs?"

Sniper #1: *"I don't have a clear shot."*

Sniper #2: *"Negative."*

"Get one, damn it," Yat said.

### Graham Street Market, Hong Kong. July 3. 6:45 p.m. Hong Kong Time.

Warren stopped and took out his phone.

Ian's gaze drifted to a nearby seafood vendor who had an astonishing assortment of fresh fish laid out on mountains of crushed ice and an array of buckets of water filled with live shrimp, lobster, crab, and other sea life. What the hell was in those buckets? Ian was leaning over for a closer look when Warren held out his phone to show them a photo.

"This is the guy," Warren said.

It was a picture of a Chinese man about the same age and build as Fung, with similar but sharper facial features, standing at the security reception desk in the lobby of a building. It wasn't nearly as interesting to Ian as whatever was swimming around in those buckets. Were those *eels*? Who brings home live eels for dinner? Are these people Chinese or Klingons?

"He's even wearing clothes like mine," Warren said.

Ian didn't know why Warren was showing them the photo. It meant nothing to him. But he did notice the battery icon on the phone was near empty.

"You've only got ten percent of your battery left," Ian said, just to be helpful.

Warren had something more to say and cast a wary eye at the fishmonger, who stood inside his stall at his cutting board, hacking at some huge fish with a cleaver. But it was obvious to Ian that the fishmonger wasn't paying any attention to them and besides, the sound of the blade smacking against the cutting board would make it difficult for him to eavesdrop. But Warren gestured them closer in a conspiratorial huddle anyway.

"The Chinese government is hiding something big and Wang is connected somehow," Warren said, powering off his phone and sticking it in his pocket. "We need to know what it is."

"We do?" Ian said.

The sudden silence in the control room was almost as startling as Fung's words, leaving them with a cliff-hanger.

"What happened?" Yat Fu said. "Where's the audio?"

"Fung must have turned off his phone," Pang said.

"Snipers!" Yat yelled, in case their attention had wandered. "Take Fung out the instant you can get a shot."

Sniper #1: *"Affirmative."*

Sniper #2: *"Affirmative."*

Yat watched the sniper scope images on-screen as both of the assassins got up and moved to new positions farther down the street.

"You've met Wang's daughter and tonight at the Big Wheel you'll meet his wife. They won't talk to me but they will talk to you," Warren said. "Why was Wang taken? Was it because of the questions he was asking? Or because of what he knows? Why is the government so eager to silence him and why now?"

"I'm a novelist," Ian said, "not an investigative reporter."

Margo stepped aside to make room for some shoppers who were passing by. "But the answers to Warren's questions could give you the inciting incident for Straker that you've been looking for to ignite your plot."

Sniper #1 took position on a rooftop. He moved his crosshairs over a break in the overlapping awnings and saw Margo standing in front of a seafood stall. Her body obscured most of Fung, except for one leg and part of a shoulder. But if she stepped just an inch to the left, he'd have a clear shot at Fung's head.

He steadied his aim and waited for his split second of opportunity.

Ian didn't buy Margo's argument. The reporter just wanted to use Ian to do his job for him. Screw that. Besides, what was Ian getting out of this? So far, Warren hadn't given him anything, just some possible motivations for the bad guys. Ian had plenty of those. What he needed was something that would get Straker moving.

"I don't feel comfortable talking to Mei about this," Ian said. "She shut me down the first time I brought it up."

"Because her bodyguards were there," Margo said.

Ian gave her a look that he hoped conveyed *shut up*. Why was she arguing for the reporter? Couldn't she tell that Ian was trying to find a polite way to say *no*?

Sniper #2 climbed up some bamboo scaffolding to a platform, hunkered down facing the street, steadied his rifle barrel on a horizontal pole, and peered through his sight at the back of Ludlow's head. He could shoot through Ludlow's skull to get to Fung's head, but it wasn't the optimal way to do it. All Ludlow had to do was take a half step to one side and he'd have a clear shot. Sniper #2 was good at waiting. Next to good aim, patience was a sniper's most valuable skill.

"Those men aren't there to protect her," Warren said. "They are there to keep her under Beijing's thumb. We'll get answers once she's free."

Why does he keep saying *we*, Ian asked himself. We don't work for him.

Warren looked urgently at Margo. "Do you understand what I'm telling you?"

Now he's giving Margo orders? Who does this guy think he is?

"Yes," Margo said.

"Not so fast," Ian held up his hands in a halting gesture. "I haven't agreed to any of this."

In that instant, three things happened at once:

1.  Some creature flopped in a bucket next to Ian and he dipped his head to look at it.
2.  Margo took a slight step aside to see what Ian was looking at.
3.  Warren Fung's head exploded like a watermelon loaded with dynamite as two .308 Winchester slugs simultaneously blasted into his skull.

# CHAPTER TWENTY-EIGHT

Nobody heard the two shots, but plenty of people saw Warren's head explode, or felt the wet gore splatter them, or saw his headless body drop to the ground, blood pouring from his neck like a dropped carton of milk.

Ian was frozen in place, unable to absorb what he was seeing and hearing. But Margo reacted immediately, grabbing Ian and pulling him down under the seafood display as screaming people scrambled away in terror. The fishmonger dropped his cleaver and ran into the back of his stall.

Now that Ian was on the ground, staring at the headless corpse, he understood what happened. "Holy shit. He's been shot."

Margo grabbed Warren's body by the feet and dragged him into the fish market. As she did, bullets hit the fish, kicking up ice. Why was somebody still shooting at them?

"Forget about him," Ian said. "He's beyond saving. We have to get out of here."

"Get his phone."

"Why?"

"Just do it!" she said with such ferocity that it startled him into complying. He couldn't think, so her decisiveness filled the void.

He reached into Warren's coat pocket for the phone and tried not to look at the soup of gore burbling from the man's neck. But he looked anyway. He vomited and yanked his arm away from the body, the phone in his hand.

Ian was still heaving when he saw Margo reach up and take the cleaver from the cutting board. She flattened Warren's right hand on the pavement, raised the cleaver above her head, and brought it down hard, chopping off its thumb.

"What the *fuck*!" Ian said.

She ignored him, yanked a plastic bag from a nearby dispenser, dropped the amputated thumb into it, and started filling the baggie with handfuls of crushed ice.

"You need to take this bag—" she began.

"The *fuck* I will," he said.

"—and run to the escalators." She tied the bag and held it out to him. "I'll catch up."

"Are you *insane*?" Ian said, but he took the bag.

Margo stood, grabbed a carp by the tail in each hand, and stepped into the street to confront two men who ran up, guns held at their sides.

Before they could raise their weapons, Margo beat the men with her fish in a whirlwind display of martial arts prowess. The men were taken down, and their weapons kicked out of their reach, in four seconds. It was something Clint Straker would do.

Ian didn't move, unable to believe what he was seeing.

She tossed the fish aside and looked angrily at Ian. "What are you still doing here? *Run!*"

Ian stuffed Warren Fung's thumb and his phone into his bag, scrambled to his feet, and dashed into the seafood stall, through a tiled room full of fish, sinks, and ice boxes, and out an open back door into a dark alley. Night had fallen while they were in the market.

Faced with a choice of which direction to run, Ian ran to his left because it was downhill and easier for a guy whose idea of exercise was lifting a full spoon of Chunky Monkey ice cream to his mouth.

He tore down the alley and barreled out onto Wellington Street beside a hardware store with rolls of bubble wrap, PVC elbow fittings, brooms, plastic planters, and buckets hanging over the open doorway. The display made no sense. *Nothing* made any sense anymore.

A roll of bubble wrap blew apart beside him with a loud pop that sounded like firecrackers, and Ian realized it had been hit with a bullet. He looked to his left and saw a man with a gun running up the street toward him.

*Shit!*

Ian bolted to his right and up the single lane of traffic toward the Mid-Level escalators, which passed over the street only a few yards away. He ran up the two flights of stairs to the bridge, crossed to the moving walkway heading uphill, and continued running, pushing past the pedestrians in his way and leaping over a wailing baby in a carriage.

At the Gage Street landing, he nearly lost his footing as he exited the moving walkway. He stopped for a moment to catch his breath and looked over his shoulder. The shooter was coming after him on the moving walkway at a fast march and with the relentless determination of a Terminator.

Ian darted onto the next inclined section of moving walkway, but it was even steeper than the one before. This was the most running Ian had done since the last time he was chased by killers. He'd be out of breath very soon and then the Terminator would be on him. He thought of Warren Fung's head exploding and got a second wind, picking up more speed.

And then Ian's chances of survival got worse.

As he neared the next landing, he saw two men running toward him down the graduated pathway alongside the next stretch of moving walkway. The men were staring at him with fierce intensity. They would all reach the landing at about the same time and it wouldn't be for a group hug.

He looked over his shoulder. The Terminator was getting closer. Ian's only chance was to get to the landing first, run down the stairs to the street, and hope to lose them in the crowd.

*Fat chance.*

# CHAPTER TWENTY-NINE

Yat Fu had watched the drama unfold with mounting frustration. He'd seen Fung go down and get dragged out of sight by the woman. But then his snipers lost sight of the targets and all he heard was heavy breathing as his agents ran toward the seafood stall to retrieve the reporter's phone and take his body away. Then he'd heard a few moist thwacks, followed by people shrieking and general pandemonium. He'd ordered his snipers to get out of there and told Pang to search nearby security cameras for any sign of Ludlow. The American spy showed up on camera seconds later running down an alley and Yat sent his men after him.

Now, Ludlow was out in the open on the Mid-Level escalators, pinned between Yat's men with nowhere to go. Soon they would have him and this farce would be over.

"Where is ground team one?" Yat asked Pang, who was now coordinating the teams along with the other operatives in the room. There were too many moving pieces for Yat to do it alone.

Pang held a finger to his earpiece, listening to a report. "Team three has arrived at the seafood stand. They say team one was attacked by the woman and she took their guns."

"Tell me they weren't beaten with another sex toy."

"Two carp," Pang said. "She's gone and so is Fung's phone."

Yat rubbed his temples. "Ludlow must have it. Get Fung's body out of there and bring Ludlow and the phone to me."

◎

There was no point in running, Ian concluded. The two men in front of him and the one behind him all had guns. He was unarmed and boxed in. So Ian stopped running and let the moving walkway carry him the last few feet to the landing and his fate.

One of the two men coming toward him smiled and said, "You're coming with us, Ludlow."

*Who were these people? How did they know his name?*

He started to raise his hands in surrender when he heard four muffled pops in rapid succession. The two guys went down, shot in the knees.

Ian whirled around to see Margo crouched in the Gage Street staircase in a firing stance with a silenced Glock in her hands. She winked at Ian, turned slightly, and shot the man behind Ian in the knees, taking him down, too. The pedestrians on the walkway began screaming and running in all directions, creating an atmosphere of general chaos on the elevated escalators.

Margo held the gun to her side, dashed over to Ian, and glanced over her shoulder. Two more men were charging toward them from the Wellington landing but their progress was slowed by the panicked pedestrians trying to run in the opposite direction on the moving ramp.

"Don't just stand there gaping," Margo said. "Run!"

Margo rushed past him onto the moving walkway and Ian hurried after her.

They were over Hollywood Road when Margo stopped abruptly, though the moving walkway still carried them along. People were still

140

scrambling and screaming everywhere. The two pursuers were catching up and not far ahead two more men were rushing toward them.

Margo peered over the railing and looked at Ian. "We have to jump."

Ian glanced down at the traffic. A big bus was just emerging from under the bridge. "It's suicide."

"Possibly," she said. "But we're definitely dead if we stay here."

A bullet hit the pillar beside Ian's head and that made the decision for him. Margo and Ian looked at each other and, in unison, jumped up and vaulted over the railing.

Ian's scream was cut short as he landed hard on the bus. He slid across the slick metal surface toward the side, unable to get a handhold on anything, certain he'd fall into the street and get run over by the cars behind. But his hand caught a protruding vent and he stopped his fall, his legs dangling over the side.

Margo landed on her back and immediately began firing her silenced Glock up at the bridge, forcing the gunmen at the railing to take cover until the bus turned a corner, out of their sight.

◎

This was an unmitigated disaster. Yat knew it and so did everybody in the room. They'd just killed a man and started a gunfight on the streets of Hong Kong, a semiautonomous region of China where the Ministry of State Security didn't have jurisdiction and wasn't supposed to be operating.

"Hong Kong police are converging on the scene," Pang said. "The corpse has been removed and we are evacuating our injured men."

Yat addressed the entire room. "I want a full cleanse. Erase all the security camera footage from the Mid-Level escalators and any public or private surveillance systems. Monitor social media and delete any photos or videos that capture the operation or any of the participants. Identify cell phones that were active in the area, access their activity, and wipe them."

The operatives in the room had engaged in this same swift, all-encompassing electronic cleansing of evidence many times before when the government's suppression of public dissent had turned excessively violent.

"We began the cleanse in real time as the operation was ongoing," Pang said.

"Excellent," Yat said.

"But the missing footage will alert the authorities that we've conducted an operation in the city."

Yat waved away Pang's concern. "This is still China. State security is more important than Hong Kong's illusion of temporary independence."

"We're not supposed to attract attention with our activities and we just killed a *Wall Street Journal* reporter in the middle of the Graham Street market."

"Nobody will know because his body will never be found."

"Ludlow and French know."

"They will never be found, either," Yat said, irritated by Pang's worries. "Where is the bus?"

"It's on Wyndham heading into Central."

"Do we have any other teams in the area?"

"They are ten minutes out," Pang said.

# CHAPTER THIRTY

Ian swung his legs back up on top of the bus and lay there, trying to catch his breath. Margo ejected the spent magazine from the Glock, tossed the magazine into the street, checked to be sure there wasn't a round in the gun's chamber, then threw the weapon overboard, too. Her casual familiarity with the gun gave Ian an epiphany that infuriated him.

He sat up and stared at Margo. "You're a CIA agent!"

"On my first assignment." She took another Glock, also equipped with a silencer, out of her bag. "So far, so good."

"How can you say that? I'm carrying around a dead man's phone and his thumb."

"We got out alive with the intel. That's a win in our business." Margo ejected the magazine and was pleased to see that it was full of bullets. She slid the magazine back into place and slipped the Glock in her bag.

While she did that, Ian began to reconsider everything that had happened to him since Margo showed up at his apartment door. It was all a lie. He'd been used from the beginning. "The night terrors, going broke. Your entire sob story was a lie. What's the real story?"

"I'll tell you later. You have to trust me now, like you asked me to trust you in Seattle," she said. "How does it feel to be on the other side this time?"

"Is that what this is? Payback?"

"No, but it's a nice perk." Margo looked ahead. Several streets converged at a wide, busy intersection with skyscrapers on almost every corner. The skyscrapers each had large department stores or multilevel shopping malls at their bases and were connected by covered second-floor pedestrian bridges that spanned the intersection and continued on toward the waterfront. "We get off here."

The bus came to a stop. Margo slid off the bus and landed on her feet on the sidewalk. She made it look easy. Ian slid off feetfirst, lost his footing as he landed, and fell hard on his side.

"Are you okay?" Margo offered Ian her hand.

"Far from it." He took her hand and she lifted him to his feet.

"Stop whining." She gestured with a nod of her head to the Marks & Spencer department store across the street. "There's a pedestrian bridge in there that will take us straight to the waterfront."

Still holding his hand, she ran across the street, dragging him along into the store, through the sales floor, and up the escalator to the bridge.

"Where are Ludlow and the woman now?" Yat demanded.

Security camera footage from a covered walkway appeared on screen and showed Ian and Margo running hand in hand down the bridge, which was packed with people going to and from the business district. Yat was amused by their hand holding. It was a pathetic attempt to blend in, to look like just another couple in a hurry instead of two spies running for their lives.

"They are in the central elevated walkway system," Pang said. "They appear to be heading to the ferry terminal."

But Yat knew that wasn't their destination. They were going to the Hong Kong observation wheel, located adjacent to the ferry terminal, for the opening ceremonies for the *Straker* movie. The area would be filled with media and sealed off by the police.

"They are going to the observation wheel," Yat said. "We need to intercept Ludlow and the woman before they get there."

As Ian ran down the elevated walkway, he looked to his left, where a massive Apple store also crossed over the six lanes of Lung Wo Road below, which was more of a waterfront freeway than a street. The Ferris wheel was up ahead, beside the ferry terminal and angled toward the harbor. Margo glanced over her shoulder. Nobody seemed to be chasing them, at least not on foot.

"Who is after us?" Ian asked. He was very aware of his hand in hers and how hard she was gripping him. She was more anxious than she appeared.

"The Ministry of State Security."

"Then they know where we are." Ian pointed with his free hand at the cameras throughout the walkway. "They're watching us right now."

He had an ominous and terrifying feeling of déjà vu. Once again, they were on the run from a government intelligence agency out to kill them.

"We'll be safe if we can get to the wheel," she said. "They won't come at us there. They aren't allowed to operate in Hong Kong."

"That didn't stop them from killing Warren Fung."

"He wasn't surrounded by Hong Kong police and the international media while standing next to one of the biggest movie stars on earth," Margo said. "We will be."

"We aren't there yet."

She led him to the staircase down to Man Yiu Street, the last exit off the walkway before it reached the Central Ferry Piers. The instant they hit the sidewalk, they saw two cars come to a screeching stop across the street.

"Run," she said.

She'd been saying that a lot lately.

They dashed across the red cobblestone plaza toward the two-hundred-foot-tall Ferris wheel with blue-lighted spokes that radiated from a massive bright-white orb in the center. Forty-two glass gondolas, capable of holding a dozen people in each, circled the wheel's inner rim. The area around the base of the wheel was sealed off with K-rails except for a single roped-off opening manned by uniformed Hong Kong police officers. More stony-faced officers were stationed at intervals along the K-rail perimeter to prevent it from being breached by the hundreds of people crowded around, hoping to get a peek at the celebrities on the other side. Inside the perimeter were dressing room trailers, studio camera trucks, catering vans, and a crowd of reporters milling around with their photographers and cameramen.

Ian and Margo pushed their way through the mob toward the entrance. Behind them, eight assassins were closing in, brutally striking and shoving people aside. But their violent approach had consequences. The crowd began to get pissed, turning to confront the aggressive intruders.

That gave Ian and Margo the extra moments they needed. They reached into their bags for the ID lanyards that Susie Yip had given them at the studio and held them up to police officers as they reached the entrance.

"We need to get through," Ian said.

"Let me see your invitation," the officer said.

Ian held up the laminated ID on his lanyard. "This is our all-access pass. We're with the crew. You have to let us in."

"We don't have to do anything," the officer said, eyeing the IDs with skepticism. "No invitation, no entry."

Margo glanced back into the crowd. The assassins were getting closer, handily overpowering the people in their path.

"I'm the writer of this movie. We're going to be late and they can't start the production party without us," Ian said. "Do you really want to be responsible for holding up everything?"

That's when Susie Yip appeared behind the officers. "Let them in. They are with us. Didn't you see their lanyards?"

The officer stepped aside without apology and let Ian and Margo through. They joined Susie, who eyed them both with curiosity.

"Did you just run all the way here?" she asked.

"We didn't want to be late." Ian looked over his shoulder.

The assassins were stopped at the police line and stood there glowering at him. They wouldn't be coming in after them but they wouldn't be leaving, either. He was sure that reinforcements were on the way. Maybe more snipers, too.

Ian and Margo had made it safely to the event. But there was another, less comforting way of looking at it: They were trapped.

# CHAPTER THIRTY-ONE

Susie escorted Ian and Margo to the dressing room trailers. Something about Margo caught the woman's eye.

"Are those fish scales on your arms?"

"It's glitter," Margo said. "Very fashionable in the States."

Susie stopped outside a trailer and faced Ian. "Your tuxedo is inside. You can clean up and change in here. The photo shoot is in fifteen minutes."

"Thanks," Ian said. "Can't wait."

He and Margo stepped into the trailer. Ian slammed the door shut, locked it, and immediately confronted Margo.

"Talk."

Margo held out her hand. "Give me Warren's phone."

Ian reached into his shoulder bag, found the phone, and gave it to Margo. She turned it on and held a finger to her lips, signaling him to keep quiet, then put her hand into Ian's bag and took out the baggie containing Warren's thumb. Most of the ice had melted, so the thumb was in water.

She opened the bag, took out the thumb, wiped the water off it with her shirt, and pressed the thumb against the iPhone's fingerprint reader, unlocking the device.

"Clever," Ian said. "But gory."

Margo put the thumb back in the bag, set it on the counter beside the sink, and then opened up the iPhone's settings app. She turned off location services and disabled the microphone.

"I don't want anyone using the phone to listen to us or track where we are," she said.

"It won't make much of a difference. There are probably a dozen Chinese agents outside already, but even if we slipped past them, there are more cameras all over the city. There's nowhere we can go in Hong Kong without being seen."

Margo opened up the phone's photo app and brought up the shot of the Warren Fung impersonator.

"Do you know him?" Ian asked.

"Nope. I'll text the photo to myself but I'm sure there's more on this phone we're going to need, like all of Fung's emails," Margo said. "I'll change the phone's password so we won't have to carry that thumb around with us."

"That would be nice," Ian said.

Margo started going through the steps on the phone to change the password and, while she was at it, the fingerprint ID. "You need to get dressed."

Ian went to the bedroom closet and found the tuxedo hanging inside. He closed the bedroom door just enough to give him some privacy while he got undressed.

"I'm guessing that you thought the bird market would be a really great place for an exchange because that's exactly what it was. The message you received there sent us to the Peak," Ian said, stripping down to his underwear. "That's where you used the telescope to get the next message, probably written in an apartment window somewhere, telling you where to meet Warren, who is a CIA source."

"Good guess." Margo dropped the reset iPhone back into her shoulder bag beside the Glock. "Maybe you should have accepted Healy's job offer at the CIA instead of me."

"Why did you take it?" He reached for the tuxedo pants.

"I had a hard time going back to my old life after what we went through together. It was too boring." Margo emptied the water in the baggie into the sink, careful not to let the thumb fall into the drain. "I missed the rush, the feeling I had when I fought off that bitch assassin."

"Fear and revulsion?" Ian pulled up his pants and adjusted the inside waistband so it fit snugly.

Margo carried the baggie to the bathroom and lifted up the toilet seat. "While we were on the run, facing certain death, I felt truly alive and present in a way I never did before. I discovered who I really am and what I was meant to do."

"Kill people?" Ian reached for the tuxedo shirt.

"No, but it sure as hell isn't singing, dog walking, or driving authors around Seattle." She reached into the baggie, took out the dismembered thumb, and dropped it into the toilet. "I have a talent for this. Healy saw it and fast-tracked my training."

Margo flushed the toilet, dropped the baggie into the trash, and washed her hands with soap and water.

Ian opened a ziplock baggie containing six onyx button studs and buttoned up his shirt with them. "Why did you have to use me as your cover to come to China?"

"Because it was too good an opportunity to pass up." Margo dried her hands and came out of the bathroom. "Wang Kang had a ton of dirt on China's ruling class that he kept secret and he was a loyal government servant. And they still screwed him over. Healy thinks Wang is probably itching for revenge and that Mei could be our way to reach him and offer him a chance to get it. Now I'm sure Healy is right."

Ian came out of the bedroom holding his shoes in one hand. "What do you mean?"

"Didn't you hear what Warren told us? Mei wants to defect."

"He didn't say that."

"Yes, he did." Margo stepped up to Ian and adjusted his loose bow tie. "In so many words."

"Words are my profession. Defection never came up in our conversation."

"It was all there, between the lines."

Ian pushed her hands away. "It's too tight, you're strangling me."

She stepped back. "You write about spies, but you don't know shit about how it really works."

"And you do?"

"I'm in it now."

"So am I," Ian said and shouldered past her. "Thanks to you."

"You won't get any sympathy or apologies from me." Margo followed Ian to the couch, where he sat down to put on his shoes. "This situation is no different than how it started with us in Seattle, back when you were a target and made me one, too."

Ian froze, midway through tying his laces into a bow. He had another epiphany, one even more shocking to him than the one he'd had atop the bus. This one scared the shit out of him.

"You're right, it's exactly the same situation." Ian looked her in the eye. "The Chinese don't care about you. It's *me* they're after."

She walked away, shaking her head in dismay. "You are so full of yourself. It's unbelievable. It always has to be about you. You know what you are? You're an egomaniac."

Ian resumed tying his shoes. "Think about it. Who did they attack after we left the bird market? *Me.* Why? To get the message that they thought was passed to me. And why were they watching us? Because of my story."

"What story?"

"The one you're supposed to be helping me research here instead of seducing publicists and playing spy."

"You mean the crazy conspiracy shit you came up with for a lousy Straker novel?" Margo laughed. "Get real. How would Chinese intelligence know anything about that?"

"Because when I logged in to the Wi-Fi at the hotel, one of their data bots hacked my computer and they read my notes." Ian finished tying his shoes and realized it was an apt metaphor for the way he was tying up the plot that had unfolded around him. "The Chinese think I've discovered their scheme to seize control of our country."

Margo stared at him long and hard before speaking again. He wasn't quite sure what to make of the expression on her face. Was it anger? Dread? Nausea? Perhaps it was all three.

"You're saying that we're being chased by Chinese assassins because another one of your fictional plots is coming true."

"I'm cursed," Ian said.

"There's no way this is happening again." Margo sat down next to him on the couch. "No fucking way. There's got to be another explanation."

There was a knock at the door. Ian got up and opened it. Susie stood outside.

"We're ready for the photo shoot," she said.

"So am I." Ian went to get his tuxedo jacket, slipped it on, and stepped outside. Margo got up, slung her bag over her shoulder, and went along with him.

# CHAPTER THIRTY-TWO

Susie led Ian and Margo to a stage that had been strategically placed to get both the Ferris wheel and the Hong Kong skyline into the background. Damon Matthews was already on the stage, claiming his spot on top of Straker's white motorcycle while several grips adjusted the lights and the photographer checked the image on his camera. Damon wore the same tuxedo as Ian and was in a heated conversation with Larry Steinberg.

Wang Mei stood beside the stage in a stunning black dress with a plunging neckline while two makeup artists made last minute touch-ups to her face and cleavage with tiny brushes and sponges. There were a lot of reporters milling around who wished they could be her makeup artists. Her two bodyguards stood off to one side, not bothering to hide on their faces the intensity of their hatred for Ian and Margo.

Margo gave them the finger.

"Don't antagonize them," Ian said.

She patted her bag to remind Ian of the Glock that was inside. "They should worry about antagonizing *me*."

Margo might as well have been giving the finger to Yat Fu, who watched her on the bodyguards' button cameras. He was so angered by her impertinence that he was tempted to give a kill order to the two snipers atop the ferry terminal.

"Do our snipers have the two Americans in their sights?" Yat asked.

"Yes, sir," Pang said. "But with all due respect, it would be a grave mistake to shoot them in front of the media."

"Thank you for stating the obvious." Yat just liked knowing the two spies were one finger twitch away from death, especially since they'd managed to get away with Fung's phone and whatever intelligence it contained. It was an infuriating failure but not a crippling one. Yat was confident that Fung knew nothing about the impending endgame or the reporter would have warned the spies about it. The important thing was that Fung was silenced. Whatever he knew probably died with him. "What do we know about the woman with Ludlow?"

"Very little. Margo French is his driver and researcher," Pang said. "They met in Seattle on his last book tour. Prior to that, she was a lounge singer at lesbian bars, a dog walker, and a cashier at a bookstore. She's a University of Washington dropout and appears to have no professional training of any kind."

"Obviously that's all false. We've seen her skills."

"If she's a spy, too, then the CIA didn't go to much trouble to create a cover for her."

"The banality of her life story is what makes it brilliant. It's designed to make us overlook her and we did," Yat said. "Clearly, Ludlow is the brains and she is the brawn."

"You think she's assigned as his bodyguard?"

"He's obviously an investigator who was sent here to corroborate the intelligence report and her job is to protect him. We need to take Ludlow alive so we can learn where that report came from."

"What about her?"

"Expendable," Yat Fu said. "Soon we'll cut off that finger and shove it down her throat."

Ian and Margo walked up to the stage, close enough to overhear Damon and Larry's conversation.

"I'm still in that tiny trailer," Damon said. "I've got no room to work. Where's my motor home?"

"It's arriving at the port tomorrow," Larry said. "You'll have it on set in forty-eight hours."

Damon pointed at him. "You'd better be right, because if it's not here in two days, then I won't be on set. So unless you want to shoot this whole fucking movie in my hotel room, you'll get me my motor home."

Larry walked off the stage, glowering at Ian as he passed.

"We're making friends everywhere we go," Margo said.

"At least Larry isn't trying to kill us."

"Suggest another script change and see what happens."

Damon spotted Ian and smiled at him from the motorcycle. "There he is, the man who made this all possible. We're living your dream, man."

And Ian and Margo were living the nightmare. Ian wished his plots would stop coming true. Maybe, if he survived this, he'd start writing westerns.

Susie stepped up onto the stage beside Damon. "Thank you for agreeing to do this publicity shoot with Ian."

"I'm glad to do anything to support the film," Damon said.

Ian whispered in Margo's ear. "Plus he gets two percent of the royalties from the tie-in editions of the book that have his picture on the cover."

"Come on up, Ian," Susie said, then looked over at Wang Mei. "You too, please, Mei. The photographer is ready."

Ian and Mei went up on the stage and stood on either side of Damon, who, by virtue of being on the motorcycle, appeared to be as tall as they were.

"You look incredible, Mei," Ian said.

"I feel like a movie star."

"You are."

"Not yet," she said.

The photographer started taking photos, giving them directions for a variety of poses and expressions. At one point, Susie handed them each copies of Ian's book *Death Benefits*, and more pictures were taken. While all of this was going on, Margo kept an eye on the two body-guards, who were having a hard time maintaining their ferocious expressions and now just appeared constipated.

Ian stood there smiling through the photo shoot thinking about Margo and how she'd lied to him, deftly manipulating his sympathy and guilt, so she could use him as her cover on a trip to Hong Kong. At least it had been an accident when he had put her life in danger, but she did it to him on purpose. It was a betrayal. And yet, somehow, he felt like he was to blame again for their predicament.

Sure, she'd used him, but it was the story on his laptop and his deadly mistake of logging in to the hotel Wi-Fi that truly put them in the crosshairs of Chinese intelligence. Of course, it didn't help that she was a spy and, by doing what spies do, made him look like one, too. But she'd done that by accident, and once he realized that, then it really was impossible to get angry with her. It was his fiction, mixed with some fate, that had screwed them both.

*Again.*

After several hundred photos were taken, the photographer declared that he was done and that he was confident one or two shots might work. The actors and Ian stepped off the stage and Susie led them, along with Margo, to the other side of the Ferris wheel, where a podium and a buffet table were set up and P. J. and the movie crew were mingling with the media.

But the mingling stopped as a gleaming two-toned Rolls-Royce drove up and parked near the podium. A bodyguard emerged from the front passenger seat and opened one of the rear doors. A bejeweled, black-haired Chinese woman in her sixties got out of the car and radiated such a regal bearing that she might as well have been wearing a crown and holding a staff.

Margo leaned close to Ian and said, "That's Wang Jing, Mei's mother. She's as much of a prisoner as her daughter is."

Another bodyguard got out of the Rolls and stared hard at Ian and Margo as he joined his partner to flank Jing.

"We know who they're really working for," Ian said.

Mei went to Jing and gave her a kiss on the cheek, then introduced her to Damon and P. J., who then escorted her to the podium. Jing tapped the microphone to make sure it was on and then faced the crowd and their cameras.

"Welcome, everyone. I am Wang Jing. I'm so proud to be here today on behalf of Wang Studios and my husband, Wang Kang, who is deeply disappointed that he couldn't attend due to his illness." She spoke English with an upper-crust, British accent. "This is an auspicious moment. The start of principal photography on *Straker* begins a new era for the Chinese film industry on the global stage. That's why it's so important that we begin by performing the traditional 'big luck' ceremony."

She went to the buffet table, where there was a cooked pig and a tantalizing assortment of fruit and cakes, surrounded by candles and incense sticks. In the center of the table was a gong. A Buddhist priest stood beside the gong, lit an incense stick, and recited a prayer in Cantonese. He pointed the incense stick in four directions, concluded his prayer, and gave a slight nod to Wang Jing.

She picked up the baton and struck the gong, and the Chinese audience and crew immediately broke into applause. Ian, Margo, and the other Americans followed their example and began clapping, too, as Jing returned to the podium.

"Thank you all for being here," she said. "I hope this film is the first of many cinematic masterpieces born from this historic collaboration of stellar talents."

Susie appeared at Ian's side. "Picture time."

She brought him up to the podium, where he joined the stars and P. J. to stand alongside Wang Jing for several group photos. When the photos were taken, the group dispersed and the journalists made a bee-line for the food.

Susie corralled Ian and Jing and waved over her photographer. "Could we get a photo with just the two of you?"

Ian stood beside Jing while more photos were taken. He tried to think of something to say to her and settled on: "I'm sorry your hus-band couldn't be here to join us."

"Thank you," she said.

"I wish there was something I could do to help."

Jing surprised Ian by grasping him by the forearm and asking, "Have you and your assistant seen the view from the wheel yet?"

"No, we haven't."

"Then I must show you before they start filming the scene."

Keeping him in her grasp, she guided him toward the ramp that led to an open cabin on the wheel. Margo moved into step beside them and the two bodyguards immediately rushed up. Jing scowled at them.

"Stay," she commanded, as if they were misbehaving Dobermans, and they obeyed. "A kidnapper can't possibly get to me on a Ferris wheel. If you really want to keep me safe, you'll make sure nobody disturbs the proper operation of the attraction."

The bodyguards stayed put and two baffled attendants opened the cabin doors for Ian, Jing, and Margo, who stepped inside. A minute later, the Big Wheel turned and the cabin rose slowly up into the air.

# CHAPTER THIRTY-THREE

Classified Location, Kangbashi District, Ordos, Inner Mongolia, China. July 3. 8:21 p.m. China Standard Time.

"Why didn't the bodyguards go into the cabin with them?" Pang asked, standing beside Yat Fu as they regarded the button-camera views from the bodyguards as well as those provided by the security cameras on the ferry building.

"It would have broken their cover to ignore her orders."

"She knows they don't actually work for her."

"But the others around her don't," Yat said. "How would it have looked to the media and the dignitaries to see her bring her bodyguards with her to talk with a writer? I believe our operatives made a wise call. It's about time one of our agents did. Do we have audio and video in the cabins?"

"Ordinarily, yes."

"Ordinarily?"

"The production crew disabled the system so it wouldn't interfere with the filming of their scenes tonight."

That was a problem. Yat needed to know what they were talking about in that cabin. "I want Jing taken in tonight for interrogation."

"Are you sure that's politically wise?"

"Are you questioning my judgment?" Yat Fu certainly would be if he were in Pang's position. Every decision that he'd made over the last two days had gone wrong. Ludlow escaped with Fung's phone and the intelligence it contained, three of Yat's agents were on choppers to the mainland for emergency knee surgery, two others had broken noses, and the Hong Kong authorities were already complaining to the Ministry of State Security in Beijing about their violent encroachments on the region's autonomy. And what did Yat Fu have to show for it? Nothing. His only solace was that none of his failures or the anger of some petty bureaucrats would matter soon.

"No, of course not, sir," Pang said, bowing his head ever so slightly in deference and obedience. "I was merely offering my counsel for you to consider."

That was the smart, suck-up thing to say and Yat Fu wanted to believe it.

"She is talking to an American spy. I need to know which is stronger, her loyalty to her husband or to her country," Yat said. "Her answers to my questions will determine that and her longevity."

"Understood, sir. How shall we proceed with the two Americans?"

With the Hong Kong authorities already irritated by his actions in the city, and his masters in Beijing also likely to be, neither abducting Ludlow and French off the street nor dragging them out of their hotel rooms was a viable option.

"We will keep them under constant surveillance and wait for an opening to detain them without creating an incident," Yat said. "If that's not possible, we'll grab them when they try to leave the country. Either way, no one in America will ever see them again."

## The Big Wheel, Hong Kong. July 3. 8:25 p.m. Hong Kong Time.

The view of the Hong Kong and Kowloon skylines from the Ferris wheel cabin was impressive and very cinematic. But Ian was too nervous to appreciate it. Something big was about to happen. He could feel it.

Jing released Ian's arm, gave him a thorough visual appraisal, and then frowned her disapproval.

Ian tugged at his sleeves. "You don't think I look great in this tuxedo?"

"I was expecting more," she said.

"More what?" Ian said.

"Muscle and strength of character. Some sense that you have the necessary capability to do what has to be done."

"Which is?" Ian asked.

"You have five days to get my daughter out of China."

"I told you she wanted to defect." Margo smiled at Ian in triumph, then regarded Jing. "But how did you know to approach us?"

Ian answered before Jing could. "Because it wasn't only the Australian bodyguard who fed Warren Fung information after the abduction. Mrs. Wang reached out to the reporter, too, because she knew he was a CIA informant. It was Fung who told her who we are."

"Mr. Ludlow is correct," Jing said. "The Chinese government needs to know there is a price to pay for betraying loyalty."

Margo eyed Ian. "How did you know that she was Fung's source?"

"Plotting is my strength," Ian said, then addressed Jing. "Why should we exfiltrate your daughter?"

"Exfiltrate?" Margo asked.

"Quietly get her the hell out," Ian replied.

"Why didn't you just say that?"

"Because this is how spies talk." And he sure felt like one now, wearing a tuxedo, facing Hong Kong, and talking about a defection.

All he needed was a martini, shaken not stirred, in his hand. He'd never felt so cool.

"I'm a spy and I don't talk like that," Margo said.

"Because you're new at this and don't know all the terminology yet," Ian said. "I've been doing it longer."

"In your imagination," Margo said. "That doesn't count."

Jing sighed with irritation. "You will get my daughter out of China because in return she will give you intelligence of extreme value to the United States. But it loses most of its value in five days."

Margo was irritated by Jing's irritation. "How do we know the intelligence you're offering isn't bullshit?"

"If it is, you can send my daughter back to Beijing. You risk nothing."

"Except our lives," Margo said.

Jing sighed again, this time with impatience. This was a woman with an entire vocabulary of sighs. "Your lives are of little significance in the grand scheme of things, unless you succeed in this exfiltration."

"What about your life?" Ian asked.

"My husband and I planned for this possibility, Mr. Ludlow. Or perhaps I should say 'eventuality.' He entrusted me to ensure our daughter's safety. That is my only purpose now."

"You are betraying your country," he said.

"They betrayed us first."

"How does Mei feel about this?" Ian said. "And what it means for you and your husband?"

"She knows we are dead already," Jing sighed with resignation. "Her purpose now is vengeance."

# CHAPTER THIRTY-FOUR

The Big Wheel, Hong Kong. July 3. 10:13 p.m. Hong Kong
Time.

A helicopter with a stuntman firing a fake automatic weapon out of the open cargo area hovered in front of the Ferris wheel cabin where Damon and Mei were performing their scene while a second helicopter, equipped with cameras, circled them all. Crowds of people massed around the ferry terminal and the K-rail perimeter erected around the Big Wheel to watch the action.

Ian and Margo observed the scene from the ground, where they sat in two director's chairs, about twenty yards away from where P. J. Tyler directed the action from a set of four video monitors mounted in a rolling stand. P. J. sat with Larry Steinberg, the assistant director, and the director of photography and used a walkie-talkie to give directions to everyone up in the Ferris wheel and choppers.

Mei's bodyguards stood near the director, where they could keep an eye on what she was doing. But every so often, the two Chinese agents would check out Ian and Margo. Margo kept her eye on them, too, and one hand near the Glock in her shoulder bag.

"Relax," Ian said. "We're safe as long as we stay with the film crew. You said so yourself."

"What worries me is what happens when filming stops for the night and the police protection around the set goes away."

"We get a ride with Damon and the director back to the hotel."

"Where assassins will slit our throats while we sleep," Margo said.

"Damon Matthews and the entire American crew are staying there, too. The Chinese won't try to snatch or kill us while we're embedded with the cast and crew for the same reasons we're safe right now."

"That means we can't leave the hotel or the studio or set foot on the street unless we're with the crew."

"Not if we want to live," Ian said.

"How are we going to get Mei out of Hong Kong alive when we can't get out ourselves?" Margo said. "And even if we could get away, she's got bodyguards glued to her twenty-four/seven."

"Except when she's shooting."

"So we're screwed," Margo said.

"It's a story problem."

"What's that supposed to mean?"

"I write Straker into no-win situations in every book and I always find a way out for him," Ian said. "I'll do the same for us."

"This isn't a novel," she said. "You can't write a solution and expect the Chinese assassins to follow your script."

"Why not?"

"Because they are real people in the real world," she said, the pitch of her voice rising as she became more exasperated with him. "They aren't fictional characters that you can control."

Ian gestured up at the Big Wheel, where Mei and Damon were pretending to dodge bullets from a helicopter. "Back in Los Angeles, six or eight screenwriters—I've lost count, to be honest—wrote that scene in a script and now it's actually happening, right here in Hong Kong. It's a Godlike power."

"But it's not real," she said, practically shrieking at him.

"I'm watching it happen." Ian pointed to the wheel. "So are tens of thousands of people on the Hong Kong and Kowloon waterfronts."

She took a deep breath and tried to calm down. When she spoke again, it was if she were explaining something basic to a child, like the importance of chewing food before swallowing it.

"You are watching actors playing make-believe characters in a fictional situation," Margo said. "If the characters get killed, the actors live. If we get killed, we're dead."

"That's the only difference."

"It's a big difference," she shrieked.

Ian stayed quiet for a few minutes, giving Margo a chance to cool off. As he did, he pictured himself back in his office, facing a blank dry-erase board, and imagined Straker in the same situation they were in. With this image still in mind, he asked Margo a question.

"Before you left the United States, you must have been briefed on emergency options," Ian said. "What was your escape plan if everything went wrong for you?"

"There's a fishing boat in Aberdeen we use to smuggle out assets as a last, desperate resort. But it won't work for you and me now," she said. "We've been exposed and there are too many eyes on us. We'd never make it and we'd burn that escape route for future ops."

Her reasoning made sense. He glanced at the crowd behind the K-rail perimeter. It wasn't hard to spot the faces of the Chinese agents. They were the ones watching Ian and not the movie action unfolding on the Big Wheel.

He shifted his gaze to the pedestrian bridge, the high-rise buildings, and the ferry terminal, knowing that there were probably dozens of cameras, and a couple of sniper scopes, trained on him right now. But watching was all they were doing, all they *could* do. He felt that familiar tickle of inspiration and he began to fill his imaginary dry-erase board with notes, story beats, plot moves.

"Perhaps all of those eyes on us can work in our favor."

"How?" she asked.

Ian didn't answer. He reached into a pouch on the side of his chair and pulled out a copy of the script with a shooting schedule attached to it. "Tomorrow night they're shooting some of Wang Mei's scenes in the taxi chase."

"Yeah, so?"

Ian flipped through the script, finding the scenes scheduled for the next day. They were shooting Eve, the character played by Mei, steering a runaway taxi from the back seat while being pursued through Kowloon by assassins on motorcycles. The scene in the script merged in his mind with the new scenes he was sketching out on his imaginary whiteboard. A story was taking shape.

"I've seen that look before," Margo said. "You've got an idea."

"Do you have a map of Hong Kong?"

"I do." Margo reached into her bag and handed the map to him. He opened it up and found the section of Lai Chi Kok Road where Mei's scenes in the chase would be shot.

"I like this," he said.

"Am I going to like this?" she asked.

"It's something Straker would do."

"What do you mean by that?"

"We're going to turn our disadvantages to our advantage."

"Rephrasing what you said before into a line from a fortune cookie doesn't make it any clearer."

"But more relevant to our setting. Do you have another CIA contact in Hong Kong who can run a few errands for us without exposing himself to the enemy?"

Margo hesitated for a moment, then said, "Susie Yip."

Now *everything* that had happened since they arrived made sense to Ian, but this was the first revelation that made him happy.

"She's a CIA agent?"

"Why don't you say it louder?" Margo said. "I'm not sure that Mei's bodyguards, the film crew, and the assassins behind the police line all heard you."

"So you didn't really seduce her ten seconds after we arrived in Hong Kong," he said. "You were already lovers."

"We met when we were both in training," she said. "Not that it matters."

"It did to you," Ian said. "You wanted me to believe that you had lesbian superpowers."

"No, I didn't. I was just protecting my cover. I'm a spy, remember?"

"You could have come up with a different story. But you chose to portray yourself as irresistible to women just to make me feel inadequate."

"You're being ridiculous. We have more pressing issues to worry about than your jealousy over my red-hot sex life. What's your plan for getting you, me, and Wang Mei out of China alive?"

Ian found a pen in the pouch and began writing on the shooting schedule. "This is what we're going to need for tomorrow and what Susie has to do for us. Don't worry, she'll never be in any danger."

"But we will be," she said.

"We already are," Ian said. "What's a little more?"

He tore the shooting schedule pages from the script and handed them to Margo, who looked over his notes, nodded to herself, and then smiled at him.

"If we're going to die," Margo said. "It might as well be spectacular."

# CHAPTER THIRTY-FIVE

The shooting didn't end until 2:00 a.m. Ian and Margo went back to the hotel with Susie, the stars, and P. J. in the studio van. During the drive, Margo slipped Susie the list and Fung's phone and kept her eye on the rearview mirror and the car that followed them.

Despite all of the bloodshed that he'd seen, the shocking secrets that had been revealed, the extreme danger that he was in, and the deadly challenges that he faced, Ian fell asleep the instant he got into bed and didn't wake up until his alarm went off at 10:00 a.m. He felt rested, with only a mild hum of anxiety running through his nerves.

It was July 4, Independence Day in America, and today he would be asserting that independence in the face of communism. It was a ridiculous notion. But thinking of what he and Margo were going to do as an act of patriotism, rather than suicidal desperation, emboldened him. He actually had "The Star-Spangled Banner" playing in his head as he went down to the lobby for a late breakfast with Margo. They ate from the buffet instead of ordering from the menu in case agents of the Ministry of State Security tried to drug their food, make them sick, and put them in an ambulance to Beijing.

After breakfast, Ian and Margo piled into the studio van with some of the other American production crew members and stunt drivers and were driven to the nearby filming location on Lai Chi Kok road.

A six-block section of the street was entirely closed off to traffic north of Boundary Street. There were wooden sawhorses and a police car barricading each intersection to make sure that no vehicles or civilians wandered into the chase area. The second-unit crew had been shooting scenes from the chase, again and again, on this same section of street for several weeks, so crowd control had become routine for the police.

The van driver steered slowly through the crowd of onlookers, who parted to let them pass, and through the police line to the production base camp at the wide Lai Chi Kok and Boundary Street intersection. The dressing room trailers, makeup trailers, equipment trucks, and other vehicles were parked there. It was also where P. J., Larry Steinberg, the director of photography, and other key production personnel would watch the chase unfold on monitors displaying the feed from the movie cameras.

As Ian got out of the van, he looked north on Lai Chi Kok and saw the stunt cars, motorcycles, and buses parked along the six-block stretch, roughly in the positions where each vehicle would come into play in the chase.

The red-and-white Toyota taxi, with the stunt driver's roll cage on top and the cameraman's platform on the passenger side, was the star of today's shoot. The stunt taxi was parked at the south end of the street, along with the three black motorcycles that the stuntman "assassins" would be riding.

The real assassins, Ian knew, were somewhere in the crowds behind the police line along the entire route. He guessed that the Ministry of State Security had probably hijacked the feeds from all of the private surveillance cameras on the six-block stretch and would also hack into the signal from the movie cameras mounted on the red-and-white taxi.

Ian saw P. J. supervising last-minute adjustments to the camera on the taxi's passenger-side platform, which would be operated by a cameraman, and the stationary one mounted on the hood of the car. Both cameras were pointed at the driver's seat, where Mei would be sitting for the chase.

There was a buzz of excitement in the air like static electricity. Something thrilling and dangerous was definitely about to happen.

Susie greeted Ian and Margo almost the instant they emerged from the van and led them to the dressing room trailers. She seemed like an entirely different person to Ian. More focused, capable, and serious. The bubbly, excited publicist persona had clearly been an act. Now she was all business.

"Everything is set. I found the container and a cargo ship. All you need to do is get to the port." She slipped Ian a set of keys and he pocketed them.

"You make it sound so easy," Margo said.

Susie pulled Margo between two of the trailers and gave her a hard, passionate kiss. Margo dropped her hands to Susie's ass and pressed against her. Ian felt bad about staring but that didn't stop him from doing it. They broke their embrace and Susie stared into Margo's eyes.

"You will make it," Susie said.

Ian asked, "What about me?"

Susie gave him a thumbs-up. "Good luck."

"Gee, thanks," he said.

"The cameraman and stunt driver were just served tea in their trailers," Susie said, checking her watch. "They should be ready."

Margo took a deep breath and let it out slowly. "Okay then. Let's do this."

Ian walked to the cameraman's trailer, knocked on the door, and when he didn't hear anything, he let himself in. The cameraman, wearing a black jumpsuit, lay unconscious on the floor, a shattered teacup beside him. Ian opened the bedroom closet, where he found a second black jumpsuit and the cameraman's helmet on a shelf. He took them both.

At the same time Ian was doing that, Margo walked to the stunt driver's trailer and knocked on the door. There was no answer. She opened the door and stepped inside. The stunt driver, also wearing a black jumpsuit, was slumped unconscious on the banquette table, his face in the plate of cookies beside his teacup.

## Classified Location, Kangbashi District, Ordos, Inner Mongolia, China. July 4. 12:07 p.m. China Standard Time.

There were dozens of live perspectives of Lai Chi Kok Road up on the control room's media wall, including a satellite view that gave them an overview of the entire street.

"We've got the location completely covered," Pang Bao told Yat Fu. "In addition to what you see here, we'll tap into the video feed from the movie cameras and the audio from Mei's microphone once filming begins."

"What ground resources do we have?" Yat asked.

"We have our operatives on foot and in cars around the base camp, where Ludlow and French will be."

"What about along the chase route?"

"There are police barricades the whole way and we have a car at each intersection. It's a tightly controlled environment to keep people out."

And it had the unintended benefit of keeping Ludlow and French in a contained space. Yat Fu liked that.

"The studio made travel arrangements for Ludlow and French yesterday," Pang added. "They are booked on the eight thirty p.m. flight to Los Angeles tonight."

"It's a ruse," Yat said. "They have no intention of taking that flight. They know we'll intercept them at customs before they can get on the plane."

"So why do it?"

"Misdirection," Yat said. "A magician's sleight of hand. We'll see them leave the hotel and head for the airport but there will be a switch somewhere along the line. They have a plan to be smuggled out."

"What is it?"

"I don't know," Yat said. "But we'll stop them."

# CHAPTER THIRTY-SIX

Lai Chi Kok Road & Boundary Street, Hong Kong. July 4.
12:18 p.m. Hong Kong Time.

Ian and Margo emerged from their respective trailers wearing identical black jumpsuits and crash helmets with visors that obscured their faces. They both headed for the red-and-white stunt taxi. The other stunt drivers were getting on their black motorcycles and into the other vehicles.

Mei was already sitting in the back seat of the taxi and getting last-minute direction from P. J., who leaned in the open window, a view-finder dangling around his neck. A dummy dressed like the cab driver was slumped in the front seat behind the steering wheel. There was fake blood and gore splattered on the driver's side window.

"Are you nervous?" P. J. asked Mei.

"Terrified," she said.

"Excellent. Don't try to hide it. Use it in your performance."

"I'm not even wearing a seat belt in this scene," she said. "How much danger am I in?"

"Less than anybody driving on the streets of Hong Kong right now." P. J. lifted his viewfinder to his eye and looked at her through it. "Beautiful. Love the fear on your face. But don't worry. Nothing that is about to happen is random. It's all in the script. We've got the entire street closed off for a mile. No outside traffic can come in."

P. J. lowered his viewfinder and nodded toward Margo, who was climbing into the driver's cage on the roof of the taxi.

"The stunt driver on top of this car has been training for this for months," he said. "Every move and impact are tightly choreographed and timed to the split second. He could do it in his sleep."

Maybe the actual stunt driver could, but this would be Margo's first time. She'd be winging it. But P. J. didn't know that.

"We've already shot the full chase sequence from multiple angles," P. J. continued. "You saw the footage. You know what's coming. So while it may seem like this taxi and every car around you is out of control, it's all just a big, well-rehearsed dance sequence."

"With speeding cars and buses smashing into me," Mei said.

"Exactly. It will be fun," P. J. said.

Ian climbed onto the platform mounted on the passenger side of the taxi, got into the seat behind the movie camera, and snapped on his seat belt. The snap of the belt got Mei's attention.

She pointed to him. "So how come he gets a crash helmet and a seat belt but I don't?"

"Because he's hanging outside the car while you're safe in a structurally reinforced cabin," P. J. said. "Think about it. If anybody should be scared of dying, it's him. One wrong move by the driver and he's roadkill. But he's got total faith in the driver and balls of iron."

Ian wished P. J. hadn't said that. It reminded Ian of how much real danger he was in. P. J. gave him a thumbs-up and Ian returned the gesture, though his balls of iron had gone into hiding.

Mei didn't seem reassured by the danger Ian was willing to face. She still looked like she might bolt out of the car at any second.

P. J. pointed to the radio on the dashboard. "The radio is tuned to my microphone so I can give you direction on your performance, though I don't think you'll need any. That's the beauty of visceral film-making. It's raw and natural."

Mei took a deep breath. "I wish I'd known that before I spent four years in London studying acting at the Royal Academy of Dramatic Arts."

"You'll just be using different muscles," P. J. said.

"Mostly sphincters," Mei said.

"That the spirit. Let's do this." P. J. walked away.

Ian's fear turned into nausea. He was afraid he might throw up, which would mean removing his helmet, which would ruin everything. So he willed himself to stay calm and keep his breakfast down. It wasn't doing the camera work that terrified him. He knew how to operate a camera and frame a shot from his years of working in network television. What scared him was Margo. She'd assured him that she'd been trained in "combat driving" by the CIA. But only a few top stunt drivers had ever tried driving a car from a roll cage on the roof.

They'd looked over the roll cage and the rudimentary cockpit beforehand. It was just a steering wheel, with a speedometer attached to the steering column, a "starter button," a brake pedal, and a gas pedal. Pretty basic stuff, she'd said. No need for an operating manual to figure it out. Besides, she'd have a wide, clear view of the three-lane road ahead and she'd studied the script, so she knew what to expect. There was no reason for Ian to worry.

There sure the hell was. Everybody drove on the left here, and that was a big enough adjustment for an American driver to handle without the unique challenges Margo would be facing driving from a cage on top of the taxi. She didn't know how hard to press the gas or how far to turn the wheel to control the taxi for the high-speed driving and the evasive maneuvers she'd have to do. And if Margo made a mistake, it was Ian who would suffer the painful consequences.

He fought down his breakfast again.

P. J. settled into his chair behind his bank of monitors. The director of photography and Larry Steinberg were on either side of him and Mei's two bodyguards looked over his shoulders.

The monitors showed the A and B camera views of Mei. The A camera view from the passenger side, where the cameraman was, showed an almost full-body view of Mei and the action happening outside the windows beside her. P. J. could give that cameraman directions and adjust the framing on the fly. The B camera mounted on the hood was locked in a loose close-up of Mei that also showed the street action behind her.

P. J. spoke into his headset. Ian and Margo heard P. J. through speakers in their helmets. Mei heard him through the dashboard radio.

"Okay, we are picking up right after the taxi driver has been shot and Eve takes the wheel from the back seat. 'A' camera, stay on Mei but just wide enough so we see the action happening outside the window. Mei, you're terrified and desperate. Are we ready?"

The three of them all said yes at the same time.

"Stunt drivers, are you ready?" P. J. stood up on his chair and looked out at all the other stunt drivers. They all raised a hand and gave him a thumbs-up from their cars and motorcycles. P. J. sat back down in his seat and yelled:

"ACTION!"

Margo stomped on the gas pedal and the taxi shot forward, pursued by three gunmen on black motorcycles.

# CHAPTER THIRTY-SEVEN

Ian got a great camera angle on Mei, capturing her character's desperate efforts to control the runaway taxi, and on the cars veering away outside her window. There was an undeniable energy to the shot but also a raw edge, an almost documentary feel, as if what he was seeing was actually happening. Because it was. It was real cars, on a real street, in real collisions, with a very real Mei trapped in the back seat, terrified for her life.

P. J. was right, Ian thought. This was how to shoot action.

Margo struggled to steer from her cage on top of the taxi. It wasn't easy. It was like trying to drive a speeding barstool. She wrenched the wheel, swerving around a truck in front of her and sliding into the right lane, putting the taxi between a bus in the center lane and the K-rail that divided the street.

Sparks flew as the taxi scraped the K-rail. There was an earsplitting screech of metal on metal, setting off another spray of sparks, as the camera platform grazed the bus. The seat belts dug into Ian's flesh, saving him from falling into the road and under the bus's tires. Mei screamed loud enough to startle Margo, who veered hard to the left, sideswiping the bus again.

The taxi hurtled down the road, pinned between the K-rail and the bus, setting off a shower of sparks on both sides, just as scripted. It was a beautiful shot, one that even Ian could appreciate despite his fear that the platform he was on would break away.

Mei leaned over the front seat, clutching the steering wheel and pretending to steer the runaway taxi as it blasted into a busy intersection full of traffic.

Margo weaved around the cars in front of her but steered too wide, plowing into a taxi and smashing it into a van in the next lane.

"What the hell?" Larry Steinberg yelled into P. J.'s ear. "That wasn't in the script."

"So what?" P. J. said. "Look at the shock and fear on Mei's face. It's gold."

"Smashing those cars wasn't in the budget."

"It is now." P. J. picked up a remote-control unit for igniting the squibs—the firecracker-like explosives that were planted in the taxi to mimic bullet strikes—and got ready for action.

Assassin #1 surged forward on his black motorcycle, firing blanks at the speeding taxi in front of him. That was P. J.'s cue to press one of the buttons on his remote.

The squibs exploded, creating the effect of bullets riddling the taxi. Mei ducked for cover as the rear window shattered, showering her with fake glass. Her scream, however, was real.

Ian felt like he wasn't there, even though he was strapped to the side of the hurtling taxi, because he was experiencing it all through the camera. He was an observer trying not to miss out on anything cool.

And he wasn't. He was getting it all. He was getting so into being the cameraman, and doing the best job that he could, that he almost forgot the real reason why he was there.

Most of the operatives in the Ordos command center were watching the car chase because it was exciting stuff. But Yat Fu was watching the *Straker* production crew at the base camp. Everybody on the crew was huddled around the director and his monitors, trying to catch a glimpse of the action . . . except for two people who were nowhere to be seen.

"Where are Ludlow and French?" Yat said.

Margo steered for the right rear bumper of the car in front of her, clipping it and spinning sideways in front of Assassin #1. The motorcycle T-boned the car and went cartwheeling over it into traffic, the stuntman landing on an inflatable cushion out of sight of Ian's camera. The assassin's spectacular demise happened outside of Mei's window, with her in the foreground, as the taxi sped past. It was a great shot.

P. J. shouted with glee: *"That's the money!"*

"It sure the hell is," Larry muttered beside him.

"Sit up, Mei," P. J. ordered. "Grab the wheel. Save yourself."

Mei rose up, reached over the front seat, and grabbed the steering wheel again, acting like she was fighting to regain control of the speeding taxi.

The stuntman playing Assassin #2 charged forward on his black motorcycle, gun out and firing at Mei, who ducked from the exploding squibs and wrenched the wheel hard, matching Margo, who did the same thing.

The taxi swerved around a car and straight into the cross traffic of a busy intersection . . . and into the path of a rampaging eighteen-wheel truck. But the taxi squeaked through and the eighteen-wheeler roared by behind it, just as scripted, creating a wall in front of the pursuing motorcycles.

That's when Margo figuratively threw out the script and began following the one that Ian had written the previous night. Instead of going straight, like she was supposed to, she made a sharp, tire-squealing left turn and rocketed toward the barricade of wooden sawhorses.

"Where the hell are they going?" Larry yelled.

P. J. had no idea and didn't care. He couldn't tear his eyes away from the screen. It didn't get more visceral than this.

Ian flicked the switch that turned off the cameras on the taxi, killing the video feed, and braced himself for impact.

Cops and civilians scrambled out of the way an instant before the taxi smashed through the sawhorses, batted aside the parked police car, and burst into traffic in a busy intersection, where nobody was following a script.

The driver of a real red-and-white taxi slammed on his brakes to avoid hitting Ian's camera platform and got rear-ended by another, identical taxi.

Ian waved his thanks and apology to the driver as Margo threaded through westbound traffic toward the elevated West Kowloon Highway that ran north along the coastline to the Kwai Tsing Container Terminals.

"What is going on?" Mei yelled and turned to her cameraman for an answer.

Ian held up a piece of paper that read:

*Be quiet. You're defecting.*

# CHAPTER THIRTY-EIGHT

**Classified Location, Kangbashi District, Ordos, Inner Mongolia, China. July 4. 12:55 p.m. China Standard Time.**

"The stunt vehicle has gone rogue and we've lost the audio and video feeds from it," Pang Bao said, stating the obvious in case anybody in the control room didn't understand what they just saw.

But they were still able to visually track the distinctive vehicle on the big screen using the satellite, storefront, and traffic cameras along the streets. It was clear to Yat Fu what was happening and he had to admire Ian Ludlow's audacity.

"Wang Mei is running. Ludlow and French are with her," Yat said. "Tell all of our units to move in and apprehend them."

Margo snaked around the cars in front of her, scraping past many of them with the now-jagged edge of Ian's camera platform, which stuck out way too far in the narrow lanes. She hoped Ian was holding on tight because she didn't have time to drive gracefully. She floored it for the tangle of freeway overpasses ahead.

*"What's happening? Where are you?"* P. J. demanded over the speaker in the taxi and in both Ian's and Margo's helmet speakers. *"Where are you going? And why the hell aren't the cameras on?"*

Nobody answered. Instead, Mei turned off the microphone transmitter clipped to her belt and the radio on the dashboard.

Now the entire production was deaf and blind to what was happening. But there were still people watching from afar.

The spy satellite's camera followed the stunt taxi until it disappeared under the West Kowloon Highway overpass and didn't reemerge on the other side.

Yat Fu swore to himself. He knew that Lin Cheung Road ran parallel, and often underneath, the elevated freeway for miles, with long stretches that were completely hidden from view from above. But there were cameras everywhere in Hong Kong.

"Show me the cameras under the freeway and on Lin Cheung Road," Yat demanded.

"I'm accessing them all," Pang Bao said.

Dozens of camera views appeared on the big screen, creating a massive checkerboard of video squares. Not one of the feeds showed the distinctive stunt taxi, even though only seconds had elapsed since it was last seen.

How was that possible?

The warehouse under the freeway was empty except for a red-and-white Toyota taxi that Susie had parked there early that morning. Margo pulled up beside the taxi and stopped the car.

Ian unbelted himself, took off his helmet, and got off the camera platform, his legs shaking so much he was afraid he might fall.

Mei got out of the stunt taxi and marched around the front of the car to confront him. He saw the shock of recognition on her face. She hadn't been expecting to see him.

"*You're* a spy?" she said.

"He's not, but I am." Margo climbed down from the cage and took off her helmet, revealing her face to Mei.

"I just write about them." Ian took Mei by the arm and rushed her over to the taxi. "You two get in the back. I'm driving now."

Mei and Margo got into the back seat. Ian got behind the wheel. There was a baseball cap and sunglasses on the dashboard. He put them on just in case his face might be briefly visible to any traffic cameras, started the taxi, and drove out of the warehouse.

Ian turned onto Lin Cheung Road and headed northbound, merging into the flow of traffic and dozens of other identical taxis.

---

There was total silence in the Ordos control center as everyone stared at the videos feeds on the big screen. All they saw was the typical stream of Hong Kong traffic. The stunt taxi was gone.

"We've lost them." Pang Bao just had to state the obvious, but this time it sounded less like a statement to Yat Fu than a recrimination.

Yat massaged his brow. "I want every operative we have in Hong Kong looking for that stunt taxi. In the meantime, we need to seal the city. Air, land, and sea. We can't let them leave China with Wang Mei and what they know."

"We don't know what they know," Pang said.

"That's the danger, isn't it?" Yat Fu said.

But that wasn't the danger that he was truly worried about. He was afraid of the reaction of his masters in Beijing if Wang Mei slipped out of China while under his constant surveillance.

⊕

Ian continued north on Lin Cheung Road, then west on Mei Ching Road, and then onto Container Port Road, which ran alongside an immense field of thousands of multicolored shipping containers. The forty-foot-long steel boxes were stacked side by side, six or eight containers high, within a system of rubber-tired gantry cranes that looked like enormous rolling staples.

He took a slip of paper out of his pocket and checked Susie's directions. He drove into the hedge maze of shipping containers, checking the numbers on the aisles and on the containers, until he found the one he was looking for and idled in front of it. The container was on the bottom of a tall stack.

"We go on foot from here," Ian said. He opened the glove box and handed them each a tiny Maglite flashlight. "Take these."

"What do we need these for?" Mei asked.

"You'll find out soon," Ian said. "But first we have to stash our ride."

Margo and Mei got out. Margo opened the container, which was empty, and Ian drove the taxi inside.

He got out of the car, helped Margo close the container, and then, following his sheet of directions, hurried with Mei to a lone container where Susie was waiting for them with her upbeat publicist smile.

"Right on time," Susie said. "But we still have to hurry."

She opened the container to reveal a motor home inside with California license plates.

"Is that Damon's rolling mansion?" Mei asked.

"Yes, it is," Susie said. "We moved it into a ventilated container."

Ian waved Mei and Margo inside the container. "Get into the motor home and buckle up."

They went in. He turned to Susie. "Thank you for everything."

"It's my job," she said. "Bon voyage."

Susie waited for Ian to get into the motor home and then closed the doors to the shipping container, locking them inside and plunging them into pitch darkness.

# CHAPTER THIRTY-NINE

Ian, Margo, and Mei turned on their flashlights, illuminating themselves and Damon's spacious motor home. Their flashlight beams played over the marble floors and countertops, leather furniture, and even a crystal chandelier. If Ian survived, he was definitely moving out of the Oakwood.

He eased into the driver's seat and found his seat belt. Margo and Mei sat in matching captain's chairs and belted in. Only a few seconds of silence passed and then they heard what sounded like a large truck approaching.

Something heavy landed on top of the container with a loud thunk, followed by the metallic snap of things locking into place. Mei gripped her armrests, anticipating what was about to happen.

The three of them remained quiet as the container was picked up by a gantry crane, transferred to a cargo ship, set gently down on deck atop a stack of other containers, and automatically secured into place with locking cables for the voyage. There were no more noises for a few more minutes and then they felt the smooth motion as the cargo ship moved away from the dock.

"I can't believe you got me out," Mei said. "How did you come up with this scheme?"

Margo said, "We decided to use our disadvantages to our advantage."

Ian gave Margo a look that she didn't see in the dark and then explained: "You were being watched constantly and the only time you didn't have bodyguards at your side was when you were on camera. So if we were going to escape, it had to be while you were filming. Once I accepted that, the rest of the plan fell into place. But that also meant we had to work within the limitations of whatever scenes you were shooting."

"Lucky for us, it was a car chase," Margo added.

"The great thing about the car chase was that the streets were closed to traffic, and everybody, including anybody working for Chinese intelligence, was held back by the police," Ian said. "That gave us a clear path."

"Most of the way," Margo said. "But after we left the controlled street, the challenge was ditching the car in a hurry and blending in to avoid surveillance."

"It's a good thing I was driving a runaway taxi in the script," Mei said, "and not a Ferrari."

"It was also thoughtful of Damon to have his motor home sent to Hong Kong by sea," Margo said. "This will be more comfortable for us than an empty container with a couple of buckets for toilets."

"All we had to do was move the motor home to a ventilated container, find the first cargo ship leaving the port, and get our container on it," Ian said. "Susie and her CIA colleagues in Hong Kong handled that."

"Where are we going?" Mei asked.

"Singapore," Margo said. "And from there to the United States."

"It's a three-day journey but we have all the comforts of home," Ian said. "There's food, water, and even some candles to conserve the motor home's battery power."

"I hope there's Dramamine," Margo said. "I get seasick.

◈

## Kangbashi District, Ordos, Inner Mongolia, China. July 4. 9:49 p.m. China Standard Time.

The ghost city was even more desolate at night, when most of the hollow structures disappeared into the darkness. Only the towers showed vaguely within the blackness. Blinking blue lights, strategically placed on top of the high-rises and within selected floors, etched loose, dotted outlines of the monoliths against the dark sky to prevent a wayward aircraft from smashing into them.

The streets were lit, but only enough to create sporadic pools of light amid long stretches of near complete darkness. Yat Fu liked to move in the shadows, avoiding the light, turning his nightly solitary strolls into a conscious metaphor for his work. But tonight, he wasn't alone. Pang Bao emerged out of the blackness into the pool of light ahead of him.

Yat Fu stopped on the periphery of the light, remaining mostly in the shadows. "Any sign of them?"

"We found the stunt car in a warehouse under the freeway. They must have had a second vehicle waiting for them."

Yat had already surmised as much. "We need to find out where they are hiding."

"You're assuming they are still in China."

"They're still here. Has Wang Jing revealed anything to our interrogator?"

"She's in a cell in Beijing," Pang said. "I'm told she's not talking."

Yat wasn't aware that Wang Jing had been taken to Beijing. He'd assumed she was taken to the same basement in Hong Kong where the bird market vendor and his granddaughter had been tortured to death. He was more troubled, though, by Pang's choice of words and the hint of contempt in his voice.

"What else were you told by Beijing?" Yat Fu asked.

"This incident in Hong Kong is a distraction that comes at a critical juncture in the longest-running and most expensive covert operation our country has ever undertaken."

"No one knows that better than me," Yat said, stepping into the light. "I played a decisive role in conceiving it and have been leading the intelligence aspect from the start."

"Beijing appreciates your loyalty and long years of service." Pang took out a silenced Glock from behind his back and shot Yang Fu in the forehead. The old man fell backward, the darkness enveloping him. "But they've lost confidence in your ability to see this program to fruition."

Pang unscrewed the suppressor from the gun. Yat Fu was a great man once but had probably been deftly masking his cognitive decline for some time, a common occurrence among highly intelligent men who recognize, but are unwilling to accept, the early symptoms of a serious neurological disorder. At least that was the prevailing theory in Beijing for the aberrant behavior of a man who was considered, until these last few days, a brilliant and visionary espionage strategist. It was certainly how he would be remembered within the Ministry of State Security.

He turned his back on Yat Fu, leaving the body to be collected by a cleanup team, and walked back to the office, mulling over what his superiors thought of the folly in Hong Kong. They didn't believe that Warren Fung or Wang Mei had presented any sort of intelligence threat. Whatever information they had was of little value.

As for Ian Ludlow, the file on his computer simply rehashed conspiracy theories that had been swirling in the American media for years and been ignored. The American public didn't care who owned companies. All they cared about was money and convenience.

It was possible that Ludlow was a spy, but it was more likely that his assistant was. She used his trip to Hong Kong as an opportunity to feel out Wang Mei's interest in sharing knowledge of her father's activities. Yat Fu's clumsy and violent effort hastened a defection that might otherwise not have happened. He was also inviting attention at the exact moment China didn't want any. Wang Mei's flight didn't jeopardize anything. It was merely an embarrassment that would soon be overshadowed by events that would shake the globe.

Nobody from the US was asking about Ludlow and French. The only screaming was coming from the American movie studio, desperately seeking reassurance that Wang Kang's financial investment in *Straker* wouldn't disappear along with his daughter. But the money was already gone. Pang had seen to that himself, transferring the cash to the secret accounts that financed the Ordos operation.

Pang entered the office building, took the elevator down to the subterranean control center, and took Yat Fu's high seat in the rear of the room. There was already a female operative, Shek Jia, sitting at Pang's former console. Nobody showed any reaction to his silent announcement of a new hierarchy.

He turned to Shek Jia. "Suspend the search for Ian Ludlow, Margo French, and Wang Mei immediately."

She nodded with a severe jerk of her head, as if she were headbutting someone instead of confirming a command. "What about the intelligence they might have?"

"It's of no concern," Pang said. "What do we hear from France?"

"Everything is going smoothly."

"Excellent," he said and started imagining what his exalted place might be in the new world order that would soon be coming.

# CHAPTER FORTY

Somewhere in the South China Sea. July 4. 10:00 p.m. Hong Kong Time.

Ian and Margo sat at the banquette table eating sandwiches, drinking beer, and playing backgammon by candlelight. The container was ventilated, but it wasn't air-conditioned. The air was blistering and thick enough to chew. Ian was shirtless and Margo had stripped down to her camisole.

Margo glanced at the closed door to the master suite. "She's been back there crying for hours."

"She got away," Ian said. "But her parents didn't. They'll pay the price for her freedom."

"Mei still has a price to pay."

"There's no hurry."

"Yes, there is," she said. "The information she supposedly has goes bad in five days. We've used up one already and we'll use up three more on the journey. And we don't even know when, where, or how we'll get it."

"There's nothing we can do to act on the information in here anyway," he said. "So you might as well take it easy and bask in your success. You just pulled off your first exfiltration."

"That's true." Margo leaned back in her seat and smiled. "Maybe now Healy will let me trade in my learner's permit for a license."

"You don't have a driver's license?"

"I'm talking about a license to kill," she said.

Ian was incredulous. "Is that really a thing?"

That's when Mei shuffled out of the bedroom, her eyes bloodshot, wearing only her bra and panties. She went to the refrigerator and took out a bottle of water.

"How are you feeling?" Ian asked, trying not to stare at her perfect body and suddenly shamefully aware of his own pudgy nakedness.

Mei sat down in a captain's chair across from them. "Adrift. Heartbroken. Triumphant. But mostly filled with sorrow for everything that I have lost."

"But you have a purpose," Margo said.

Mei drilled her with a harsh look. "That's all you care about, the secrets that you were promised."

Margo met her gaze with one that was just as hard. "We aren't doing this for fun."

Mei looked at Ian. "What about you?"

Ian crossed his arms under his chest, hoping it would have the effect of bulking up his soft pecs. "I wasn't given a choice. I don't know you or what you've done. I have no idea if you or your family deserves saving or sympathy. I engineered our escape to save myself and Margo."

Mei mulled his answer for a bit, then got up, opened a drawer in the galley, and pulled out a steak knife. Ian and Margo immediately tensed up.

Margo leaned forward, and Ian wondered if she was calculating how fast she could get out from behind the table and grab Mei's knife.

"What are you doing?" Margo asked.

"Giving you what you want." Mei sat down in the captain's chair and spread her legs apart.

Ian's eyes were inexorably drawn between her legs and he noticed a tiny scar on her left inner thigh. And just as his gaze landed on the scar, Mei used the knife to slice open the old wound in a spurt of blood.

The unexpected action made Ian jerk back, but he couldn't tear his eyes away from what she was doing with cold efficiency. Grimacing, Mei used one hand to splay open the wound and her other hand to insert the tip of the knife into the cut and pry up something with it, blood dripping onto the floor.

What she retrieved from her flesh was a flake of plastic, about the size of a fingernail, coated with blood. She wiped the object on an unbloodied part of her leg and passed it to Margo in the palm of her hand. The object was a microSD card in a tiny clear case.

"Jesus," Margo said. "You're hard core."

"This is definitely going in my next book," Ian said.

Mei got up, blood streaming down her left leg, tossed the knife in the sink, took a dish towel from the counter, and pressed it against her wound. If she was in any pain, she wasn't showing it.

Margo opened the case, removed the microSD card, and went to the large flat-screen TV mounted on the wall. She peered at the many inputs on the back of the screen, found a microSD slot, and inserted the card.

Ian searched several nearby drawers, found the TV remote, and turned on the TV, scrolling through the various external input options until the menu of the SD card came up on-screen. There was only one file, a 2GB MP4 video, but the name was written in Chinese characters. Ian glanced over at Mei for more details. She sat in the chair, holding the towel to her thigh, and gave him a blank poker face.

"Play it," Mei said.

Ian did.

The picture was in crisp high-definition and filled the entire screen. The camera was pointed at a king-size bed in an upscale bedroom with silk wall coverings, fresh flowers on the end tables, an empty bottle of champagne in an ice bucket, and three naked Chinese women writhing around a naked man.

All Ian could see of the man were his pale, hairy legs and the bottoms of his curled, dry feet. A woman with her back to the camera was straddling him, moaning and thrusting rhythmically, while the other two women were on either side of his body, kissing and stroking him.

So far, it could have been any porn movie downloaded from the internet. But then the man let out an enormous fart, startling the women, particularly the one on top of him. Even before the woman practically leaped off the man, Ian knew the face he was going to see. Because the fart, with its volcanic bass and sonorous cadence, was as instantly recognizable as it was infamous, one that had been replayed, analyzed, and mocked on countless news programs and talk shows. It was the historic fart that rocked the vice-presidential debates.

"Pardon me, ladies," Vice President Willard Penny said, sitting up, a sheepish expression on his red face. "I guess I had a little too much bubbly."

But his embarrassment didn't dim his desire. He reached for the nearest woman and clapped her on the butt.

"Bend over," he said.

She smiled slyly and got on her hands and knees. He grabbed her by the hips, his wedding ring catching a glint off the lights, and entered her from behind, his flabby belly slapping against her firm butt as he went at it.

"Yuck," Margo said. "That's something I can never unsee."

Now that Ian had a good look at Penny, more than he would have liked, he noticed that the grunting vice president's hair wasn't entirely gray and that his double chin wasn't nearly as pronounced as it was these days.

"How old is this?" he asked Mei.

"This was shot ten years ago in a Beijing hotel owned by my father. He was following an order from President Xiao, who wasn't president yet but everybody knew that he soon would be," she said. "It's just one of many videos Xiao has of Penny indulging his desires with multiple prostitutes."

"I thought Penny and Xiao were friends," Margo said.

Mei smirked at that. "Xiao's idea of a friend is someone he can use to grab, retain, or expand his power. My father and Xiao were friends since childhood and Xiao still betrayed him."

Ian used the remote to turn off the TV. They'd seen enough. "Your father must have known betrayal was a possibility or he never would have kept a copy of this for himself."

"You don't become a billionaire without intelligence, foresight, and cunning." Mei removed the towel to examine her gash. The blood had congealed, but the cut was still wide and moist, the skin around it a deep red.

"It runs in the family," Ian said.

Margo stepped forward to inspect the wound. "You're going to need disinfectant and stitches. There must be a first aid kit in here somewhere." She started rooting around in the cupboards for it. "How long have you had that disc under your skin?"

"Years," she said.

"Jesus," Margo said. "Did you put it in your leg yourself?"

"My mother did. She said it would keep me safe."

"Did you know what was on the disc?" Ian asked.

Mei shook her head. "My mother told me after my father was kidnapped and jailed."

Margo found the first aid kit under the bathroom sink, came back over to Mei, and got on her knees beside the chair to tend to the wound. "What about Penny? Does he know these videos exist?"

Mei laughed ruefully. "He's been doing China's bidding since he was governor of Ohio."

Ian and Margo shared a look. He said, "Do you know what this means?"

"Hell yeah," Margo said, soaking a cotton swab with disinfectant. "The vice president of the United States is a traitor."

"No, not that," Ian said. "I finally have the inciting incident that propels Straker into action in my next book."

"Oh good, now I can finally sleep at night," she said, and started gently dabbing Mei's wound with the swab. But despite her sarcasm, her curiosity soon got the better of her, as Ian knew it would.

"So what's his mission going to be?"

"The same as ours," Ian said. "Saving the president of the United States from assassination."

# CHAPTER FORTY-ONE

Jules Verne Restaurant, Eiffel Tower, Paris, France. July 4. 6:00 p.m. Central European Summer Time.

The man who called himself Warren Fung in Hong Kong and Simon Chen in Turkey was now Maurice Kwok in Paris. He'd used so many names in his life that he'd forgotten his real one. If he had to pick a name, though, it would be Death. And tonight, Death had a reservation for two at the Jules Verne, the exclusive restaurant wedged between the girders of the Eiffel Tower like a bird's nest, forty stories above the City of Light.

His date for the night was Chinese spy Tan Yow, who affectionately held his hand as they emerged from the restaurant's private elevator into the elegant chocolate- and amber-hued dining room. The only French people in the restaurant were the staff. All the diners were tourists who'd reserved tables weeks in advance for the panoramic view of Paris, framed by the distinctive *belle époque* lattice of the Eiffel Tower's wrought-iron girders. The gourmet cuisine was an added benefit, though Kwok believed that most of the diners would have been just as satisfied with Big Macs.

Kwok and Tan were greeted by a young French hostess in a crisp Lanvin 15 Faubourg suit who led them to a coveted window table. The chairs were custom made in carbon fiber with orange leather by Pininfarina, the Italian car designer, allowing tourists to experience what it might be like taking a Ferrari to the drive-through window of a French restaurant.

The table had a spectacular view across the Champ de Mars, a grand carpet of grass lined with elms, to the fifty-eight-story Tour Montparnasse, the only skyscraper in central Paris, sticking out of the historic fifteenth arrondissement with the vulgarity of a beggar standing outside the window and flashing his erection.

"Does the table meet your expectations?" the hostess asked.

"It's perfect," Kwok said, pulling out Tan's seat for her.

"It's also presidential," the hostess said.

"I don't understand," Kwok said, taking his seat.

"This is the view the president of France and the president of the United States will have at dinner," she said proudly. "They're eating here in two days."

Tan reached across the table and took Kwok's hand. "You told me this was a special place, darling, but I had no idea how special." She looked up at the hostess. "Will they be sitting at this table?"

"Not this exact table, but in this general area. Are you celebrating a special occasion?"

"We are," Tan said, sharing a smile with Kwok.

"The end of a major project," he said. "One for the history books."

"That's wonderful," the hostess said. "We're always glad when people make lasting memories here."

"That's definitely our intention," Kwok said.

The hostess walked away.

Tan kissed Kwok's hand. "Excuse me for a moment, I need to freshen up."

She rose from her seat and went to the restroom, where she washed her hands and pretended to check her makeup. On her way back to the table, she paused in front of a wall and several banquettes that faced the windows. She sprayed some perfume on her neck but most of the mist went on the wall, coating the surface with microscopic RFID particles. When she returned to the table, a bottle of champagne was waiting. The waiter popped the cork, filled their flutes, and walked away.

Kwok raised his glass to Tan in a toast. "To a killer view."

## Somewhere in the South China Sea. July 4. Hong Kong Time.

Margo wasn't a nurse, but as part of her CIA training, she'd been taught how to treat wounds, particularly her own, while in the field. Having a first aid kit handy to clean and dress Mei's self-inflicted wound almost felt like cheating.

"The Chinese are going to kill the president," Ian said. He was repeating himself but it had been several minutes since his dramatic revelation, and Margo hadn't responded.

"Yeah, I heard you," Margo said, focusing her attention on treating Mei's ugly gash. "But I'm a little busy right now. It sounds great."

"No, I mean *really*. That's what they are going to do. They are going to assassinate the president unless we can stop them."

"Relax," Margo said. "You're not God. Not every story you come up with becomes reality."

"Don't you see? Killing the president makes perfect sense." Ian stood up and walked over to her. He didn't want to talk to her back about something this important. "Now they'll own the one thing left that they need to take over the United States: the White House."

"An assassination may be the missing piece you need for your novel but there's no evidence that it's going to happen in the real world." Margo glanced up at Mei, looking for an expression of agreement, but got nothing. The actress was lost in her own thoughts.

"You're right," Ian said. "All I have are my novelist's instincts and a strong sense of story, both of which have proven right so far."

"Let's be realistic about this," Margo said. "You don't know if Chinese intelligence read your story, or if your story is true, or if that's how or why they were onto us from the get-go. I know you want it all to be true, but that doesn't make it so."

"Why would I want it to be true?"

"So you can save the world," she said.

"I don't want to do that," he said. "I'm a writer, not a spy. I want you to do it."

"You want me to tell CIA Director Healy that the Chinese are going to assassinate the president of the United States because that's what they'd do in your book."

"What good is owning the vice president if you can't put him in the Oval Office?"

"There's a lot you can do with a vice president in your pocket," she said.

"Like what?" Ian asked.

"Influence the president, influence Congress, influence public opinion in favor of legislation, trade deals, and military actions that help China. He could eventually use his position to get himself elected president."

"Why would the Chinese wait for him to be elected president when they can make it happen now?"

Margo stood up and looked down at Mei, who had been sitting quietly throughout the conversation and the bandaging of her wound.

"What do you think?" Margo asked. Mei didn't reply. Her eyes were staring off into nothing. So Margo leaned forward and snapped her fingers in Mei's face.

"Hello? Anyone home? I asked you a question. What do you think?"

Mei blinked, met Margo's gaze, and sounded very tired when she spoke. "None of it matters. Whether Penny becomes president or not, China doesn't own him anymore. You do."

That aspect hadn't occurred to Ian. Now they also had leverage over the vice president. But the Chinese didn't know that and it didn't change the fact that the president's life was in danger. So that meant Mei was implying something else, something truly insidious. "You're suggesting that we should let the president get killed."

"You may not want to," Mei said, "but perhaps the CIA would like it. That way they can own the Oval Office."

"I got news for you, honey," Margo said. "This is the United States you're talking about, not China or Russia. Our intelligence agencies don't undermine our elected officials or our democracy."

"Really?" Ian said. "Have you forgotten how you became a spy?"

Margo looked at Ian for a long moment as she thought about that. "It's a good thing the assassination is only a plot for your novel and not reality."

"And what if you're wrong?"

"We're screwed," she said. "Because for all you know, he's dead already."

# CHAPTER FORTY-TWO

Tour Montparnasse, Paris, France. July 4. 9:40 p.m.
Central European Summer Time.

After Tour Montparnasse was built in 1973, with a façade like the front
grille of a Ford Torino, the French were so repulsed by it that they
banned buildings in the city center from being higher than fourteen
stories. The only thing that Tour Montparnasse had going for it was
a fantastic view, particularly on the northwestern side, where every
office above the tenth floor could see the Eiffel Tower without any
obstructions.

That was why Death rented an empty office on the forty-fifth
floor and why he'd furnished it with the laser-guided antitank missile
launcher that he'd brought back as a souvenir from Turkey.

Kwok and Tan walked the two and a half miles back to their office
at Montparnasse after dinner. Kwok wanted to check whether they'd
accomplished their task at the restaurant. Tan thought it was unnecessary, but she indulged him because she enjoyed walking through Paris
and holding hands like they were two people in love. And she wanted
to burn off the rich, decadent meal.

The vacant office was lit by a few fluorescent light bars that dangled on wires from the exposed ceiling rafters. The floor was plywood and the walls were exposed to the studs. It had been stripped like this for years, ever since a botched asbestos removal project in the building spread the highly toxic carcinogen everywhere instead. Most of the tenants who fled during the cleanup eventually came back, but not the guy in this office. He died on the operating table while having a malignant tumor the size of a plum removed from his sinuses.

The modified 9K135 Kornet missile launcher was mounted on a tripod facing the window and centered on the Eiffel Tower. The tripod was bolted to a wooden platform to clear the windowsill and so the operator could sit in a chair to fire the high-explosive warhead. A wide opening would be cut in the glass shortly before the two presidents arrived at the restaurant.

Tan had retrofitted the weapon with an Android tablet with a timer app that would fire the missile if necessary. The tablet was purely a backup measure, insisted upon by Yat Fu, in the unlikely event that they were arrested, killed in a car accident, abducted by aliens, or binge-watching *Game of Thrones* and couldn't be there to pull the trigger.

Kwok sat down behind the launcher, turned on the laser-targeting system, and peered into the viewfinder. Tan stood behind him, feeling her pulse quicken and her mouth go dry. There was something unbelievably erotic about watching a predator prepare for the kill.

"Tagging the target with RFID flakes wasn't necessary," she said. "The laser-guidance will do the job. You just wanted to leave your mark on the kill zone."

"I like the insurance. The tags will help the missile find the mark if my aim is off." Kwok made some adjustments with the dials. He might as well have been twisting Tan's nipples. She almost gasped.

"You're right," she said, her voice husky. "We should definitely check the targeting."

Tan slipped off her dress and removed her panties. She didn't know whether it was the desire in her voice that Kwok heard or the sound of the fabric sliding down her naked body. But he leaned back from the weapon and unbuckled his pants as if responding to a spoken demand.

She straddled his lap and pulled his face to her chest. He squeezed her breasts, pinched an erect nipple with his teeth, and sucked hard. It brought tears of pleasure to her eyes. She opened his pants, grabbed his throbbing erection, and squeezed him as tight as she could, making him wince.

"The weapon is ready, the aim is true." She took him deep inside her. "Target acquired."

She began thrusting and gyrating against him as forcefully and as fast as she could. He rose to his feet, lifting her up with him. But she didn't stop moving. She clutched his neck and wrapped her legs around his waist and slammed herself against him with a savage intensity.

"We're going to change the world," she said between heavy breaths. "Right here. Can you feel it?"

Kwok's secret was that he felt nothing except physical sensation, and even that somehow felt distant this time. He carried her to the floor and laid her on some plastic sheeting.

Tan spread her legs and eased her hold on his erection, allowing him to choose his own rhythm, to penetrate her as deeply, and as hard, as he could. He pounded into her, supporting himself with one hand while his other hand slid up her sweat-slicked stomach, over her taut nipples, and settled on her throat.

Locking eyes with her, he slowly squeezed her throat, giving her just enough oxygen to stay barely conscious while creating a buildup of carbon dioxide in her brain that would heighten the intensity of her climax. He'd done this to her many times before, not so much to give pleasure but to get her used to submitting to him, to completely lowering her guard.

They came together, but her orgasm was much stronger than his. She was so deep into her intense climax when she died that she probably never realized that he was strangling her. At least he hoped so, for her sake.

He stood, pulled up his pants, and got to work. While she was still warm and pliable, he broke her neck, arms, and legs, arranged her in a compact fetal position, wrapped her in the plastic, taped her up, and stuffed her into a large rolling Samsonite suitcase.

Kwok liked Tan and admired her abilities, professional and otherwise. He didn't want to kill her, or Lucio and Fina, but he had no choice. His orders were to completely wipe his trail. He knew what that meant for his future. After the mission was completed, there would be an assassin waiting somewhere to kill him. It would be a freelancer, most likely a native European, simply fulfilling a contract to murder some nameless Chinese man and dispose of the body.

But as patriotic as Kwok was, he had no intention of sacrificing himself for his country. He'd evade or kill the assassin and spend the rest of his days in luxury, anonymity, and constant travel, watching and appreciating the profound impact he'd made on the world.

But for now, Kwok powered down the missile launcher, took the suitcase, and left the office with a sense of accomplishment, a full stomach, and a nice ache in his groin.

# CHAPTER FORTY-THREE

Somewhere in the South China Sea. July 5.

Ian had a sense of motion but, since they were in perpetual darkness, didn't have any sense of time. They didn't have smartphones or clocks to tell them what time it was. They could have been traveling for hours or days, it was hard to know, especially since they were all taking a lot of short, unsatisfying naps. The darkness and boredom made them tired, but the hot, suffocating air made it difficult to sleep.

He was also tormented by frustration, the thought that the president might already be dead, or could be in the crosshairs right now, and he was helpless to do anything about it.

At one point, the three of them were sitting around the banquette, water bottles in front of them, flipping through a stack of old gossip magazines that Damon had kept for the articles about himself.

"You must hate me," Mei said after studying for some time a photo of Damon emerging from the surf in Hawaii, sucking in his gut all the way back to his spine, pretending he didn't know he was being photographed.

Ian lifted his head from a photo collage of actors who'd fathered children out of wedlock. Damon wasn't among them. "Why do you say that?"

"I've killed your movie and probably the American studio, too. All the Chinese money will be pulled out after what I've done."

"The movie's chances for success are better now than ever. The studio wouldn't dare shut it down with all the publicity you'll be getting," Ian said. "You're the beautiful daughter of a billionaire fleeing from Chinese oppression."

"What oppression?" Margo asked without raising her eyes from a photo array of known and rumored bisexual Hollywood actresses under the headline THEY SWING BOTH WAYS.

Ian ignored the question. "You're going to be a sensation and the studio will want to exploit that. They'll rewrite *Straker*, set it someplace like San Francisco's Chinatown, and you'll be back in front of the cameras in two months."

Ian's words were like a hot shot of caffeine delivered straight into Mei's bloodstream. She perked up immediately. "Do you really think so?"

"Even if I'm wrong about *Straker*, you'll still be a big star," Ian said. "If that's what you want."

"As a billionairess, I have become accustomed to a certain standard of living," Mei said. "Celebrity strikes me as the best way to get it."

"You're going to love America," Margo said and began browsing a photo array of enormous female butts, in tight pants and workout sweats, under the headline CAN YOU IDENTIFY THESE KARDASHIAN BOOTIES? "You'll fit right in."

⌖

The motor home stunk. They had a working toilet but not much circulating air, so the combined body odor from the three of them was becoming a fourth presence, another person to avoid bumping into in the dark. The motor home fit snugly into the ventilated container, so they really didn't have the option of getting out and walking around.

After what seemed like weeks, not days, they felt the ship slow and get pushed into port and then it became a matter of waiting for the container to be lifted off the deck. Because of their impatience, the wait seemed even longer than their journey, but they used the time to get dressed and clean up the motor home as a courtesy to their host. Finally, they felt the shake of the crane clutching the container and the rapid elevator-like ascent as they were carried into the air and onto the dock. It seemed to take another eternity before they heard someone working the latches on the container door.

Ian, Margo, and Mei moved apprehensively to the front of the motor home to see what awaited them. They'd literally been in the dark for days, so they didn't know if they'd arrived in Singapore, or returned to Hong Kong, or had been rerouted somewhere else. They could be facing allies, pirates, or a firing squad.

A blinding bright light illuminated the inside of the container. Ian held up his arm in front of his face to shield his eyes and squinted into the light. There were four dark, vaguely human silhouettes framed in the container's entrance. The figures looked like the aliens leaving the mother ship in *Close Encounters of the Third Kind*. One figure stepped forward from the rest. He was a rotund silhouette with a hat and walking stick.

"We might as well go out and see who they are," Ian said. "There's nothing gained by staying in here."

The three of them stepped out of the motor home and were greeted in front of it by a middle-aged man in a Panama hat and a white seersucker suit that strained to contain his large, round belly. But his most prominent feature was a thick mustache with flamboyantly curled ends that dramatically underlined his bulbous drinker's nose and rosy, round cheeks. He leaned on a pearl-handled walking stick for style rather than balance.

"Welcome to Singapore, my friends. I'm Terrence Trafford, CIA head of station here in this lovely island city-state." Trafford had the vaguely British accent of monied East Coast Americans popularized by Cary Grant and John Hillerman as Higgins on *Magnum, P.I.*

Ian rushed up to Trafford. "How is the president of the United States?"

Trafford raised a bushy eyebrow at the strange question. "As presidential as ever. Today he tweeted that a CNN reporter's brain couldn't fit in a flea's scrotum."

Ian was relieved to hear that but that didn't ease his anxiety. The president needed to be warned that his life was in immediate danger.

Trafford peered past Ian at Damon's rolling mansion. "A luxury motor home in a shipping container. What a remarkable way to travel. I can see this catching on among the well-heeled Asian refugee class."

"Is there such a thing?" Margo asked.

"There will be if China keeps jailing their billionaires," Trafford said. "I foresee a whole new class of boat people driving their Rolls-Royces into one of these things and sailing them to freedom in a new shopping mecca." He raised his walking stick and pointed it at Mei. "You're the first."

"What happens to me now?" Mei asked.

"There's a private jet waiting to whisk you to the land of In-N-Out Double-Doubles, shiplap, and *Real Housewives*, where you'll be deplaned, debriefed, debugged, detoxed, depleted, and, finally, deposited in the city of your choice," Trafford said. "Toodle-loo!"

And with that, two of his men dutifully stepped forward to escort Mei out to a panel van with GULLIVER TRADING COMPANY and a Singapore address inscribed in elegant script on the sides. Parked beside the van was a Mercedes-Benz S-Class, undoubtedly Trafford's conveyance, as Trafford would have put it.

Mei got into the van without so much as a wave or a smile goodbye to the two people who'd whisked her to safety from Hong Kong. Ian was sure that he'd catch up with her again at the *Straker* premiere.

Trafford turned to Ian and Margo. "I imagine you'd both like a shower, a fresh change of clothes, and a nice meal, all of which await you at the legendary Raffles Hotel, where I've reserved rooms for you. Afterward, we can debrief over a refreshing Singapore Sling in the Long Bar and toast the ghosts of Somerset Maugham, Ernest Hemingway, Joseph Conrad, and Rudyard Kipling."

"We don't have time for that," Margo said. "We need to talk to Healy right away on a secure line."

"It's three a.m. in Langley and you both look and smell like vagrants," Trafford said. "Surely a few hours won't make a difference."

"You're wrong about that," Ian said. Wang Jing had told them they had five days before the intel Mei gave them lost most of its value. To Ian, that meant the president would be dead within the next two days. They didn't have a second to waste. "Those hours could determine the fate of our nation for the next century."

"Well, we certainly wouldn't want that," Trafford said. "Come along. I'll pinch my nose and roll down the windows."

He turned and waddled off toward the Mercedes-Benz.

# CHAPTER FORTY-FOUR

**Singapore. July 6. 4:10 p.m. Singapore Standard Time.**

If Trafford felt any urgency, it wasn't expressed in his driver's leisurely speed or the station chief's relaxed travelogue as they drove from Tanjong Pagar harbor to the Gulliver Trading Company's office in Boat Quay on the southern bank of the Singapore River.

"Singapore is a former British colonial trading post that's half the size of Los Angeles, but with much better cuisine," Trafford said. "There are twenty thousand food stalls offering every kind of dish you can imagine, all of it absurdly cheap and wonderful. The 5.6 million people who live here love to eat, mostly because there's nothing else to do. I'm proof of that. When I was assigned here thirty years ago, I was as thin as the soggy rattan cane the authorities use to whip people for breaking their countless petty rules. Get caught chewing gum or, God forbid, spitting on the streets and it's twenty-four lashes on your bottom. Of course, if your bottom likes that sort of thing, there are men and women on Geylang Road who will gladly cane you, and so much more, for a reasonable fee. It's all totally legal, because second to eating, indulging your erotic desires is all that's left to do. This is not a place you want to live if you are given to gluttony."

Their short journey took them west through the cluster of office towers in the city center and gave them a view of the Marina Bay Sands hotel and casino, Singapore's new defining landmark, which looked to Ian like a giant surfboard across the top of three skyscrapers.

"It's an abomination," Trafford said, following Ian's gaze. He told them that he much preferred the last remaining vestiges of colonial Singapore like Boat Quay, a densely packed neighborhood of nineteenth-century shophouses tucked between the new glass towers of the financial district and, across the mouth of the Singapore River, the neo-Palladian Old Parliament House, the Raffles Hotel, and the Padang cricket field.

"Foreign spies have been working out of Boat Quay since the early 1800s, when it was the port of Singapore," Trafford said as they threaded down Lor Telok in Boat Quay and parked at the corner. "That changed in the mid-twentieth century when the port moved to Pasir Panjang on reclaimed land west of here. Now this is where the Singapore soccer moms go for Pilates and boba."

They got out of the car. The Gulliver Trading Company, the cover for the CIA station, was on the second floor of a colonial-style shophouse with a Thai restaurant below. The shophouse next door, with a more Asian flair, had a noodle house on the first floor and the Rope, Hardware, and Paint Merchants Association on the second floor. Which intelligence agency, Ian wondered, was hiding behind that association?

Trafford led them to a side door and typed a code into a keypad, and they went up a steep staircase to a small office where four ceiling fans with rattan-mesh blades pushed the air over several unoccupied desks. Either the agents were all out spying, Ian thought, or there wasn't much need for spies in Singapore.

"Can you set up the call?" Margo said to Trafford.

"This way." Trafford opened a door that had a red light mounted on top. They entered a cramped, windowless conference room dominated by a long table, its far end pushed against the wall below a flat-screen TV and camera. Six chairs were squeezed between the table and the walls, which were lined with stacks of bulging cardboard boxes labeled "Top Secret" with a Sharpie.

The station chief closed the door, went to an ancient desktop computer tucked into a corner, and leaned over it to type some commands on the keyboard.

"The videoconference will commence on an encrypted line as soon as Healy answers on the other end." Trafford started to pull out the seat at the head of the table—not simply because it was the customary seat of authority but also because it was the only chair that he could pull out far enough for him to fit into. But before he could sit down, Margo spoke up.

"I don't know if you have the security clearance to hear this."

Trafford straightened up, blinked hard, and regarded her with disdain. "I've been in the spy game for thirty years. You're a glorified trainee and he's a novelist. My stapler has a higher security clearance than either of you do."

Margo wasn't impressed or intimidated. "When was the last time you or your stapler exfiltrated the daughter of a Chinese billionaire from Hong Kong?"

Trafford smiled. "You'd be surprised what me and my stapler have done. But you certainly deserve a round of applause for the Wang affair." He turned to the door. "I'll be right outside if you need me."

"With your ear to the door?" she asked.

"This room is secure. That's what the red light above the door means." Trafford pointed to the red bulb, which was illuminated. "Or did you think you were in Amsterdam?"

He opened the door and the red light went off, and when he stepped out, closing the door behind him, the red light went on again.

"What did that crack about Amsterdam mean?" Margo took Trafford's seat at the head of the table, facing the TV and the camera.

Ian squeezed into one of the seats wedged between the table and the wall. It was a tight fit. He decided that he needed to go on a diet as soon as he got back to Los Angeles. "In Amsterdam, hookers looking for business sit in storefront windows lit with red lights. It's where the phrase 'red light district' comes from."

"Clever prig, isn't he?" Margo said.

The flat screen flashed on and Healy appeared, sitting at a desk against the backdrop of a bookcase full of leather-bound editions. He was wearing a bathrobe over pajamas. Despite how Healy was dressed, he reminded Ian of one of those gasbag cable news pundits, reached at home on Skype to offer their analysis of the president's latest tweet.

"Good evening," Healy said, not getting the time right for his corner of the world or theirs. "I'm glad to see you're both safe and unharmed."

Ian wanted to punch the screen. "No thanks to you."

"I'm sorry we deceived you, took advantage of you, and put you in danger," Healy said, "but it was for the greater good."

Now Ian wanted to punch the screen even more. He looked for something heavy he could throw at it, but there wasn't anything handy. "You aren't sorry. This is what spymasters do. They manipulate people to get what they want."

"You should be proud of yourself, Ian. Your exfiltration scheme was brilliant. You have a real affinity for this work," Healy said. "Instead of writing books about spies, you should be one."

"Fuck you, Mike."

Healy shifted his televised gaze to Margo. "What was the intel that Wang Mei gave you?"

"A video of Vice President Penny banging three Chinese prostitutes in a Beijing hotel room," she said.

Every muscle in Healy's face stiffened. He was either constipated and experiencing a painful cramp or was very displeased. "I obviously made a mistake recruiting you. This isn't some game or a big joke. Warren Fung was killed in this operation."

Ian was afraid Margo might say something she'd later regret, so he spoke up before she could. "She's telling you the truth. We have it on a microSD card."

Margo held up the card for Healy, though Ian doubted he could see it pinched between her fingers. It was about the size of a dime.

"I apologize," Healy said. "How long has Penny been compromised?"

"This romp was shot while he was still governor of Ohio," Margo said.

"My God," Healy said.

"That's not the critical issue," Ian said. "Where is the president now?"

Healy looked confused. "He's in Paris for the G8 summit. He comes home after dinner at the Eiffel Tower tomorrow night with the French president. Why do you ask?"

Ian turned to Margo. "Paris. That's where Wang Studios opened a production office for a movie that doesn't exist. It all fits."

"No, it doesn't," she said.

Now Ian wanted to punch her, too. "How can you say that? Of course it does."

Healy raised his voice. "What are you talking about?"

Ian looked back at the TV. "The Chinese are going to assassinate the president while he's in Paris."

"You say that like it's a fact," Margo said.

"It *is* a fact," Ian said to her, then turned back to Healy. "You've got to get him out of Paris now."

"Convince me," Healy said.

"Me too," Margo said.

# CHAPTER FORTY-FIVE

Ian explained to Healy how China was buying up companies in key industries to take over the US economy, how they were using products made in their country to steal data and spy on Americans, and how it was all a plot to take control of the United States and subjugate its people, though he thought the CIA probably knew all of that already or they weren't much of an intelligence agency.

"That conspiracy theory has been around for decades," Healy said. "It's a cliché. I thought writers hated them."

"It's real and now the only thing the Chinese need to finalize their plot is to take control of the White House," Ian said. "If they kill the president, then Penny steps up and they own the Oval Office."

"What makes you think it's going to happen in the next forty-eight hours?"

"Because Warren Fung told us that Wang Kang was snatched right after he discovered that his studio opened a production office in Paris for a movie that doesn't exist and was sending money to fake vendors in Turkey. Wang Jing told us we had five days to get Mei out of Hong Kong or the intel would lose much of its value. That's when the G8 summit ends. The timing and the location all match up."

"That's it?" Healy said. "That's what you have?"

That seemed like more than enough to Ian. "What more do you need?"

"Some concrete evidence or actionable intelligence would be nice," Healy said. "But even if you're right, it's all moot. We have the video. We own the vice president now."

"The Chinese don't know that."

"That's the beauty of it," Healy said.

Ian got a sick feeling in his stomach. Mei's prediction was coming true. "In other words, you're willing to let the president get killed so you can own the Oval Office."

"That's the problem, Ian. Your theory about the Chinese assassination plot is based on wild conclusions like that one," Healy said. "Wild conclusions are safe to make in fiction but reckless in reality."

"You want to know what's really reckless? Gambling with the president's life."

"The vice president might be the biggest traitor in American history, even bigger than Wilton Cross," Healy said, referring to the man who'd taken Ian's terrorism scenario for the CIA, made it real, and then tried to kill him. "We can turn this disaster to our advantage, feeding Penny false intel to pass along to the Chinese, turning them into our unknowing puppets."

"Meanwhile, the president gets killed," Ian said.

"I deal in facts. The tape and Penny being compromised are facts. Your assassination scenario is pure fantasy."

"Speaking of facts," Margo said, "were you able to get anything interesting from Warren Fung's phone?"

"Not much more than what Ian just told me about your conversation with Fung," Healy said. "We've run the photo of his imposter through all of our databases. We didn't get an ID, but we have been able to track his travel. We know that he went through customs at Atatürk Airport in Istanbul on June 28 and again in Marseille Provence Airport on July 2."

"Turkey and France," Ian said. "Those are the same places that Wang Kang discovered money was being sent from his studio to fake vendors. What does that tell you?"

"It tells me that the man in the photo, Fung's imposter, is a Chinese intelligence operative who is investigating the corruption in Wang's company," Healy said. "And it strongly suggests that Wang was apprehended for legitimate reasons, not a political power play."

"Or it suggests the man in the photo is actually an assassin on the move," Ian said.

"What was he doing in Turkey and Marseille?" Healy asked.

"I don't know," Ian said. "But I know how the story ends. We're running out of time."

"I'm unconvinced," Healy said. "Margo, I want you on the next flight back to DC. Right before you go, I want you to ingest the microSD card."

"Excuse me?" Margo said.

Ian explained: "He wants you to swallow the card and shit it out when you get to Langley."

Her eyes widened. "I never saw that mentioned in my job description."

"At least you aren't the one who has to dig the disc out," Ian said.

"Are you sure?" Margo said, then looked at Healy for confirmation.

"Trafford has a protective capsule you can put the card in before ingestion so you won't scratch your throat and your stomach acid won't damage the card," Healy said, notably not answering her question. "Ian, thank you for your service to our country. A plane ticket to Los Angeles will be delivered to your hotel tonight as well as a reimbursement form for you to fill out for any losses or expenses you incurred."

"Fuck you, Mike." Ian reached back to the computer, hit the escape key on the keyboard, and was pleased to see that it cut off the transmission. He faced Margo. "Thanks for the support."

"You sounded like a crazy person."

"I can't turn my back on this," he said. "If I do, then I'll be responsible for the president's assassination."

"What are you going to do?" she said. "Tell your story to the media?"

"They'd just write me off as a crackpot," Ian said. "Unless you want to make me a copy of that SD card before you swallow it."

"Think again. I signed the Official Secrets Act. I could be tried for treason."

That didn't leave Ian with many options. "Okay. Then there's only one thing I can do."

"Go home and write your book?"

"Go to Paris tonight and find the assassin."

Margo laughed. "Assuming he even exists, and that you can find him, then what will you do?"

"Whatever Clint Straker would do."

"I knew you would say that," she said. "But what does it really mean? You have no hand-to-hand combat or weapons training. You can't even beat me arm wrestling."

"I'll think of something," he said.

"You'll get yourself killed," she said. "I'm going with you."

Ian wasn't expecting her to say that. "Why? I thought you weren't convinced by my argument."

"I'm not. But I'd rather go to Paris with you than swallow this card," she said. "What if I need to crap on the airplane? Then what?"

"That's a noble motivation," Ian said. "I'll be sure to change it in the book."

# CHAPTER FORTY-SIX

Ian and Margo stepped out of the conference room to find Trafford sitting at his desk, having a cup of tea and some shortbread cookies with his driver. It didn't seem very spylike to Ian. He couldn't picture James Bond or Jason Bourne having tea and cookies.

"Do you have a diplomatic pouch to DC?" Margo asked.

"It leaves daily," Trafford said.

Margo snatched a blank Gulliver Trading Company envelope off his desk, dropped the SD card into it, stapled it shut six times, and wrote "Super Secret Classified Stuff" on it with a Sharpie. She passed it across the table to Trafford. "This goes in the pouch. For Healy's eyes only. Put a rush on it."

He regarded the envelope with amusement. "Very well. Would you like a ride to your hotel now? I'd strongly advise it. Our paint is beginning to peel."

"I can't wait to get in the shower," Ian said, though he was more eager to get away from their CIA minders.

Trafford opened his desk drawer and handed them their keys, which were actually electronic cards made to resemble old-fashioned keys, their room numbers written on the fobs. "Leave your dirty clothes in a bag outside your room and we'll see that they are incinerated."

Ian wasn't sure that Trafford was joking.

Trafford's driver took them the short distance to the 130-year-old Raffles Hotel, which was named for Stamford Raffles, the British statesman who established Singapore as a trading post in 1819. The hotel was built on the waterfront but now, due to Singapore's relentless expansion onto reclaimed land, it was a third of a mile inland.

The driver dropped them at the front door and they walked into the grand lobby, an all-white, three-story marble arcade. Ian felt like a walking smudge set against all that whiteness and expected one of the security people to escort him out. But waving his room key got Ian and Margo past a disapproving staffer to the portion of the lobby, and the rest of the hotel, reserved exclusively for hotel guests.

Margo went straight to her room. Ian went to the business office, where he used one of the guest computers to find the first flight to Paris. He booked two premium economy seats on a Qatar Airways flight that left Singapore at 8:45 p.m., had a two-hour layover in Doha, and arrived in Paris at 6:25 a.m. Hopefully, they'd be in Paris before Trafford even realized they were gone.

He made arrangements with the concierge to have a driver take them to the airport at 6:45 and then he called Margo on the house phone.

"You have forty-five minutes to shower and change before we go to the airport to catch our flight to Paris," Ian said.

"What's the big rush?"

Ian lowered his voice and cupped a hand over the receiver so no one could hear him. "We have to save the president's life, remember?"

"Even if you're right, we have no chance of succeeding."

"We have to try," Ian said.

"Only if you promise that if you're wrong, we'll stay in Paris for a week at your expense."

"Agreed," Ian said. "But until the president leaves France safely, you have to pretend you're taking this seriously."

"I can do that," she said.

Ian hurried to his room and was pleased to find fresh underwear and socks, blue chino slacks, a white Tommy Bahama silk twill camp shirt, a windbreaker, a pair of leather loafers, and a small carry-on suitcase waiting for him in the closet.

He took a quick scalding-hot shower, shaved, and spritzed himself with copious amounts of cologne as a preventative measure against the stench of a seventeen-hour flight to Paris and another day without bathing.

He got dressed in the new clothes, made sure he had his wallet and passport, and checked the bedside clock. It was 6:35. That gave him just enough time to stuff his windbreaker and some food from the minibar into his carry-on bag and hurry down to the lobby.

### Singapore. July 6. 8:55 p.m. Singapore Standard Time.

Margo looked out the airplane window at Singapore slipping away below them. "It won't take long for Healy to figure out we're gone and where we're going."

She wore a sleeveless red Tommy Bahama polo shirt, a buttonless blue cardigan, and white boyfriend jeans. Their identical carry-on bags were in the overhead bin and made them look like a couple to ticket agents and airport security, though that probably wasn't Trafford's intention when he bought them.

"What difference does it make?" Ian said. "I'm free to travel wherever I please. Besides, what harm can I do?"

"They'll want me."

"What for?"

"Going AWOL," she said.

Ian turned and whispered in her ear. "It's the CIA, not the military."

"It's like a branch of the military."

"No, it's not," Ian said.

"So I'm in the clear."

Ian leaned back in his seat. "Of course you are. You exfiltrated Wang Mei and sent them the microSD card. Mission accomplished. They'll look at this as a much-deserved vacation after a job well done."

"No wonder you write fiction," she said. "You live in a dream world."

"That's true," Ian said. "But between the movie getting made and my stories actually coming true, it's getting harder and harder for me to tell the difference lately."

"That's a good argument to make when they're dragging you into the mental institution." Margo reclined her seat and extended her footrest. "What's your plan when we land?"

"I don't know yet," Ian said. "I figure I can use the next seventeen hours to come up with one."

"Or you could binge the last season of *Duck Dynasty* on the inflight entertainment system."

"That won't help us save the president," Ian said.

"It might help you understand him," she said.

# CHAPTER FORTY-SEVEN

The airport was a colossal metal-plated luxury shopping mall with an undulating roofline that was designed to evoke sand dunes and ocean waves.

In the center of it all, surrounded by stores selling solid gold bars and Hermès scarves, was a giant yellow cast-iron teddy bear impaled on a desk lamp that went up its ass and out through its head, illuminating its button-eyed, dead face. Ian knew exactly how that teddy bear felt.

When Ian and Margo emerged from the plane, they were greeted by a Qatar Airways ticket agent who informed them that the 1:05 a.m. flight to Paris was canceled due to mechanical problems with the plane. They were given tickets for Qatar's 7:35 a.m. flight to Paris, which would arrive at 12:50 p.m.

Ian immediately checked the departure board to see if there were any other flights that could get them to Paris sooner, but there were none. They were going to be stuck in Doha for six and a half hours.

Margo didn't think it was a bad place to be stuck for a few hours, especially after being trapped for three days in a shipping container.

But she wasn't feeling the same urgency to get to Paris as Ian. So while she roamed the terminal, having coffee at the Qataf Café's gold-plated counter and a BBQ Bacon Whopper at Burger King, Ian spent fifty dollars for access to the Oryx airport lounge so he could keep an eye on CNN for any breaking news from Paris and use one of their guest computers to do some research.

He learned from CNN that the president was still alive and would spend the final day of the G8 conference at the Élysée Palace, dine at 7:00 p.m. with the French president at the Eiffel Tower, and then fly back to Washington, DC, immediately afterward.

Ian decided that the president was probably safe while he was inside the Élysée Palace. That meant that the only time the president was in danger was in his motorcade going to the Eiffel Tower, while he was eating at the restaurant, and on the way to Orly, where Air Force One was parked.

The Élysée Palace and the Eiffel Tower were only a couple of miles apart on opposite sides of the Seine. Google Maps gave him three possible driving routes to the Eiffel Tower, depending on which one of three bridges the president used to cross the river. For the drive from the Eiffel Tower to Orly, Google Maps gave him only one likely route: the freeway. But the president might avoid the streets entirely and make both trips by chopper. He could land on the lawn of the Champ de Mars, the park in front of the Eiffel Tower, and depart from there after dinner.

The president would be traveling either in his nearly impregnable Cadillac limousine or a chopper that was fortified against all kinds of attack, so Ian ruled out an assassination attempt in transit. That left only one place for the killer to make his move.

Ian left the lounge and went to WHSmith, the English-language bookstore, to buy a Paris guidebook by Rick Steves. He'd watched so many episodes of Rick's TV show as research that it felt like they were close friends. Rick would have his back in Paris. He tracked down

Margo at the duty-free mall, found a seat under the teddy bear, and shared his reasoning with her.

"If the Chinese are going to take a shot at the president in Paris," Ian said, "it's going to be at the Eiffel Tower."

"I'm sure the Secret Service and the French authorities came to the same obvious conclusion and are taking extreme security measures," Margo said. "But let's say that they missed something. How are you going to discover that flaw, track down the assassins, and stop their plot in six hours?"

"I'll use my imagination," he said.

"That's all you've got?"

"That's all I've ever had."

"Then you better hope that you're wrong," Margo said. "Because we don't stand a chance."

✺

## Classified Location, Kangbashi District, Ordos, Inner Mongolia, China. July 7. 8:00 p.m. China Standard Time.

Pang Bao was at the computer in his office, deep into the time-consuming and tedious task of personally confirming the deletion of all the incriminating video and data files from the Hong Kong debacle, when there were two sharp knocks on his door. He recognized the knocks, delivered like body blows. It was Shek Jia, his subcommander.

"Come in, Jia," he said.

Shek Jia opened the door and approached, her upper body slightly bowed in ingratiating supplication. "I'm so sorry to disturb you, sir."

He knew from his own experience in her position that she wouldn't be intruding unless the news was grave, potentially disastrous for him, and beneficial for her.

"What's wrong?" he asked.

"We halted our surveillance on Ian Ludlow and Margo French, as you ordered. But we neglected to disengage our bots from automatically tracking data related to them, like their credit card purchases. We know where Ludlow and French are."

"Back in the United States, I presume."

"They were in Singapore yesterday and they are arriving momentarily in Paris."

Upon hearing that last word, Pang fought back the urge to vomit. The implications of what Shek Jia said were so poisonous that his body instinctively wanted to purge for self-preservation.

*Yat Fu was right all along.*

If Yat's perceived mistake was punishable by death, what penalty would Pang have to pay for causing the failure of China's most ambitious covert operation in history? The asset in Paris had to be warned, but he was unreachable.

The same wasn't true for the freelancer they'd hired to kill him.

"Get word to our freelancer," Pang said. "Tell him to make contact with the asset and warn him that he may be exposed."

The problem was that, by design, there were several layers of people between Pang and the freelancer. It could be hours before the freelancer got the message.

"You're taking a big risk," Shek said. "We have no idea how the asset will react to the message or the discovery that a freelancer was tracking him and the obvious purpose of it."

"We have no choice. The asset needs to be warned," Pang said. "The freelancer needs to be taken off the field immediately after delivering the message and replaced with another player."

"Of course."

Shek Jia walked out and Pang immediately vomited into his trash can.

# CHAPTER FORTY-EIGHT

Paris, France. July 7. 12:50 p.m. Central European Summer Time.

The Qatar Airways flight to Paris departed Doha promptly at 7:35 a.m. Ian fell asleep within minutes of departure and awoke when the plane touched down at Charles de Gaulle Airport at 12:50 p.m. They didn't have checked luggage, so they made it through customs in thirty minutes. In the arrivals terminal, Ian went to a newsstand and bought a burner phone with cash rather than a credit card in case the CIA or anybody else wanted to track them in Paris.

Ian and Margo waited another twenty minutes outside the terminal for a taxi to take them to the Eiffel Tower.

The traffic on the freeway was slow and it took them over an hour to get into the city, where the congestion was even more nightmarish than usual, the taxi driver complained in broken English, due to street closures related to security for the G8 summit. The Eiffel Tower, and much of the area around it, was already closed to traffic in preparation for the presidential dinner. So were the Palais de Chaillot and the Jardins du Trocadéro, directly across the Seine from the Eiffel Tower, as well as Pont d'Léna, the bridge that connected the two shores.

The taxi driver thought the early street closures were overkill and cursed the foreign leaders for snarling Paris traffic. Why couldn't they meet at the Palace of Versailles or, better yet, in a different city?

The closest their driver could get Ian and Margo to the Eiffel Tower was Place Joffre, the street that ran along the southeastern end of the Champ de Mars and the front of the École Militaire, an ornate building from the 1700s that, according to Rick Steves, was still an active military training institution.

Ian and Margo got out of the taxi, retrieved their matching carry-on bags from the trunk, and faced a postcard-perfect unobstructed view of the Eiffel Tower at the northwestern end of the Champ de Mars.

The borders of the tree-lined park were closed off with K-rails and patrolled by armed soldiers and officers with bomb-sniffing dogs. Police and military personnel vehicles were also parked along the gravel paths on either side of the park. But people were still permitted to wander through the Champ de Mars, at least for now.

Ian and Margo started to join the flow of people walking to the Eiffel Tower but they were immediately stopped by a pair of armed soldiers, who asked them to open their small rolling suitcases for inspection. Ian and Margo unzipped their suitcases, which only contained his jacket and her sweater.

"Why are you traveling with empty suitcases?" one of the soldiers asked in a heavy French accent that immediately reminded Ian of Inspector Clouseau.

"We aren't. Our luggage is back at the hotel," Ian said. "We brought these with us because we're going on a shopping spree and we don't want to lug around a bunch of bags."

The soldiers seemed satisfied with Ian's answer and continued their patrol.

Ian and Margo zipped up their carry-ons.

"See?" Margo said. "Tight security."

Ian couldn't argue about that and they resumed their walk. It was possible, he thought, that the assassins might be masquerading as police officers or soldiers, but he couldn't think of a way that he could flush out any imposters, so there was no point in trying, especially given his own absurdly limited time and resources. He had to narrow down the potential assassination scenarios to one that he and Margo could reasonably handle.

They reached the Bassins du Champ de Mars, a fountain in the roundabout in the center of Avenue Joseph Bouvard, a wide boulevard that crossed the park but was now closed off to traffic. Tall, temporary cyclone fencing and K-rails prevented people on foot from getting any closer to the Eiffel Tower, which was two hundred yards away, so hundreds of people filled the empty street, angling for position to take selfies with the Eiffel Tower in the background.

The trees that lined the park were so densely packed that they were like tall hedges. Ian could imagine a camouflaged sniper hiding in the trees, but he doubted a man could get up there now or go unnoticed by the patrols or their dogs. The security teams were probably even using heat-seeking technology to find anybody who might be hiding in or near the park. The apartment buildings on either side of Champ de Mars had certainly been searched and locked down and had police snipers posted on the rooftops watching for trouble. So Ian ruled out those obvious assassination scenarios.

He looked back the way they came and saw only two buildings: the École Militaire and farther beyond, a monolithic office tower. Both buildings had completely unobstructed views of the Eiffel Tower. But the École Militaire was full of military personnel. There was no way a sniper could sneak inside. So that left the skyscraper.

Ian checked his guidebook and learned from Rick Steves that the building was Tour Montparnasse, the only skyscraper in central Paris. If Ian were writing this story, that's where he'd put his killer. His story instincts hadn't failed him yet.

"Come on," Ian said and led Margo back the way they came. "We need to catch another taxi."

"Where are we going?"

Ian pointed toward the skyline in front of them. "There."

"The big, ugly skyscraper."

"Tour Montparnasse. It has a direct line of sight to the Eiffel Tower. The only other buildings that do, the military school in front of us and the Palais de Chaillot behind us on the other side of the Seine, are locked down."

"That building is miles away," Margo said. "Do you honestly believe a sniper can shoot somebody sitting at a table in the Eiffel Tower from there?"

"Anything is possible," Ian said.

"No, it's not. Can a dog write a novel? Can you rub two sticks of butter together and make a fire? Can a fish live without water, grow a beard, or sing show tunes?"

"What does any of that have to do with our current problem?" They reached Place Joffre again and Ian scanned the traffic for an unoccupied taxi.

"I'm trying to inject reason and rationality into the discussion."

"By asking if a fish can grow a beard and sing show tunes? What's reasonable about that?"

"You're missing my point," Margo said.

"I certainly am." Ian spotted a taxi and waved to the driver, who saw him and angled toward the curb.

"What makes you think that building isn't locked down, too?"

"That's what we're going to find out."

# CHAPTER FORTY-NINE

The Louvre, Paris, France. July 7. 4:30 p.m. Central European Summer Time.

Maurice Kwok couldn't understand why the *Mona Lisa* was the most famous and valuable painting in the world. She was a drab woman in dull clothing. There was nothing physically appealing about her. In fact, she was freakish, missing her eyelashes and eyebrows. The only possible reason Leonardo da Vinci could have painted this portrait was for the money. However, that didn't explain why it was so revered by everybody else.

He'd met a hooker in Bangkok with an elaborate snake tattoo that wrapped around her entire torso, its head nestled between her breasts, its forked tongue flicking one of her nipples. Her skin deserved to be in a bulletproof case, hanging in the Louvre, admired by millions, instead of mounted on a wall in a back-alley apartment in Macau where only Kwok could gaze upon it. She was a true work of art far more beautiful than Mona Lisa, which was why he'd kept her skin rather than let it decay with her corpse.

But Kwok couldn't visit Paris and miss the most celebrated painting on earth. He was glad he'd come to the Louvre, not because he got to see the dreary hag up close, but because it allowed him to spot the man tailing him, a pallid Frenchman with a hook nose. The man inadvertently revealed himself after Kwok passed through a large tour group to get to another gallery. Hook Nose had to rush through the crowd not to lose him.

Kwok strolled through the museum, pretending to admire the works of art while actually checking to see if more than one person was shadowing him. After a few minutes of wandering through the gallery, he was convinced that if anybody else was watching him, it was from the security cameras. To test that theory, he left the Louvre and went to the Metro station, where he caught the subway train toward Porte d'Orléans. Hook Nose stayed with him, but loosely, taking a seat in a different car. Nobody else paid any attention to Kwok, who was satisfied now that he had only one man on his tail.

Who ordered the surveillance? Surely it wasn't a law enforcement or intelligence agency. If they suspected what he was here to do, they would have mounted a more robust effort and certainly wouldn't have used someone as careless as Hook Nose. So that left only one possibility: This was Kwok's assassin, the man hired to kill him later tonight, keeping an eye on his eventual target.

Hook Nose was an overeager fool, but getting somebody like him was the risk you took when you hired a freelancer. And Beijing knew that, so Kwok assumed there was redundancy. There were probably two or three backup freelancers waiting in the shadows for him if he eluded this idiot. And he would. The only question was whether to kill Hook Nose now or later.

## Tour Montparnasse, Paris, France. July 7. 4:45 p.m. Central European Summer Time.

The driver dropped Ian and Margo off at a bus stop at the Rue de l'Arrivée entrance to Tour Montparnasse.

The office tower was in the center of a large plaza, an island amid several intersecting boulevards, that had a Galeries Lafayette department store at one end and the Gare Montparnasse train station on the other.

Ian eyed the people streaming in and out of Tour Montparnasse. "The building doesn't look locked down to me."

"That should tell you something," Margo said. "Do you really think you're the only person in Paris who has noticed that this building has an unobstructed view of the Eiffel Tower? The French and American Secret Service know it, too, and obviously aren't concerned."

"They don't have my imagination."

"But they know that two miles is the longest distance ever recorded for a sniper kill shot."

"How do *you* know that?"

"Because a Canadian sniper in Iraq made the shot while I was in weapons training at the Farm. All the instructors were talking about it," Margo said. "I watched the taxi driver's odometer on the way here. We're 3.5 kilometers from the Eiffel Tower, which is over two miles. So your imaginary sniper would have to match or break a world record to make that shot, and that's assuming he can even get the president in his crosshairs."

"Maybe he's not using a rifle," Ian said.

"What else is there?"

"A missile," Ian said. "The sniper wouldn't need to get the president in his sights. The president would just have to be in the restaurant."

"A missile," Margo said.

"It's possible."

"Only in a Straker novel."

"We'll see." Ian headed for the Montparnasse lobby.

Margo tagged along after him. "What do you intend to do? Search the entire building for a rocket launcher?"

He ignored her question and went inside. The stark lobby was clad in marble but had the sterile, austere ambiance of a post office. The elevator banks were behind a counter, where four uniformed guards checked people's IDs against the visitor list on their computers. A dozen visitors were lined up in front of the security counter in a lane marked by two velvet rope barriers. There was a separate line for people going straight up to the observation deck and restaurant on an express elevator.

Ian went to the tenant directory and scanned the names. What he saw gave him a chill.

"We only have to visit one office," he said and pointed to the bottom of the list. "Look who's on the forty-fifth floor."

She did and her body stiffened when she saw the name.

*Wang Studios.*

# CHAPTER FIFTY

"Shit," Margo said.

"Are you convinced now that the president is in danger?"

She didn't have to say yes. It was written all over her face. Ian took out his phone and started taking pictures of the tenant list.

"What are you doing?" Margo asked.

"Getting the names of every tenant on the forty-fifth floor."

"Why?"

"We have to get up there and we can't do it without an appointment," Ian said. "We need to find somebody who will invite us up."

"What are we going to do when we get up there?"

"I don't know yet." Ian put his phone back in his pocket and walked outside. Margo kept up with him as he crossed the plaza to Rue de l'Arrivée and stopped at the curb.

She held her hand out to Ian. "Give me the phone."

"What for?" Ian spotted the Hotel Parisian Montparnasse at the corner of Rue de l'Arrivée and Place Bienvenüe.

"I'm going to call Healy."

"And tell him what?" Ian waited for a break in traffic.

"That Wang Studios has an office in the Montparnasse tower with a clear view of the Eiffel Tower and there could be an assassin in there with a rocket launcher."

Ian didn't say anything. He just looked at her, giving her a moment to think about what she'd just said.

"Okay, scratch that," she said. "Healy won't believe it and even if he did, he probably couldn't convince the French or US Secret Service in time."

"Exactly." He dashed across the street and she followed, joining him again on the sidewalk.

"We could call in a bomb threat to Montparnasse and tell them the explosives are in the Wang Studios office," Margo said.

Ian walked up to the door of the Hotel Parisian Montparnasse. "We don't know how many assassins are in the office or what measures they've taken to protect themselves to get the job done. All we may end up doing is getting a lot of people in the building killed along with two presidents. We have to do this ourselves."

She tilted her head at the hotel door. "So what are we doing here?"

"Research," he said and walked in.

The lobby was tiny and contemporary, the front desk doubling as a coffee and snack bar. There were two dining tables, a couch, and an office nook in the far corner with a desktop computer, printer, stationary, maps, and tourist brochures for hotel guests.

Ian went up to the counter, booked a room with the bored, balding clerk, and got the key while Margo sat waiting on the arm of the couch. When Ian was done, he tossed her the key.

"You can take our bags to our room."

"What will you be doing?"

"I'm going to use the guest computer to look up the phone numbers of the tenants on the forty-fifth floor and get us an appointment with someone up there."

"And then what happens?"

"I haven't plotted that far yet."

"Take your time. It's not like we're in a rush." Margo took the key and the two suitcases, squeezed into an elevator that was barely large enough to hold her, and rode it up to their fifth-floor room.

Ian sat down at the computer, took out his phone, and scrolled through the photos of forty-fifth-floor tenants in Tour Montparnasse. The tenants on either side of the Wang Studios office were an accountant and a psychologist, Dr. Alex Barlier. He looked up Dr. Barlier on the internet and gave him a call.

A man answered on the first ring. "*Bonjour*. Dr. Barlier."

"Hello, do you speak English?"

"Yes, I do," he replied.

"Thank God," Ian said. "I'm an American tourist here with my wife and we have a marital emergency."

"How did you find me?"

"We're staying at the Hotel Parisian Montparnasse across the street. I saw the huge office building and figured there must be at least one psychologist inside. I got your name off the tenant list in the lobby."

"*Incroyable,*" Barlier said. "What is your emergency?"

Ian looked up and saw Margo walking across the lobby toward him. He maintained eye contact with her and said, "I just walked in on my wife in bed with a woman! We weren't even here a day! Our entire marriage is based on a lie."

Margo gave Ian the finger.

"Is your wife willing to see me, too?" Barlier asked.

"Yes and no," Ian said. "I told her to come with me or I'm calling my lawyer to file for divorce right now. So she's coming."

"I can see you tomorrow morning at ten."

"No, no, no, I can't wait that long, or one of us will take a flying leap out of our window. The question is will it be me or her."

Barlier sighed. "All right. I can see you at six thirty tonight."

"What's wrong with right now?"

"I have other patients. You're lucky I'm squeezing you in at all. I'll need your names for the visitors list."

"Ian Ludlow and Margo French."

"Bring your passports. You'll need them at the security desk. Try to calm down in the meantime," Barlier said. "Perhaps it's best if you two remain apart until we talk."

"That will be no problem. I can't stand to look at her." Ian disconnected and smiled at Margo. "We have an appointment at six thirty with the shrink in the office next door to Wang Studios."

"Good, because you need professional help," Margo said. "I can't believe that you're still upset that I got Susie into bed."

"I'm not," Ian said. "I needed a story to tell the shrink and the best lies are based on truth."

"So what's the truth? Do you feel betrayed that I slept with her and not with you or are you upset that I got her and you didn't?"

It was both. "Neither one."

"Then what is it?"

"You lied to me so you could go on the trip to Hong Kong and jump into bed with Susie Yip."

"That wasn't why I lied to you," Margo said.

"Save your excuses and rationalizations for the shrink," Ian said and checked the time on his phone. It was 5:00 p.m. "We have bigger issues to resolve."

"We certainly do. Like how the hell are we going to get into Wang's office and what are we going to do after that? We have no idea how many people are in there or what weapons they have."

"Besides a missile launcher," Ian said.

"Yeah, and that, too."

"What do you know about missile launchers?"

"Nothing," she said.

"They didn't teach you anything about them at the Farm?"

"I was training to be a spy, not a soldier," she said. "Spies don't typically go around firing rockets."

"Did they teach you how to play baccarat, or fly a fighter jet, or choose the best wine to go with fish?"

"No, they didn't."

"James Bond wouldn't have survived thirty seconds if the CIA had trained him," Ian said. "Their curriculum needs a total rethink."

Ian thought about the obstacles the two of them were facing. They were unarmed and in ninety minutes they might be confronting a group of well-armed killers with rocket launchers. They were doomed. What would Straker do in a situation like this?

Straker was never doomed but he'd often helped people who were. That got Ian thinking about how Straker had evened the odds for some innocent, wholesome, unarmed civilians facing an army of gun-toting, bloodthirsty, merciless killers. Straker's plan had worked for them. There was no reason, besides being entirely fictional, that it couldn't work for Ian and Margo.

Ian stood up. "Come on, we have some shopping to do."

# CHAPTER FIFTY-ONE

Paris Metro, Paris, France. July 7. 5:15 p.m. Central European Summer Time.

Andre Le Roux's assignment was simple and specific: kill a Chinese businessman named Maurice Kwok anytime after 9:00 p.m. on July 7, preferably when Kwok returned to his apartment or his car, and dispose of the body where it wouldn't be found.

He was given a picture of Kwok, the address of the Airbnb apartment where Kwok was staying, and the make, model, and license plate of Kwok's van, which was parked in the Alésia-Maine underground parking structure beneath L'église Saint-Pierre de Montrouge.

But Le Roux was a big believer in *Le monde appartient à ceux qui se lèvent tôt*, which translated to "The world belongs to those who get up early." So Le Roux was outside Kwok's apartment this morning and had followed him around all day on what appeared to be a Paris sightseeing tour.

Kwok got off the train now at the Raspail station, so Le Roux figured the Montparnasse Cemetery was the next tourist stop on the businessman's checklist.

Le Roux's phone vibrated with a call as he was following Kwok up the steps to Boulevard Raspail. The harsh computerized voice on the other end of the line said in French:

"The job has changed. Contact the target right away, tell him 'you have been compromised,' and then walk away. No other action is necessary. Confirm completion of the assignment by text. You will be paid your full fee."

In other words, whoever ordered the hit had second thoughts. That was usually the reason why a kill order became a warning without even a good beating to underscore it.

Le Roux was disappointed. The anticipation of the kill had already started to build up in him, like sexual desire, and now he had no way to release the sweet tension. After he gave Kwok the message, perhaps he'd indulge himself and stab the first person he saw who let their dog crap on the sidewalk. He hated the dog shit all over Paris.

Kwok emerged from the Raspail Metro station and walked around the corner, past a café, and onto Boulevard Edgar Quinet. It was a wide tree-lined street that ran along the northern wall of the Montparnasse Cemetery, where over forty thousand graves were crammed into forty-six acres, and ended half a mile away at Tour Montparnasse.

The cemetery was a housing tract for the dead, with row after row of elaborate family mausoleums. The bodies inside these small marble-and-limestone structures were stacked on shelves, the coffins emptied and consolidated to make room for each new generation of corpses. But if a family stopped paying for their mausoleum's upkeep, the bones were cleared out and the crypt was left to fall into ruins until someone came along to buy the plot, clear away the rubble, and build their own monument to their dead. Lately, most of those buyers were cash-rich Chinese, who knew a cemetery wasn't just a place to bury bodies but also their money, figuratively speaking. Unlike the dead, money could be resurrected.

He glanced at the windshield of a parked car to check on his pursuer and in the reflection he saw Hook Nose, the impatient imbecile, picking up his pace, moving in for the kill at least two hours early.

Kwok pretended not to notice and casually entered the cemetery. He stayed a few steps ahead of Hook Nose, while making sure he was easy to spot, as he snaked around the various tombstones, until he found an abandoned mausoleum and slipped inside. The dark space smelled of urine and the ceiling was a blanket of spiderwebs. It was only seconds later when Hook Nose moved past the doorway. Kwok charged out of hiding, grabbed the killer in a headlock, and dragged him into the crypt.

Hook Nose tried to speak, but Kwok broke his neck before any words came out. Kwok laid him down and searched the man's pockets. What he found was a stiletto, a garrote, a wallet, and a burner phone. There were no saved text or phone messages on the phone, so Hook Nose wasn't a complete idiot. Kwok ignored the cash and the fake ID and credit cards in the wallet. All that mattered was that he hadn't found a badge or a wire. Hook Nose was a lone wolf. He pocketed the man's weapons and slipped out of the crypt.

The encounter was unexpected but helpful. Now he knew for certain that he was targeted for death that night, just like the president of the United States. The difference was that Kwok would survive. He strolled out of the cemetery and up Boulevard Edgar Quinet to Rue du Départ and his date with destiny.

# CHAPTER FIFTY-TWO

The destiny that Kwok was thinking of probably wasn't the one that occurred without him noticing.

Kwok crossed Rue du Départ to Tour Montparnasse at the same moment as Ian and Margo, only going in opposite directions, neither of them aware of the other. Kwok was going to Tour Montparnasse while Ian and Margo were going to the Monoprix, the French equivalent of Target.

As soon as they were inside the store, Ian and Margo each took a shopping cart and split up. He hurried through the aisles, filling his cart with household cleansers, several bottles of water, a box of sugar cubes, an instant cold pack, a table salt substitute, and a roll of aluminum foil. He nearly collided with Margo ten minutes later at the cash registers.

She smiled when she saw what was in his cart. "That's the finale from *Death Benefits*."

In the book, the basis for the movie in Hong Kong, Straker used common household items to help the simple Texas townsfolk make bombs to fight back against the well-armed, ruthless Mexican drug cartel.

"It seemed fitting to go back to that book for this," Ian said.

"More like destiny," Margo said. Her cart contained a box of steak knives, several rolls of masking and duct tape, and eight hand-painted porcelain souvenir tiles, two each of the Eiffel Tower, Notre Dame, the Arc de Triomphe, and l'Opera.

"What is that stuff for?" he asked.

"Protection," she said. "I'll explain later."

Ian paid for their items and they rushed out, carrying their shopping bags. But they didn't go far. Two doors down was a Relay, essentially a storefront version of an airport newsstand, and Margo hurried inside.

She went straight to a display of hardcover bestsellers. Mixed among the titles was *Le Ciel de la Mort*, the French edition of Ian's Straker novel *Death in the Sky*.

Margo took all eight copies. "We have to get these."

"I'm flattered," Ian said, "but we can buy them after we've saved the president."

"No, we can't," Margo said, moving past Ian and heading for the cashier. "Our lives may depend on these books."

"That may be the best blurb I've ever received," Ian said.

They got back to their hotel room at 6:00 p.m. Margo dumped her bag out on the bed.

"Have you come up with a plan?" Margo asked as she pulled down her socks and folded up her pant legs.

"We use the bombs to create a diversion, break down Wang's door, and subdue the assassin before he can fire the missile."

"That doesn't sound very imaginative to me." Margo opened up the box of steak knives. "But sometimes simple is better."

"What are those knives for?"

"Killing," Margo said and began using the masking tape to secure a knife to each ankle. She was definitely not the same woman he'd met in Seattle.

"I'm not killing anyone," Ian said. "It's not that I'm unwilling to—it's just that I probably suck at it."

"I'm sure you do. Killing is my job. Yours will be disabling the rocket launcher," Margo said. "I'll buy you the time. No matter what happens to me, that is your mission. Are we clear?"

"Yes, but I hope it doesn't come to that."

"Me too." Margo pulled up her socks and folded down her pant legs hiding the knives. "Okay, let's go save the president."

Clint Straker couldn't have said it better.

Ian and Margo approached the security desk in the Tour Montparnasse lobby. He was holding the shopping bags with most of the stuff from Monoprix and she was wheeling a carry-on suitcase containing his books and the souvenir tiles.

Ian told the guard they were there to see Dr. Barlier and handed over their passports. The guard verified they were on Barlier's guest list while another guard examined the contents of Ian's bag and Margo's suitcase, ending his inspection without comment.

The counter guard handed Ian and Margo their passports along with two visitor pass stickers. "Place these on your shirts. You are restricted to the forty-fifth floor. You will have to come back down here if you want to go to the observation deck or the restaurant."

Another guard walked Ian and Margo to an elevator, swiped a card key over a pad on the wall, and typed "45" on a keypad. The elevator doors opened and the guard waved them in. Ian and Margo stepped inside, the doors closed, and up they went. They were alone in the elevator but they were silent in case there was a microphone in the cabin. But somewhere around the thirty-fifth floor, Margo reached for Ian's hand and gave it a squeeze. They looked into each other's eyes for ten floors.

"God, I wish you weren't gay," he said softly as the doors slid open. She abruptly let go of his hand. "You just had to ruin the moment."

"How did that ruin anything? I was speaking from the heart."

"You were speaking from your crotch." Margo marched out of the elevator.

They rounded a corner and headed down the hall toward Dr. Barlier's office. Margo gestured to a standpipe and fire extinguisher in a glass box in the wall across from the psychologist's door. Ian nodded to show her that he'd seen it, too. He also saw the door to Wang Studios and thought about what terrors might be behind it.

Ian took a deep breath and opened Dr. Barlier's door, and they stepped into a small, unoccupied outer office with four chairs and a coffee table covered with a selection of magazines.

Dr. Barlier stood in the doorway directly across the room. He was younger than Ian expected, maybe in his early thirties, with a carefully curated two-day beard that diminished his slight overbite and pointed nose. He wore glasses, a turtleneck sweater, corduroy slacks, and tasseled loafers and held a notepad.

"You must be the Ludlows," he said, stepping aside to usher them into his office.

"Thank you for making time to see us tonight." Ian walked past him to the floor-to-ceiling window and the incredible view of the Eiffel Tower. Even from this distance, he could see that the Champ de Mars had been cleared of people. Police cars lined each side of the park and barricaded the streets all the way up to the tower.

Ian turned to the door as Margo came in, rolling her suitcase behind her. The doctor's desk and a file cabinet were in a corner, to one side of the outer office door. A couch was angled diagonally to face the window and a painting resembling a multicolored inkblot was on the wall. The doctor's armchair was also at a diagonal, putting his back to the wall and the view so he could focus all of his attention on the patient.

"I apologize for wasting your time, Doctor," Margo said.

Ian dropped his bag beside the couch and confronted Margo. "You don't think this marriage can be saved?"

She smirked. "All you want is someone to take your side against me."

"Who wouldn't take my side? I caught you fucking a woman!"

Barlier stepped between them and held up his hands in a halting gesture. "Please, sit down, and let's try to talk about this calmly and without recrimination."

"Easy for you to say," Ian said. "You're French."

Before the doctor could reply, Margo grabbed his right arm, pinned it sharply behind his back, and covered his mouth with her other hand.

"Make a sound or try to struggle," Margo said, "and I will break your arm."

She removed her hand from his mouth. Ian pulled a roll of duct tape out of his Monoprix bag and tore off a piece.

"I'm sorry about this," Ian said. "There's a man in the next office who wants to assassinate your president and ours. We're trying to stop him."

"You're crazy," Barlier said.

"You could be right." Ian covered Barlier's mouth with tape. "We'll know in a few minutes."

# CHAPTER FIFTY-THREE

Maurice Kwok picked up a pair of binoculars, went to the window, and looked out at the Eiffel Tower. Police snipers were on the observation deck and more were on the rooftops of the nearby apartment buildings. French and American Secret Service agents, police officers, and soldiers patrolled the grounds around the tower and along the Champ de Mars. Their vigilance was all for nothing. But he was wearing a shoulder holster and carrying a Glock just in case the police came charging in.

He lowered his binoculars and wheeled over the glass-cutting device, an enormous metal octopus with suction cups on five of its six outstretched tentacles. He hit a button, awakening the beast. The five tentacles reached out and stuck against the glass. The sixth tentacle, with a high-powered laser at the tip, reached over the other tentacles and began to slice the glass in a large circle. The crackle of the laser was so low that nobody besides Kwok could hear it.

Kwok took a few steps back to watch the beast work.

Duct tape covered Dr. Alex Barlier's mouth and bound his hands and feet. He was lying against the wall and behind the couch, which had been flipped over to give him cover from what Ian hoped was about to happen.

Ian had emptied out four water bottles and was now carefully filling two of them with a mixture of cleansers, the potassium chloride salt substitute, and other chemicals. He was saving the other two bottles for the activating compound he'd pour into the other pair of bottles to create an explosive reaction. At least that was the theory. He'd never actually tried what he'd written because he wasn't a crazy person. Now, apparently, he was. Just ask the shrink behind the couch, Ian thought.

Margo had laid out Ian's books and the porcelain souvenir tiles on Barlier's desk. She placed two tiles between two books and bound them together into a sandwich with duct tape. She repeated the process three times. When she had the four book-and-tile sandwiches completed, she lined two of them up spine to spine and taped them together. She did the same with the other pair, ending up with two packets comprised of two sandwiches.

Ian was rolling scraps of aluminum foil into gumdrop-size balls when some movement outside caught his eye. A police helicopter flew over the Seine, its spotlight illuminating the presidential motorcade as it crossed the bridge. They didn't have much time. A few minutes, at best.

"I need your help." Margo placed one of the packets she'd created over her chest and stomach.

Ian picked up a roll of duct tape and secured the improvised body armor to her, rapidly winding the tape around her midsection and over her shoulders.

"Not too tight," she said. "I need to be able to breathe."

"Can my books really stop a bullet?"

"They'd better," she said. "Or next time I'm using Janet Evanovich's novels."

The beast finished its work.

Kwok hit a button and the beast's tentacles retracted, its suction cups lifting out a round section of glass the size of a tractor tire from the window. Cold air blasted into the room, whipping up dust and dropping the temperature by ten degrees. He wheeled away the beast, and the glass it held, to the other side of the room, leaving a hole in the window large enough for a missile to pass through.

He walked back to the window and stood in front of the hole, the wind buffeting him. The presidential motorcade was pulling up to the tower. Police boats moved into position on the Seine. A helicopter circled the Eiffel Tower and swept the area with a spotlight.

It was 6:55. They were right on time.

Kwok went over to the missile launcher, took his seat, and peered into the viewfinder, lining up the restaurant windows in his crosshairs. He honored Tan Yow's memory, and Yat Fu's wishes, by activating the timer on the rocket launcher just in case something went wrong.

## Classified Location, Kangbashi District, Ordos, Inner Mongolia, China. July 8. 1:55 a.m. China Standard Time.

It was the next day in Ordos.

The news feeds from the French television networks covering the presidential dinner were up on the big screen. Pang Bao, Shek Jia, and two dozen operatives watched as the French and US presidents and their much younger second wives, both ex-fashion models, arrived at the Eiffel Tower and emerged from their limousines.

Shek Jia hadn't received any confirmation that their asset had been warned but Pang assured her that there wasn't any real reason for concern. If Ludlow and the CIA knew about the assassination plot, or where the assassin was, the spy wouldn't have been traveling to Paris on a commercial flight booked with his own credit card. At most, Ludlow was chasing a hunch that had come up empty—otherwise they would have heard radio chatter by now about major police activity at Tour Montparnasse.

At least that's what Pang kept telling himself. And when that didn't reduce his anxiety, or his urge to vomit, he told himself something else that did:

In five minutes, the United States would become a Chinese province.

# CHAPTER FIFTY-FOUR

Tour Montparnasse, Paris, France. July 7. 6:55 p.m. Central European Summer Time.

Margo finished taping the improvised body armor on Ian, who looked down at her handiwork.

"This would make a great author photo," he said.

Margo looked past him and out the window. The motorcade was at the tower. "We're out of time."

Ian overturned Barlier's desk to create a barricade, then went over to the coffee table and dropped tiny balls of aluminum foil into two of the bottles of chemicals.

Margo dashed into the waiting room, picked up a magazine from the coffee table, swiftly wrapped it around her left wrist like a sleeve, and duct-taped it into place. She did the same with another magazine on her right wrist.

Ian came in and handed her two bottles. One bottle was half-full of brown liquid and a ball of aluminum foil. The other was a third full of a bubbling concoction similar to Alka-Seltzer. "It's a binary explosive. Pour the bottle with less stuff into the one with more stuff, seal the cap, shake it, and run."

She skeptically regarded the two bottles. "Are you sure this is going to work?"

"Hell no, and if it does, there's a good chance we'll blow ourselves up."

"Thanks for the pep talk."

"Give me ten seconds," Ian said. "And then go for it."

Ian gave her a tender kiss on the cheek, ran back into the doctor's office, and slammed the door behind him. He picked up the two bottles from the coffee table, added the bubbling mixture from one bottle into the other, sealed the cap, shook it like he was making a martini, and placed it against the common wall Barlier shared with Wang.

He knew the explosions would be heard by everyone on the floor, and noticed by scores of people on the street, but that didn't concern him. The only people he worried about were on the other side of the wall and he hoped the element of surprise would give Margo and him an edge. It was why they didn't just go charging through the Wang Studios door in the first place.

He took cover behind the overturned desk and saw Barlier behind the couch, staring at him with wide-eyed fear. Ian gave him a thumbs-up, hoping it would give the doctor some false reassurance, and covered his ears.

Out in the hall, Margo combined the two mixtures into one bottle, closed the cap, gave it all a shake, and placed the bomb on the floor at Wang's door. She ran down the hall and around the corner to the elevator banks for cover. She prayed that no innocent bystanders working in offices on that floor walked into the hallway at the wrong moment—but it was a risk she had to take and one that would be over in a few seconds.

The two presidents and their wives were riding the elevator from the ground-floor lobby to the Jules Verne.

Kwok waited for a glimpse of the president in the window. He didn't need the man in his crosshairs. All he needed to know was that the president was in there. The missile would obliterate everyone in the restaurant.

He was imagining the blast when a wall in his office exploded and blew him out of his seat.

The fire sprinklers burst on, creating a rainstorm in Barlier's smoke-filled office, and an alarm began to bellow. Ian peered over at Barlier, who was fine, then rose from behind the desk and saw a jagged opening in the wall, large enough to step through into the next office.

He moved to one side of the hole, peered around the mangled, exposed metal framing, and saw a rocket launcher on a wooden platform, aimed through the window.

*Holy shit, I was right.*

Margo was flat against the wall by the elevators, getting drenched with water. People would be running out of their offices at any second and her bomb hadn't exploded yet. She peeked around the corner and down the hallway. Her bottle was still sitting at Wang's door, its contents bubbling, the plastic swelling.

*Come on, blow!*

Kwok sat up, his ears ringing, and squinted into the smoke and rain. There was a ragged opening in the wall that exposed the interior of the adjacent office. He drew his gun, got to his feet, and took aim at the hole.

Ian didn't see anybody in the smoke and darkness. But he did see a tablet computer screen on the weapon, and it was ticking down seconds, the numbers glowing.

*47, 46, 45 . . .*

*What happened to the second bomb? Where the hell was Margo?*

He couldn't wait for her, not with the seconds ticking down on a timer attached to the rocket launcher. It could only be counting down to one thing.

Ian took a deep breath and stepped through the opening into the next office.

Kwok fired three times at the man coming into the room, hitting him in the chest, center mass. The man went down.

Ian lay on the floor, struggling to breathe, all the air pushed out of his flattened lungs. It felt like he'd been hit with Thor's hammer.

The shooter was coming back to finish him off. It was the man in the photograph on Fung's phone. At least Ian would die knowing he was right.

The man was still alive and squirming, a cluster of three bullet holes in the center of what Kwok surmised was improvised body armor. The whole situation puzzled Kwok, but not nearly as much as the flash of recognition he saw in the man's eyes.

*How could this man possibly know me?*

He aimed his gun at the man's head for the kill shot and—

Blam!

—another explosion blew him off his feet. His gun flew out of his hand and right out the window.

The bomb that destroyed Wang's door detonated at just the right moment. A second later and it would have exploded into the crowd of people that was now pouring out of the offices into the smoky, showering hallway.

Margo pushed through the panicked crowd, smashed the glass standpipe case in the wall, removed the fire extinguisher, and blasted the spray into Wang's office as she charged in.

She saw the rocket launcher and Ian lying wide-eyed and squirming on the floor, trying to speak but unable to draw the air to do it. But there was no sign of anybody else. She caught movement from the corner of her eye and turned just as Kwok slashed at her throat with a stiletto.

Margo blocked the knife's edge with her magazine-wrapped left forearm and slammed him in the side with her fire extinguisher.

He took the painful blow and stabbed the knife into her exposed midsection, the stiletto sticking deep in her body armor.

Margo head-bashed Kwok, breaking his nose, and took another swing at him. He ducked it and drop-kicked her into a pillar. She smashed hard into the iron and lost hold of the extinguisher.

While Margo and Kwok fought, Ian crawled to the rocket launcher and, still gasping for breath, climbed into the seat. The seconds were ticking down on the screen.

*21, 20, 19 . . .*

He tried to pull the tablet off the machine but it was welded tight. The only buttons on the screen were in Chinese and he was afraid of what might happen if he touched the wrong one.

*15, 14, 13 . . .*

If he couldn't stop the damn thing from firing, he'd have to find a different target.

Margo yanked the stiletto out of her armor and charged Kwok with it. He grabbed the wrist of her knife hand and yanked her to his side, twisting the stiletto out of her hand and tripping her over his outstretched leg. She fell to her knees and he pounced like a lion, wrapping a garrote around her throat and attempting to strangle the life out of her.

Ian studied the launcher, noting the viewfinder and the two control wheels, and realized it operated just like a Panavision camera. The wheel on the left panned the firing tube from left to right, and one in the center tilted it up or down. He glanced at the timer.

*10, 9, 8 . . .*

He wiped the water out of his right eye, put his hands on the wheels, and looked through the viewfinder at the Jules Verne. The window and the foursome at a table beside it were in the crosshairs and at the end of a laser targeting beam.

Margo's vision went black and she couldn't breathe. Who did she think she was kidding? A lesbian folk singer and failed dog walker was no match for a professional assassin. In a few seconds, she'd be dead and she deserved it for being so stupid.

*5, 4, 3 . . .*

The only open space Ian could see was the Champ de Mars in front of the Eiffel Tower. He used the control wheels to point the crosshairs and the laser beam into grass, just past the fountains in the center of Avenue Joseph Bouvard.

Margo's reflexes told her to grab at the wire around her throat. Instead, she reached down for the steak knives taped to her ankles and yanked them loose.

She stabbed one knife deep into Kwok's left leg. Kwok cried out and stumbled, his hold on her throat going momentarily slack. She used the instant of freedom to twist to her right and plunge the other knife into his kidney.

Kwok staggered backward, pulled the bloody knife from his side, and turned toward the window. He realized two horrifying things in that single, crucial instant: The timer count was down to 2 and he was standing right behind the firing tube.

拉屎！

The missile shot out with a deafening crack and the scorching back-blast from the firing tube blew Kwok apart like a hand grenade in a piñata.

Ian kept the crosshairs pointed at the grass and saw the missile riding the targeting laser beam like a bullet train.

The missile smashed into the grass at five hundred miles per hour, igniting a blast that was the equivalent of twenty-two pounds of TNT, shooting up a roiling, dirt-filled fireball, and sending out a wave of concussive force that snapped tree limbs, shattered windows, and threw dozens of soldiers off their feet.

# CHAPTER FIFTY-FIVE

The air in the office was thick with water, smoke, and dust. Ian stood up, barely able to hear, and was joined by Margo. Together they went to the window and, through the settling dirt and smoke, saw a charred impact crater in the Champ de Mars. A helicopter banked behind the Eiffel Tower and came racing toward them.

"The cavalry is coming and we have to get out of here," Margo said. "But we can't go looking like this."

Ian didn't hear what she'd said. She didn't try to explain again—she simply cut the body armor off him with a few deft swipes of the bloody knife, did the same with her own armor, took his arm, and led him quickly out of the room. The two of them darted into the hall just as the office was floodlit by the helicopter's searchlight.

They mixed in with the hundreds of panicked office workers pouring into the stairwells to evacuate the building. They let the human stream carry them out of Tour Montparnasse and spill them out into the plaza, where everyone was looking up at the hovering chopper, its spotlight illuminating the gaping hole in a forty-fifth-floor window. The wails and shrieks of hundreds of approaching sirens sounded to Ian like the onslaught of a rampaging army of robot hyenas.

"Follow me." Margo took his hand and they darted through the crowd, across Boulevard du Montparnasse, and into the warren of streets leading to Boulevard Raspail.

"Where are we going?" Ian asked. They were both soaking wet.

"The US embassy," she said.

"I'm not sure that's the best idea."

"It won't be long before they figure out we were the terrorists," Margo said.

"We weren't."

"But that's not how it will appear when they look at the security video and talk to Dr. Barlier."

"We might be able to get out of Paris before that happens."

"Don't count on it," she said. "We're going to need the CIA to keep the French government from taking us to the guillotine."

"The guillotine doesn't exist anymore."

"They might bring it back just for us."

"We just saved the French president's life," Ian said.

"You know that, and I know that, but I'm not sure if it's clear from the damage we left behind. It might look like you fired the missile and simply missed. The real story is going to be a hard sell."

"Selling stories is my business," Ian said. "Leave it to me."

"I'd rather leave it to the CIA."

"You should know better than that," he said, but he went along with her without putting up a fight.

They walked two miles up the boulevard, over the Seine at the Pont de la Concorde, past the Ferris wheel at Place de la Concorde, and to the US embassy on Avenue Gabriel. The building was on high alert, marines scrambling all over the grounds, and the only reason they got past the front gate was because Margo gave some magic code word to the guards.

Once they got inside the building, Ian began shivering. He wasn't sure whether it was because he was soaked or whether it was from the fear he'd held back during those crucial minutes in Tour Montparnasse.

Margo gave another code word to the harried young female bureau-crat who met them at the door and they were immediately hustled to a command center in the basement, where dozens of people were work-ing phones and computer keyboards. A wall of flat screens monitored local and international news programs as well as live surveillance feeds from outside the embassy, from the Eiffel Tower, and from choppers following the presidential motorcade that was speeding on the freeway to Orly, where Air Force One was waiting.

Ian and Margo were led to a frantic, disheveled man in his forties who was giving orders left and right and took a good two minutes before he acknowledged the two wet, bloody, and dusty Americans standing behind him.

"I'm Markham, the fucking CIA station chief," the man said. "Who the fuck are you and what the fuck do you have to do with this clusterfuck?"

Margo got right in his face. "You know the fucking rocket that nearly hit the fucking president? We're the fucking reason it fucking didn't, so go fuck yourself."

"It was a Chinese plot," Ian said. "You'll find the assassin on the forty-fifth floor of Tour Montparnasse. He's the gore splattered everywhere."

Markham ordered a couple of marines to separate Ian and Margo and take them away. They were individually debriefed over the next four hours by interrogators. The more Ian talked about the experience of the last forty-eight hours, the less real and more fictional it became in his mind. That's because he was telling a story, and when he did that, he found himself narrowing the focus, highlighting the drama, downplay-ing the details, exaggerating the action, and speeding up the pace for maximum entertainment.

Ian and Margo were given dry clothes and flown back to Washington, DC, on a private jet that same night.

◎

## Classified Location, Kangbashi District, Ordos, Inner Mongolia, China. July 8. 10:37 p.m. China Standard Time.

Pang Bao sat in the vacant control room, unable to tear himself away from the hundreds of video streams of TV news broadcasts from around the world on the big screen. His console was splattered with vomit. He didn't care to clean up his involuntary reaction to the day's events. All of the broadcasts said essentially the same thing:

A lone assassin attempted to kill the presidents of France and the United States while they were dining at the Eiffel Tower by firing a modified Russian-made antitank missile at the restaurant from an office building two miles away. The missile fell short of the target, slamming into the grass of the Champ de Mars. The presidents were unharmed but dozens of officers on the ground suffered minor injuries in the blast. The assassin blew himself up with an improvised explosive.

ISIS claimed responsibility for the attack.

The botched assassination was definitely a disappointment and a lost opportunity but Pang could argue, at least to himself, that it wasn't a disaster for China. They still could spy on millions of Americans through their electronic devices and could readily access enormous amounts of their private medical, financial, and social data. They still owned major American companies in vital industries. And they still controlled the vice president of the United States, who could win the Oval Office in a few years.

Not only that, but ISIS did them a big, unexpected favor by proudly taking credit for their failure, ensuring that the investigation and retaliation would be directed far away from China.

But Pang was aware that none of that logic would spare him. His superiors knew the truth. It didn't matter if their assassin bungled the kill or was thwarted by the police. Someone had to be held responsible for the fiasco. With Yat Fu gone, Pang was the obvious scapegoat.

That's why everyone had gradually slipped out of the control room over the course of the last few hours, leaving the pariah alone to vomit until there was nothing left in him but regrets. Shek Jia was probably talking to Beijing now, arranging for his detention or immediate execution.

Pang was resigned to his fate. There was nowhere to run. He was in a ghost city in the middle of a barren desert.

Soon he would be a ghost himself.

# CHAPTER FIFTY-SIX

The White House, Washington, DC. July 11. 10:00 a.m. Eastern Daylight Time.

Ian arrived at the White House in a Jos. A. Bank two-for-one dark-blue suit and carrying a hardcover copy of *Death in the Sky*. The suit and the book were provided by the CIA, who'd been holding him "incommunicado" at a safe house in Charlottesville, Virginia, since his return to the United States.

All he'd been told was that, in the aftermath of the Paris assassination attempt, the president had tweeted that America could use a man like Clint Straker in our nation's fight against ISIS and other enemies of freedom.

It was an odd tweet, but no stranger than the one, for example, that the president had sent months earlier calling a couple on HGTV's *Love It or List It* "dimwits who don't have the mental capacity of an amoeba" for choosing to live in their renovated house rather than sell it.

This time, however, the tweet was all part of a carefully orchestrated publicity stunt to justify Ian's presence at the White House. It was also a tangible expression of the president's gratitude. Ian was there to give the president a signed copy of the latest Straker novel, which the tweet had instantly propelled to number one on every bestseller list, earning Ian hundreds of thousands of dollars in royalties.

Ian was led by a Secret Service agent to the Oval Office, where he was greeted at the door by the president with a campaigner's smile and a hearty handshake.

"It's an honor to meet you, Ian. Thank you for saving me, my wife, and our country from a shocking act of Chinese aggression."

"You're welcome, sir," Ian said and stepped into the office. Margo and CIA director Michael Healy were sitting on one of the two facing couches. He hadn't seen Margo since they'd landed at Andrews Air Force Base.

"Please sit down, Ian." The president closed the door. Ian took a seat on the other couch. "I'm sure you're wondering what's been going on in the world since you left Paris."

"It's crossed my mind," Ian said and looked at Healy, "though I've enjoyed catching up on the last three seasons of *The Walking Dead*."

"First, let me take care of two formalities." The president picked up one of two slim leather boxes from his desk. He brought it over to Ian and opened it for him to see what was inside. The box contained a blue ribbon with white edges attached to a ring of five golden eagles around a white enamel star with thirteen gold stars in the center. "I'm secretly awarding you the Presidential Medal of Freedom, our highest national honor, for your heroism."

Ian smiled at Margo. "I wasn't alone, sir. Margo deserves as much, if not more, credit for what we did."

"She's already received her medal," the president said.

"I'm glad to hear that." Ian reached for the medal and the president snapped the box shut.

"It's a secret award. It will be declassified in seventy-five years."

"I'll be sure to save a spot on my mantel for it," Ian said.

The president went back to his desk, picked up the other box, and brought it over to Ian.

"The French president has secretly presented you with the Legion of Honour, *their* highest award." He opened the box and Ian admired the red ribbon and the gold medal, which resembled a royal crown. "You may view this again in private, for as long as you live, at the Élysée Palace, where it will remain in perpetuity."

"I suppose it's the thought that counts," Ian said.

"They've been very thoughtful," the president said, closing the box and returning it to his desk. "They've completely erased, through the destruction and suppression of evidence, your entire involvement in the incident."

"What about the psychologist we assaulted?" Ian asked.

Healy spoke up. "The doctor is very appreciative of what you and Margo did for his country. In fact, he invoked doctor-client confidentiality to protect you before he was even asked to keep quiet."

"He also got a secret Legion of Honour," Margo added.

"It's nice that every contestant is getting a prize," Ian said. "But why hide what we did?"

"It doesn't serve our national interest." The president sat down in an armchair that faced the two couches. "There are other narratives that offer us more benefits."

In other words, Ian thought, they had a better story. That was a way of thinking that he understood. They were rewriting history like it was a novel that needed work.

"While you were flying home," Healy said, "ISIS claimed responsibility for the assassination attempt."

"You mean you claimed it for them," Ian said.

Healy shrugged. "They aren't denying it. They're running with it because it makes their capabilities seem far greater than they actually are."

"The dumb shits," the president said. "They're doing it even though it justifies us going nuclear on them and any nation that ever supported them, directly or indirectly."

Margo went pale. "You're going to use nuclear weapons?"

"It's a figure of speech," the president said. "I simply mean we can be far more aggressive militarily than Congress, the United Nations, or the EU ever had the guts to be before. It's freed up billions in defense spending."

That was one of the benefits of the new narrative, but Ian thought it ignored the real threat. "What about retaliating against China? They're the ones who actually tried to kill you and put their puppet in this office. It was the last step in their ongoing plot to take over our country."

"As far as the Chinese know," the president said, "we are completely unaware of all of that."

"We're opting to take a more covert approach," Healy said. "We confronted the vice president with the tape."

"That was one titanic fart," the president said. "Worse than the one at the debate."

"Now he's working for us," Healy said. "He'll be feeding false intelligence to the Chinese that will impact every aspect of their foreign policy."

Margo looked at the president. "What if something happens to you? He's still next in line for the presidency."

"If I'm forced to leave office for any reason, Penny will immediately resign or Mike will release the tape and reveal his decades of collusion with the Chinese."

"What happens if he decides to run for president when your term expires?"

"Same thing," Healy said. "He'll never occupy the Oval Office, not even for a minute."

"I don't even want the gasbag in the White House," the president said. "That's why he left today on a friendship tour of Madagascar, to be followed by an extended diplomatic visit to Antarctica. We've neglected the people living on our ice caps for too long. I might even send him to the International Space Station. His farts could actually keep the Goddamn thing in orbit."

It wasn't how Ian would have handled the situation, but he wasn't running the country or the CIA. It would be different in his book. On the page, he was God.

"What about the rest of China's plot against the United States?"

"Now that we know what they are doing," Healy said, "we can leverage that to our benefit, too. Their ignorance of how much we know gives us a huge tactical advantage and a means to manipulate them."

"You'll be using their own weapons against them," Ian said. "You'll put Trojan horses into the data they're mining and get a back door into their global surveillance system. You'll see what they see."

Healy smiled. "You should be a spy."

"That brings us to the real point of this get-together, Ian," the president said. "I didn't invite you here just to show you your medals, give you an intelligence briefing, and do a photo op with your book. Your country needs you."

Ian looked at Healy. "You're offering me a job again?"

"This is the second time you've uncovered and destroyed a conspiracy to cripple our democracy," Healy said. "You have a gift."

"It feels more like a curse," Ian said.

"You love it," Margo said. "Maybe even more than I do."

"We want you to keep writing thrillers and traveling the world researching and promoting your work," Healy said. "While spying for us at the same time."

The idea was exciting, but it was also terrifying. He'd barely survived these last two experiences. Seeking out this kind of danger might be pushing his luck. "I don't think I'm cut out to be an action hero. I'd never survive the training."

"That's where I come in," Margo said. "I'll be the tough guy."

She'd be his full-time author escort . . . with a license to kill. The idea amused him even if the reality would be very different.

"We want you to use your imagination to uncover plots we might not otherwise see," Healy said. "Your role with us will be loosely defined to allow your creativity to guide you. It's worked so far. You'll report directly to me."

"And Mike will keep me in the loop," the president said. "Nobody else will know that you're a spy."

It was dangerous. On the other hand, he'd be a spy.

*The name is Ludlow, Ian Ludlow.*

"Will I get an Aston Martin with an ejector seat?"

"No," Healy said, "but you'll get a Hertz Gold Plus membership card."

"I'm in," Ian said.

"Thank you, Ian." The president stood up and everyone rose with him. "I need a word with Mike. I'll meet you and Margo in the Rose Garden in a few minutes for that photo shoot."

The president opened the patio doors to the garden. Ian and Margo walked out onto the grass.

It was hard for Ian to believe he'd just met the president of the United States and that he was now strolling through the White House Rose Garden as a newly minted secret agent.

"I guess this makes us partners," Margo said.

"Except I'm in charge."

"No," she said. "I am."

"I have the imagination."

"But I have the actual professional training to do this shit."

"It was literally *my books* that saved our lives in Paris," Ian said.

"I'm sure John Grisham's would've done just as well."

"Don't be ridiculous," Ian said. "He writes legal thrillers."

"What difference does that make?"

"How long do you think we would have survived if we'd been thinking like a lawyer instead of Clint Straker?"

"You may have a point," she said and reached for his hand.

He took her hand and they kept walking.

# AUTHOR'S NOTE AND ACKNOWLEDGMENTS

I'd like to thank Hunter Rawlings, Chuck Knief, and Rich Colabella for sharing their expertise. I'm responsible for any technical and geographical errors you may have noticed and there's a good chance I made them on purpose to serve the needs of my story.

# ABOUT THE AUTHOR

*Photo © Roland Scarpa*

Lee Goldberg is a two-time Edgar Award and two-time Shamus Award nominee and the #1 *New York Times* bestselling author of more than thirty novels, including the *Washington Post* bestseller *True Fiction*, *King City*, *The Walk*, fifteen Monk mysteries, and the internationally bestselling Fox & O'Hare books (*The Heist*, *The Chase*, *The Job*, *The Scam*, and *The Pursuit*), cowritten with Janet Evanovich. He has also written and/or produced scores of TV shows, including *Diagnosis Murder*, *SeaQuest*, *Monk*, and *The Glades*. As an international television consultant, he has advised networks and studios in Canada, France, Germany, Spain, China, Sweden, and the Netherlands on the creation, writing, and production of episodic television series. You can find more information about Lee and his work at www.leegoldberg.com.